Outstanding praise for Lynn Lipinski
GOD OF THE INTERNET

A deadly and exhilarating game of cat and mouse that has all the makings of an engaging series about fighting terrorists.
—*Kirkus Reviews (starred review)*

Five Stars. *God of the Internet* is a delightfully frightening, completely realistic fictional depiction of a new face of terrorism.
—*IndieReader*

Five stars. In a real thrill ride of a read, *God of the Internet*…will grab readers from the very first pages, and keep them obsessively turning…all the way through until the very end.
—*Readers' Favorite*

Five stars. Lipinski has constructed a thriller based on elements that are intricately intertwined today—the internet, the family, and terrorism. In this fast paced potboiler, digital derring-do shares page space with familial obligations and international intrigue.
—*Pacific Book Review*

ALSO BY LYNN LIPINSKI

Bloodlines

GOD OF THE INTERNET

Lynn Lipinski

Majestic Content Los Angeles

Trade paperback edition, August 2016

Cover design by Seven25.
Inside page layout by Polgarus Studio.

Trade paperback ISBN: 978-0-9964676-2-9
eBook ISBN: 978-0-9964676-3-6

Library of Congress Control Number: 2016910987

http://majesticcontent.la

For my mother, Rosemary Lipinski,
whose love and curiosity inspires me.

Acknowledgements

Thanks first of all go out to my technical beta readers, particularly Leo Vegoda, for helping me understand how every hack in this book is possible. Change your passwords often, dear readers, and don't open email attachments from people you don't know.

I'm in awe of Darcy Burke, whose ongoing battle with her beautiful daughter's hydrocephalus provided real world inspiration. I hope my characters convey half of the strength, humor and love I've seen between Darcy and her daughter.

My deep appreciation extends to editors Laura Anne Gilman and Julie Wood for their diligence and their eagle eyes, to Isabelle Swiderski for the brilliant cover art, and to Jason and Marina Anderson at Polgarus Studio for the interior design.

On a personal note, I'm profoundly grateful for the love and support of my mother Rosemary Lipinski, my sister Laura Kane, and my good friend Priya Kapoor, who were with me from the very start of this journey. And my special thanks to Stephen Arakawa, my anchor and my love, for his unyielding support.

Chapter 1

The screen of the disposable laptop flickers as though it trembles with as much excitement as the man sitting in front of it. He calls himself G0d_of_Internet online, a sacrilegious joke he shares with only one other person. And that person had expressed his dislike of it so vehemently that G0d_of_Internet keeps using it just to toy with him.

He knows the time has come to send his baby out into the world, yet like any parent, he holds on for a few more moments, his eyes caressing the programming language he has been working on for months. He'd written the worm's coding lean and tight, then hidden it like a tiny pearl in a series of those *matryoshka* dolls from Russia where ever-smaller dolls nest inside one another.

He checks his TorChat instant message account and sees one message from his humorless client and counterpart, who goes by the innocuous online handle Proxyw0rm. Tor uses five thousand relays to bounce instant messages and online activity around the globe, all to keep his work wrapped in secrecy.

This is the beauty of the internet. It had been created by academic utopian idealists who believed in free information and had an abnormal amount of trust in the human capacity for good. No

1

one actually controls it. The internet had been built from the start as a distributed, resilient network, a completely decentralized system that draws its greatest power from the fact there is no head to cut off. At its core are thirteen root servers that route and relay traffic all over the world. If one root server goes down, no problem. The internet just routes itself around that one.

He thinks of the internet like the starfish he used to see wash up on the Red Sea shore during his boyhood vacations. If a starfish loses a leg, it grows a new one. And the coolest part is that the leg itself grows a new starfish. Every part of the starfish holds the capacity to regenerate.

That resiliency, combined with the lack of centralization, opens the door for untold innovation and allows for the internet's rapid takeover of commerce, social interactions and entertainment.

But, he thinks, *those hippie-dippie techies forgot one thing.* If no one is in control, then who polices and defends its use from the bad guys?

He remembers the private dinner in Singapore eight months ago with Abdul al-Lahem, leader of the Islamic Crusade, and his closest advisors. The comfort and ease he had felt at being among others like himself had been intoxicating after so many years living among the Americans, always on the fringes of their frenetic pace and constant consumerism.

"Imagine how the American people would feel to have their financial accounts wiped clean, even if you are only able to keep it so for a few days," al-Lahem said to him over a steaming pot of chili crab. He pulled the crab legs off ferociously, splattering red sauce on the tablecloth then gnawing on the sweet white meat inside.

"Money is so important to them," he said, and G0d_of_Internet nodded. Money is the main thing he has cared about for a long time. Even though his re-commitment to Islam helped him see past money to a greater goal, he still wants to be comfortable. Living in poverty may be noble, but he never wants to depend on others' charity.

"I cannot continue to live in the United States once this attack is underway," he said, and al-Lahem and his advisors nodded like they had understood that all along.

"We will make sure that you have safe passage to the Kingdom," al-Lahem said. "Though you may need to live with brothers in Yemen for a while."

G0d_of_Internet imagines the living conditions he might expect in Yemen. Concrete houses on narrow alleys, filled with brothers fighting for the cause, breathing dirty air and walking through piles of trash on the streets. He knows he should erase his pride, but instead his mind keeps churning, thinking of ways to hide money for his use once he is on the run. Some habits are hard to break.

He places his hands on the computer keyboard to type in the commands that will execute the worm he's named *Chrysalide*, then pauses. He thinks of home: the smell of cardamom and coffee, the olive trees in his uncle's courtyard, the azure waters of the Red Sea, the *muezzin's* melancholy call to prayer. Soon he would be there.

He types in the commands, then holds his breath while he waits for launch confirmation.

Launch confirmed.

He tips his head back and closes his eyes, slowly expelling the air from his lungs.

He types into the TorChat interface:

G0d_of_Internet: *Chrysalide* is launched. The game has begun.

Proxyw0rm: Well done, my friend. Soon we will awaken the world to our honorable fight.

G0d_of_Internet: May our work reflect the glory of Allah. Peace be upon you.

And G0d_of_Internet rests.

Chapter 2

Juliana doesn't bother to go into a stall in the ladies' room to hide her tears. Plenty of the female employees in UCLA's Information Studies Department have seen her crying in here before, so why hunch over a toilet seat for the pretense at privacy?

Mahaz, her husband of eighteen years, had humiliated her again. She needs to think, but she just feels like crying. She feels trapped by their marriage, unable to see another path for her life, but equally unable to visualize being with Mahaz for twenty or thirty more years. Hell, she isn't sure she wants to be with him twenty more minutes. At some point this marriage—and her life—has drifted far off course and she is tired of pretending that everything is still going according to plan.

Today's embarrassment came during a meeting with a consultant he'd hired to advise on his Center for Information Technology's social media strategy.

"Let me show you some of our past social media efforts," he said. One of the profiles Juliana had set up on a video- and photo-sharing site appeared on the big flat screen mounted to the conference room wall.

"Pretty pathetic, huh?" Mahaz said. "Look at this, only five followers. It's so obvious we don't know what we are doing, right, Juliana?" His voice was low and convincing. She had nodded because he'd always had this power over her. To persuade her to change her mind, to acquiesce to his wishes, to follow him. And following him was what she had done her whole adult life, an act as routine as breathing or blinking. His certainty used to make her feel protected and safe, but lately it only makes her feel vulnerable and small. A fish swimming in the wake of a shark, pulled along by its force but dangerously exposed.

At forty-six years old, Mahaz Al-Dossari is an exceptionally skilled computer network security specialist and a professor at UCLA. But the biggest feather in his cap is the enviably endowed chair he received, courtesy of His Royal Highness Prince Abdul Fahd bin Aziz, a schoolboy friend. That ensures not just his long-term employment, but also an overflowing coffer of money for his research. Mahaz uses the money to fund his Center for Information Technology at UCLA, where he hired her as his communications manager four years ago.

She once heard Mahaz describe her job to a colleague as a perk he had earned for bringing such a big donor to the university.

"I consider it another way to supplement my income. I put her in communications where I figured she could do the least harm," he said to a visiting professor from Egypt. The other man laughed and looked at Juliana like she was a prize calf at the fair. Back then, she told herself that Mahaz was only showing off for his friend, and that he hadn't intended to hurt her. Rationalizations that shepherded her through the dinner and the next day without confrontation. But his words still stay with her years later, growing a toxic mix of resentment, shame and rage like poisonous mushrooms in a terrarium.

If she were totally honest with herself, the pain of those words stems from how they expose her deepest fear that she is an imposter in her job. A college dropout, Juliana wishes she could be as confident about her work as she is about being a mother. But the bottom line is that she has more experience as a housewife than in the working world. She'd put in serious effort to tip the balance, taking classes on marketing and public relations at UCLA Extension, and joining the local chapter of the Public Relations Society to beef up her skills. But some days, she feels the deep chasm between her and the bevy of young, educated professionals who stream through Mahaz's office having deep conversations on intricate information security matters she knows little about.

Funny how life works. She had started talking to Mahaz about finding a job because she wanted out of the San Fernando Valley homeroom mom crowd. In wealthy and competitive Sherman Oaks—where bumping into pop stars like Miley Cyrus or Britney Spears could happen at the nail salon or the organic farmer's market—people were constantly trying to outdo one another. Whether it was private school tuition that cost more per year than Harvard University or equestrian lessons or birthday party movie screenings in private home theaters, the relentless beat of one-upmanship had worn her out. Juliana had thought working in an office would be a sanctuary from it, but the escape turned out to be an even swap of one set of problems for another.

She daintily tries to dab her eyes dry without smearing her mascara, all that was left of the make-up she had applied this morning. She grips the granite countertop with one hand and looks in the mirror. The face that looks back at her could be her ghost. Pale lips and cheeks punctuated by her red nose and dark, deep circles under watery eyes. She studies herself in the harsh light for a moment before closing her eyes so she no longer has to see the humiliation in them.

A toilet flushes. She thought she was alone. She blinks and tries to take a deep breath but she only shudders with the effort.

Allyn Carriaga, one of her husband's teaching assistants, traipses her way to the sink with her eyes on the floor. *She is avoiding eye contact*, Juliana thinks. *She's embarrassed for me. Or by me.*

Juliana pats the skin under her eyes with the rough paper towel while Allyn rubs soap on her hands with a surgeon's thoroughness under a stream of running water.

"I'm sure it will get better," Allyn says, finally meeting her eyes in the mirror. "I pray for your son all the time."

My son? Juliana is startled by the sudden intimacy, even though she knows that her seventeen-year-old son Omar's hydrocephalus, better known as water on the brain, is no secret among the staff and faculty. Sure, let Allyn think that she was crying about Omar. There is certainly enough sorrow and pain there to last a lifetime. She'd cried a thousand rivers over him in emergency rooms and hospital beds. But on a daily basis, she blinks back those tears and does everything she can to make her son's life as normal as possible. And today is one of those wonderful, ordinary days, with Omar happily at school, doing the ordinary things that teenagers do.

What does it matter what Allyn thinks anyway? These co-workers aren't confidantes or friends or even lunch buddies, just fellow travelers in a shared workplace. Let her leave the restroom and plop down at her cubicle and tell the other research assistants that poor Juliana is sobbing in the restroom about Omar. Better that than the more salacious gossip about the health of her marriage, how Mahaz treats her, and why she puts up with it. These twenty-something graduate students know nothing about the compromises you have to make in marriage and life. The messiness of life is still theoretical to them, so they can afford to shake their heads and proclaim they'd never stay with a man who cheated on them.

"Thanks for your prayers, Allyn," she says, because her role as Mahaz's wife is always to be graceful and kind to his staff. "We appreciate them." She sniffles and runs the corner of the paper towel under her lower lashes to capture the last of the tears.

Allyn slips out the door and Juliana counts to ten to let her make her way down the hallway. She gives herself a big smile in the mirror, throws the crumpled towel in the trash bin and swings the door open. As her daughter would say, you've got this.

But her humiliation isn't over yet. She hears Mahaz's laugh and turns toward the sound. He walks down the hall with Kendall Sage, away from her. The woman leans into him. You couldn't fit a cell phone between them as they stride toward his private office, footsteps echoing on the travertine floor. A rock lodges in Juliana's chest as she watches them enter the office, Mahaz's hand on her shoulder, guiding her inside.

She thinks of that song about setting the one you love free and wonders if in fact she still loves him at all. If she did, wouldn't she chase after them, leveling accusations and telling that woman to stay away from her man? How had she arrived at this bitter, sad place of resignation?

Chapter 3

Ken Oakey downs the tiny can of an energy boosting drink in one swallow. It is his second one of the day. His heavy lunch is making him sleepy. Very sleepy. He considers stretching out on the black leather sofa that spans a bank of windows overlooking the Los Angeles National Cemetery in Westwood, but he suspects he'd sleep too long and then be awake all night.

"Let's go looking for trouble," he says out loud, to no one but himself. He turns his attention to one of four computer monitors sitting on his desk to see which spammers or malware proponents he has trapped today in his corner of the world wide web.

He makes his living doing a variety of odd jobs related to computer network security and stability: managing computer systems for a few small businesses, playing security expert on the witness stand for different law firms, and doing a little of what they call "white hat" security on a freelance basis. He likes the white hat work the best because it allows him to use for good the skills he developed as a pimply-faced teenager hacking into Pacific Bell phone lines.

He runs his eyes over the white text flickering on his black screen where Honeynet Two, or Edith as he likes to call her, lists out the day's infections. The average computer user has become accustomed to spam mail over the years and knows to ignore the emails from Nigerian princes and the fake Viagra ads. But still, enough of them click on the links to keep the bad guys in business. And that in turn keeps guys like Ken in business, fighting what some have estimated as 82,000 malicious software, or malware, threats a day.

Criminals, Ken likes to say, only have to get it right once in a while. White hats like Ken have to get it right one hundred percent of the time. That's twenty-four hours a day, holidays included. The black hats are rattling doorknobs around the clock from anywhere in the world, ready to exploit that one door left unlocked or that one window left open.

The honeynet today has recorded eighty-seven rattles on the doorknob and the day is far from over. A quick check of the time code at the top of the screen shows it isn't even two o'clock in the afternoon yet in Los Angeles.

He scans the list of entries in the intruder log and sees one that grabs his interest. It has an internet protocol address from Moldova. That is notable, but not interesting to Ken. Moldova borders Ukraine, one of the world's most notorious countries for cyber crime and production of malware. It is such a haven for black hat hackers and fraudsters that its third-largest city, Odessa, is known as the premier marketplace for stolen credit and debit card information.

What is interesting about the entry is how *new* it is. One of the characteristics Ken tracks about each invader is how well it is known to the slate of antivirus companies that combat malware. Most of the intruders are what security people call the usual suspects. Exploit and FakeAV are two of the newer names, but some of the big viruses like Melissa, ILOVEYOU, Storm and others have been around for years.

This new one isn't recognized by any of the big companies that track malware. And this is what wakes Ken up out of his afternoon torpor.

He swivels to look at the third computer monitor to the right, where his email box is filling up with messages from several of the security-geek lists he subscribes to. "Anyone else under attack?" reads the subject line of one from his friend Niels Jansen who runs a security consulting firm in Amsterdam. "Moldova invasion" reads another from Henri Braga, security director at a big internet service provider in Brazil.

He shoots off a response to Niels that he'd seen it too, and by the time he swings back to take a look at Edith, his pretty little honeynet is covered in entry after entry of this same worm. If regular malware reproduces like a bunny rabbit with a hundred bunnies a year, then this new one has reproductive rates closer to a flea laying five thousand eggs in the same year.

Ken leans into the ergonomic back of his desk chair and takes a deep breath. It is going to be a long night.

He makes three phone calls in quick succession. First is to his mother asking her to feed and walk his neurotic dachshund, Tilly. The second call is a voicemail message to his buddy Jack cancelling their tennis game that night. And the third reaches Mohamed "Mo" Mansour, data analyst.

"Mo," he says. "Edith has an intruder and we need you to strip him down."

Chapter 4

With some relief, Juliana pulls off of congested Vanowen Boulevard and into the valet parking for Valley Presbyterian Hospital's emergency room. People talk about the San Fernando Valley as though it is suburbia with picket fences and strip malls but it is easily as crowded and hard to find parking as any part of downtown or west Los Angeles. Juliana and Omar walk through the sliding glass doors of emergency, with fifteen-year-old Leila trailing behind, her fingers flying over her smart phone as she texts someone. Where Omar is saddled with chronic pain and dozens of surgeries to relieve the pressure of fluids on his brain, Leila is the picture of health and youth. Juliana no longer tries to understand why.

Mothers are supposed to fix things. The fact that she can't help Omar with this, other than hold his hand and shuttle him to endless appointments with doctors and specialists, has broken her heart every single day since his diagnosis at five years old.

The nurse at the intake desk greets each of them by name with a smile. Juliana smiles big to cover up that she doesn't remember his name.

"I think the shunt's not working properly," Juliana says. She doesn't say the word "again." It isn't the nurse's fault, or the doctor's, or Omar's that the shunt needs constant adjustment.

"We'll get you right back, Omar, don't you worry," the nurse says.

Omar tries to say thank you but it comes out slurred. Difficulty speaking is one of the symptoms that the shunt doctors had inserted six months ago isn't operating correctly. Often he also suffers acute headaches, dizziness, vision problems and vomiting. He never complains about the headaches, Juliana reflects, but they must be terrible. He's told her that the sensation is like waves of pain crashing over him. When she sees his eyes glaze during those times, she thinks of it as him turning inward to see his brain under pressure, squeezing tiny veins and soft grey cells and holding them down tight so they can't function properly.

"He wants to know if Dr. Godin is here?" Leila asks. Juliana wonders if Omar persuaded Leila to ask if the prettiest young ER doctor is working tonight, or if Leila anticipated his request. Her two children have a tight connection, going back as far as Juliana can remember. When they were very young, before Omar was diagnosed with this condition, he used to do all the talking for Leila. "Leila wants some milk." "Leila wants to wear her red T-shirt." He talked for her so much that she never really learned how to answer for herself. She lagged in development behind the other kids in her age group and had to go into special education classes for a while.

Now, a decade later, she speaks for him.

Juliana has a similar bond with her little brother, Drew. As far back as she can remember, Drew has been her biggest fan. He is serious, smart and fiercely protective of her. She is so glad her children have developed the same kind of relationship. It makes the world easier to deal with to have an ally and a sidekick.

They slide into adjacent vinyl covered seats and each pulls out their smart phones and starts tapping and sliding the screens. Omar puts headphones on to listen to music. Juliana dials Mahaz.

Five rings, no pick up. She leaves a message that they are at Valley Presbyterian in emergency and hangs up without asking where he is. He'd texted her a few hours before she left the office that he would work late tonight on the social media strategy for the Center. She didn't need to be a part of it, he said. He'd fill her in later.

She certainly doesn't want to be a part of it. Kendall flicking her hair and fluttering her eyes and laughing at his jokes, and him eating up the attention. It has been years since she and Mahaz have turned that kind of attention on one another.

Juliana remembers the pleasures of being seduced by him all those years ago. God, he could be so charming. He used to look at her like she was the only woman in the world. In those early days, he had asked her questions about her childhood, her dreams, her favorite foods and where she liked to shop. She had been ready to sleep with him on the first date but he deposited her in her dorm room with a chaste kiss, extracting a promise from her for a second date the next night.

When exactly did he stop loving her like that?

She glances at Leila and Omar. Omar's eyes are shut and his body is entirely still. He looks like his father with the straight nose, impossible good looks, infectious smile. Leila types furiously with two thumbs on her smart phone, biting her lip. Her long eyelashes nearly touch her high cheekbones as she narrows her eyes with concentration.

Juliana's mind falls into a well-worn groove. *When they're in college, and if things haven't gotten better with Mahaz, then I'll leave him.*

"Omar Al-Dossari, come on down!" A blond nurse in polka-dot scrubs gestures at the wheelchair before her. "You're our next contestant!"

Juliana nudges Omar and the three of them head to the door.

"How many times have we been here?" Leila says.

"Too many to count," Juliana replies.

"Fifteen," Omar says.

Chapter 5

Ken wakes roughly, from a dream where he was walking through an endless set of corridors, to see Mo's face above his. Mo has dark rings under his brown eyes and his brown curly hair is disheveled and standing up straight in a few patches.

Ken rubs his eyes and sits upright. Mo hands him a cup of a coffee, warm and fragrant, and he takes a sip.

"Let me show you what I've got," Mo says. He sits down on the couch next to Ken and opens his laptop.

"Edith's intruder is a nasty little fellow," he says. "I'm going to have to break it down in object code."

Ken's eyes widen in a subtle show of admiration for Mo and for whoever is behind the worm. Most program analysts work within one of many computer programming languages like C, Ada and FORTRAN, and Mo does that too. But he is also a master at object code, the most basic layer of computer programming where commands are stripped down to the ones and zeros that form the language of machines. To put it simply, Mo speaks "machine."

"Whoever designed this is very smart," he says. "They covered their tracks very neatly so it took me some time just to find the file buried in services.exe."

Ken gives a low whistle over his coffee cup. Edith's intruder has not just broken in to her house, but he has made himself a sandwich, sat on the couch with his feet on the coffee table and taken control of every system.

"They used three layers of encryption, so that's going to take me some time to break through. But it's clear to me we are dealing with somebody very good. Could be state-sponsored hacking. I mean, it's really state of the art."

"There's an SSRWG call today, so give me what you got and I'll see what the others have," Ken says. In the land of computer security and all things internet, acronyms are as essential as coffee. SSRWG stands for Security, Stability and Resiliency Working Group, and is a loose affiliation of security geeks who meet to discuss the latest happenings in their field and to write policy advice papers to governments and other internet geeks. Spread out all over the world, the group works virtually for the most part and comes together in person only a few times a year.

A few hours later, Ken is dialed in with the faces of eight other security guys, including Henri in Brazil and Niels in the Netherlands. All of them have been trading information about the worm for the past fifteen hours. None have gotten more than a few hours sleep in the past day.

"You think the end game is a botnet?" Niels asks the group. Criminals use bots and botnets, or groups of these computers, to send out spam and malicious software. The typical computer user at home may be infected and never discover it.

"At the rate it is spreading, it's going to be an army, maybe of millions," says Dan Kowalczyk, head of digital crimes for PersonalPro, one of the world's biggest software companies. Their operating system runs seventy-five percent of the world's computers. "We're infected too." Dan is the most corporate of them all. Where the rest of them wear T-shirts emblazoned with superhero characters or geek jokes, Dan sports a crisp white button-down shirt with a striped tie. The last time Ken had worn a tie was high school graduation, and only then because his mother had insisted.

"Whoever it is walked in through the barn door your software security left open," Henri says, leaning into the camera as though he wants to jump out of the monitor at Dan.

Ken shakes his head. Henri tends to say whatever is on his mind with no filter, which makes him a lively conversationalist but also tends to offend others right and left. Everyone on the call knows the worm is exploiting a well-known security hole in PersonalPro software, but no one thinks that is Dan's personal fault.

"Hey, no pointing fingers here, Henri," Ken says. "Not productive."

Henri leans back from the camera. He is used to being told to cool it.

"Anyone cracked it open yet to see what it does? Mo said it has three layers of encryption," Ken says.

"We're close," Dan says. "We have learned one thing."

He pauses to shift the call from his speaker phone to his personal handset. "We think it's set to go off in six days."

Six days. Whoever has created this thing has given it just six days to spread before it goes active.

"We need to get more people involved," Ken says. "I'll put a call out on some of the mailing lists, and let's regroup in twelve hours."

Chapter 6

Juliana stands by the hospital room window, watching cars whiz by on Vanowen, while she listens to the deep, restful breathing of Omar and Leila sleeping. Omar has been admitted and scheduled for a shunt revision the next morning at five a.m.

She is emotional and tries not to think too much about what might happen if this time, Omar doesn't pull through the now-routine procedure. Brain surgery, no matter how common, brings with it a panoply of risks such as swelling, infection, coma, loss of speech, seizures or stroke. Most days, she stuffs the terror of these worst-case scenarios deep below the surface, showing only optimism and cheer. At least while her children are awake. But at this late hour, with them asleep, with Mahaz God-knows-where, the surface has been nicked. Anxiety and fear pour out of her like blood.

When Omar was born, she'd held him nearly constantly those first four weeks, the neonatal period they warn you about, when your baby is at his most vulnerable. She'd worried so much about Omar dying in his crib—needlessly, it seems now—while simultaneously fretting about losing her own life and leaving this precious, tiny creature behind. No mother wants to disappear from her children's lives when they are young.

But no mother wants to outlive her child either. She has been facing that particular horror show since his dizzy spells and headaches and that first terrifying seizure were named hydrocephalus by the pediatric neurologist. The year Omar started kindergarten.

After that diagnosis, she blamed herself, obsessing over a running tally of things she had done wrong during her pregnancy and after he was born. That glass of white wine in the first trimester. How often she forgot to take her pre-natal vitamins. The time she had clumsily let Omar's head hit the changing table. Mahaz had been her rock then, holding her tight and assuring her that it wasn't her fault that their beautiful baby boy was suffering. More importantly, he made sure she knew they were in it together.

She had been afraid of so many things. First and foremost, she had been terrified of losing Omar, or that he would struggle to speak, think, walk or take care of himself. She also feared that her marriage wouldn't endure the stresses of having a seriously ill child. But Omar had endured and even excelled in most of his classes at school. As for the marriage, she had not given Mahaz enough credit all those years ago. He had come to every doctor and specialist appointment. He had scoured the internet for information as much as she did, reading the books she ordered by the dozens about the disease and how other families coped with it. They had been a team.

Maybe things haven't been good between them lately, but she won't forget his strength and love those weeks and months after Omar's first hospitalization and diagnosis. Those actions—kind, caring—conflict with the scene still replaying itself in her head: Mahaz and that woman, leaning into each other, laughing.

She leans into the windowpane, resting her forehead on the glass. Her breath fogs the cool surface. She and Mahaz need to clear the air about the marriage. She knows it deep in her heart. But knowing you need to have a conversation, and actually doing it are two very different things. You have to go into a conversation about the state of the marriage ready to hear what the other person has to say, and she doesn't know if she can face that right now. She has to find the right time, and the courage.

Her phone pings, a soft bell. It can only be Mahaz at this late hour. She picks her phone up from the bedside table. It is a little after midnight. "I'm parking," his text reads. "I'll take Leila home so she can go to school tomorrow."

Years of taking Omar in and out of hospitals means they have the process down to a science. He knows without asking that she will stay with their son, and that Leila should get back on her regular schedule as soon as possible.

She slumps into the chair, gripping the phone. She forces herself to concentrate on her breathing so she can present a calm front to Mahaz. Someone somewhere had taught her a technique for calming the body with breath, by inhaling for five seconds, holding the breath for six seconds, and exhaling for seven seconds. If she can force herself to do it more than five times in a row, it will calm her down. One-two-three-four-five. One-two-three-four-five-six. One-two-three-four-five-six-seven.

She hears the ding of the elevator, followed by fast footsteps in the hall. Mahaz has changed from work clothes into dark grey sweatpants and a black hoodie sweatshirt with the UCLA logo on it. In the darkened room he looks like the graduate student she fell in love with all those years ago. One-two-three-four—

He kisses Juliana on top of her head and she smells the cloying vanilla scent that the social media consultant had been wearing when they met earlier. She stops breathing and flexes her jaw, feeling the anger rise in her like bile in her throat. So much for a calm presence.

"How's he doing?" he whispers.

"Tired," she says, her tone clipped. She feels the strong urge to push him away. "Where have you been?"

"Working late, I told you," he says. Her eyes search his for the truth but find only walls of deflection. He doesn't even flinch. He pulls out his phone and fiddles with it for a moment, its screen lighting his face. "I'm trying to put together my presentation for the Internet Unique Identifiers Authority meeting next week in Brussels."

The IUIA runs the internet's phone book, or domain name system, collecting money every time a domain name is sold. Mahaz loves being invited to speak about info security at their meetings because they are nearly always in five-star hotels in major cities around the world. He had taken her to one in Prague, back when things were still good between them. A romantic getaway. She tries to remember it but now she only sees that woman's face instead of hers, this time on the streets of Brussels.

The question swirls in her head for a few moments before leaping out of her lips. "With Kendall Sage?"

Her voice leaks bitterness. Even she can hear it. Tears spring to her eyes. *You're tired*, she thinks. *Stop this.* But still the words come out. "Why did you have to embarrass me like that today in front of her?"

"Embarrass you how?" he says, narrowing his eyes like a cat playing with a mouse it has cornered.

"Making fun of the social media page I had set up," she says.

Juliana is sweating despite the chill of the hospital room air. She feels exposed and petty. Ill-equipped for a badly-timed fight. Why did she start this conversation with their children sleeping just three feet away? This isn't how she'd wanted to do this. She wants to sound pulled together, logical, an adult woman expressing her feelings to her husband. Instead, she is a shaky, emotional wreck, blurting out feelings like a teenage girl.

Mahaz stares at her, his thick eyebrows knitting together in concern. His head tilts to one side. "I was just being honest with her. If we're going to pay for her expertise, then we should be honest about our needs. You are the first to admit you don't know anything about social media."

There it is. His dismissal of her, done with such practice and skill that she barely feels the knife go in. He waits for her to agree as she usually does, but tonight her brain and her mouth won't go along with it. She is too furious, not just that he'd belittled her but that he'd actually picked the social media consultant over his son in the hospital tonight. That is a new low in their strained relationship.

"You didn't have to say it like you did in front of her, Mahaz," she says.

He suddenly laughs. "Oh, I see what is happening here," he says. "You are jealous of Kendall Sage. It's because she's pretty and young, yes? You are threatened by her."

Fury clouds her eyes and blood pounds in her ears. She suddenly knows exactly what the phrase "seeing red" means. She wants to pummel him with her fists and wipe the arrogance off his face. Her breath comes in short bursts as her body prepares for fight or flight.

"Do you want a divorce, Mahaz?"

The words come out of her in a whisper, without her conscious consent. Something in her has broken free and taken control, urging her to take their troubles head on.

His palm hits her cheek with a loud slap. Her skin burns like a thousand bee stings. His eyes go icy cold, and she drops her gaze to the floor, stunned, not sure what to do.

"Do not think of it. You do that and I will take the children to Saudi Arabia," he says, his voice a low hiss. "You will not see them again."

His words ricochet around her brain and slam into her chest like bullets. She stumbles back a few steps, away from him. It is as if she stepped off a cliff, and can do nothing to stop her fall. There is no going back.

Mahaz steps to where Leila sleeps in the reclining armchair and shakes her awake. Juliana watches, horrified, as he smiles sweetly at their daughter and guides her out of the room without looking at his wife. As though she didn't exist.

Chapter 7

The programmer is delighted to see how quickly the discussions on the various cyber security fora have turned to his creation *Chrysalide*.

More than four hundred messages have accrued in the worm's new discussion string about how quick the worm has burrowed her way silently into their computers. He expected them to figure this out quickly. Even as skilled as he is, there is no way to conceal such a massive infection. *Chrysalide* is performing her first job, and that is to infect and link together as many computers as possible into his army of obedient bots. It is hard to do this without someone in the security world noticing. But thousands and thousands of botnets exist, most used by criminals for money-making schemes.

His botnet has a different purpose. It will take the security community some time to figure this out.

And by then, if everything goes as he planned, it will be too late.

Chapter 8

Shunt adjusted with no complications, Omar was discharged from the hospital the day after his surgery and is comfortably resting in his bedroom. Home for the first time since his hospitalization, Juliana sits at the kitchen table and reads the email from Mahaz for a second time. It still doesn't make sense to her. Addressed to someone she has never heard of named Ken Oakey, the email is a word salad of acronyms and techie lingo that she is only somewhat familiar with. By reading the full chain of back-and-forths between Mahaz and this Ken Oakey, she gets the gist of a request. Some kind of computer virus-type thing that they call a worm is spreading fast and they want Mahaz to join a global task force to stop it.

The request to Mahaz makes sense, of course. Mahaz is one of the world's experts on security.

What doesn't make sense to Juliana is why Mahaz would direct them to work with her. His email to her to "handle it" is one of few communications they've exchanged since his threat at the hospital. Is this another of Mahaz's games to humiliate her? It has to be. It also has to be a slap to this Ken Oakey, whoever he is, that Mahaz isn't taking his warning of the worm's dangers very seriously. After all, Mahaz has research assistants and graduate students studying malware and worms and viruses just like this. One of them is the obvious choice for the task force, not his non-techie wife.

But she isn't inclined to push any further with Mahaz. She does not doubt for a minute his threat to take the children to Saudi Arabia and out of her reach. She finds herself only surprised she hasn't foreseen it happening. The possibility has always been there, she knows it now. And she, an American who couldn't put a sentence together in Arabic, would be completely ineffective in navigating the Saudi legal system for custody.

Her husband's close friendship with Prince Abdul, and all his connections in the Royal Family, would make it even harder for her to find an attorney to represent her, or any allies in that country. So, if Mahaz carries out his threat, she would join the hundreds of other non-Muslim women who struggle against the country's laws and customs for the privilege of supervised visits with her children. Any kind of split custody would be out of the question.

She had thought Mahaz was different, but he is using their children as pawns. And though she hates him for it, she doesn't see what she can do right in this minute except for nothing at all. To act is futile, anything that looks like victory would be the opposite. She pictures Leila's face, frantic and demanding, asking her over and over again, how could you let this happen to me?

How could she? Is there even one answer? The laws are against her. She has no money, no influence. She realizes she is scared of Mahaz, and this empties out her heart. The children she loves more than anything in the world are half his. She is trapped. And she has no one to blame but herself.

She tries to concentrate on the email and put the threat out of her mind but the anxiety wins out. She leaves the laptop on the table and walks into Mahaz's office to look for Leila's and Omar's passports, thinking she will hide them away.

Sunlight streams through the French doors and onto the hand-stitched silk carpet. His maple desk looks as clean as one in a furniture store showroom. No papers litter its surface or the black leather blotter. His monitor and wireless keyboard sit in one corner of the desk, rendered useless by the fact he's taken his laptop with him to work. A fat, heavy black pen is the only other object allowed to rest on the surface.

It smells like him in here, so much that icy fear creeps into her stomach. She imagines him popping out from behind the potted plant or rising up from the sofa and demanding to know why she is snooping around. After years of partnership, he has become her enemy.

She takes a deep breath and slides open the top drawer where they keep the family's passports. Only hers is in the drawer. In a panic, she pulls all the papers and cords and pens and little bits of junk and throws them on the floor, then sifts through them on her hands and knees.

He is a step ahead of her. She opens the lower desk drawer and flips through the neatly filed bills and private school tuition invoices and insurance statements. The passports aren't there either.

She already knows it is hopeless but she goes through the other drawers methodically only to get the same result. She considers pulling the dozens of books on computer coding, security, leadership and management off the shelves and flipping through the pages of each, like a detective in a novel, but something tells her not to bother. Mahaz probably has the passports with him, or has hidden them in his office at UCLA. He was home yesterday. And he knows her. He knows how fiercely she loves her children. He knows she would do anything for them. She would lay her life down for them. And he is using that against her.

She returns the papers to the drawer without caring if he notices the disarray and takes her own passport and puts it in her purse. She'll leave a sign for him that she knows what he's done. And could she really trust him not to destroy her own, just to delay her from following him if it in fact comes to that?

Juliana returns to the kitchen and types a fast email to her brother Drew, inviting him to lunch tomorrow or the next day. She would give him her passport for safekeeping, but more importantly confide in him about Mahaz's threat. She has to tell someone. The therapist she'd seen a few times for depression after Omar started kindergarten comes to mind, but is quickly rejected. All she'd wanted to do was to "smooth things out" by putting Juliana on anti-depressants, an option Juliana thought was extreme at the time.

No way she'd tell her parents yet. She loves her parents but she can't bear to disappoint them or worse, make them fearful. Too much history. All of the conversations they had had about cultural differences and how hard it could be to build a life with a man from a strict Islamic upbringing are so far in the past they are nearly forgotten. They had accepted Mahaz with open arms as a son-in-law and finally as father to their grandchildren, and if there had been a sigh of relief that he didn't insist on raising the children as Muslim, they had never said so to Juliana. Mahaz had been eager to acclimate to all things American when they were first married and this had put Juliana's family and friends at ease because they could understand that desire. It was familiar and welcome.

She clicks back to the email from Mahaz and hits reply-all.

Dear Ken: I'm happy to help however I can. Let me know when the first meeting is and I'll be there.

She signs it Juliana Wareham Al-Dossari, Communications Director, taking care to include her job title so this Ken Oakey would realize she is more of a layperson than a techie. She figures he'd realize that Mahaz is giving him the brush-off, then he would write her off and not even send the invitation to the meeting.

She clicks through the rest of her emails to see if there are any from reporters looking for quotes from Mahaz on either this worm or other security issues, but no one has reached out.

A new email pings the inbox. From Ken Oakey.

Juliana-glad to have someone from UCLA's Center for Info Tech on board. We'll meet at 21:00 UTC.

She does the mental math to convert the time zone and figures out the meeting is in four hours. Even though it would make the day rushed, she responds that she'll be there. Then she shuts the laptop and checks on Omar. She'll just keep putting one foot in front of the other, having realized a long time ago that that is the only way to get through the day.

Chapter 9

Juliana stands uneasily in the door frame and watches Omar sleep. His chest rises and falls with warm breath, his legs are tangled in the sheets. His computer tablet rests on his thighs. In this moment, he is not in pain. She closes her eyes and smells his teenage boy scent of sweat and body spray and dirty socks.

She knows Omar's room better than her own, the one she shares with Mahaz. She'd spent so much time in here, nursing her son, holding his hand, reading him stories, that she'd memorized every corner of his room. She opens her eyes to find the place where the green-striped wallpaper had started to peel off the wall. Underneath, she knows, is the secret drawing of a dinosaur that Omar did when he was seven. On the bookshelf, a finger-sized action figure named Stanley lies face down on a stack of graphic novels. A lei of bright purple silk flowers hangs from the headboard, a remnant of his eighth grade graduation party. The relics of a boy's life, but none of it, not one thing, untouched by a memory of his sickness.

She's prepared his whole life to lose him to this disease. But now, the threat comes from his father.

She runs her hand over his brown curls, pressing her fingers lightly on his forehead to check for fever. No sign.

The home phone rings, jolting her out of her reverie. She grabs the cordless handset from Omar's dresser and answers on the first ring, walking quickly into the hallway and down the stairs so as not to wake Omar.

Her brother Drew wants to come over for a cup of coffee. He was in her neighborhood at one of the city's water pumping stations when he saw her email, he says.

"Yes, yes," she says, curling both hands around the phone and feeling her brother's calm and safe presence. Hearing his voice makes her feel better, and she needs a distraction.

"What are you doing in the valley anyway?" she says, not wanting to hang up yet. In fact, she wants to talk to him until he arrives at her door.

"Weird computer network problems today," he says. "Some of the pumping and treatment systems are acting oddly. Probably some kind of glitch or virus or something."

"Huh," she says. She tells him about the task force, wondering aloud if the two are related.

"I don't know," Drew says. "We get hit with technical issues all the time. I feel like I'm a servant to the computer systems as it is. I'm just waiting for them to develop a consciousness and come to life like in that movie. What was that computer's name? Hal?"

"Hal," she says. "Yes, *2001: A Space Odyssey*. One of Mahaz's favorite movies."

"How is Mahaz?"

"Let's talk about that when you get here," she says. "I'm home with Omar. He had another surgery to adjust the shunt. He's home recovering. Sleeping now."

She goes into the kitchen to make a fresh pot of coffee, taking pleasure in the slow steps of rinsing the pot, grinding the beans, pouring the water. Routine comes easy. She switches the coffee maker on just as she hears the knock on the door.

"Drew!" she says, then promptly bursts into tears on his shoulder.

He stands there for a moment in her doorway, absorbing her sobs and shaking shoulders before he squeezes her shoulders and whispers they should go inside.

"I'm so glad you came," she says into his crisp cotton shirt.

Drew hugs her tightly then steps back to see her face. He gently wipes a tear from her cheek with his thumb. "I'm glad I was nearby, Julie," he says. Her family still calls her by her childhood name. Mahaz had been the one to persuade her to use her full name, Juliana, instead of Julie. He thought it was more regal.

"I made a fresh pot of coffee," she says, walking to the kitchen as he follows.

He sits down at the breakfast table and rat-tat-tats his fingers on the wood. Drew is one of those people who has to be in constant motion. His hands and feet tap staccato rhythms on whatever surface they contact. His legs shake and bounce as though driven by electrical currents. If there were a pen on a table, he would flip it endlessly.

Most people who don't know him associate the shaking with nervousness, but Juliana knows better. The shaking is unconscious and more a sign that he is deep in thought or absorbed in a task than that he is distracted or anxious.

"What is going on with you and Mahaz?" he asks her.

Juliana feels her body stiffen as she pulls mugs out of the cupboard. She takes a deep breath one-two-three-four-five, and then places them on the dark granite countertop with a clang. Too tense to hold her breath, she skips right to exhale. One-two-three-four-five-six-seven.

"I asked him if he wanted a divorce. Then he told me he would take the kids to Saudi Arabia if I did that." Juliana speaks with her back to Drew. She doesn't want to see his first reaction. She leaves out the slap he had delivered to her, and the calculating fury in his eyes. Her brother and her parents can't know about that, not yet. They need her to be safe in her home, dealing only with the challenges of a marriage that is ending, not dealing with an abusive husband. She isn't ready to take that step yet.

"A divorce," Drew repeats. "Has this been brewing for a while?" He is careful in his word choice, Juliana notices. Has he seen this coming?

"Of course," she says matter-of-factly as she pours coffee into the mugs and brings them to the table. "These things don't happen overnight, do they?"

Drew's blue eyes skitter from hers and focus on the coffee mug. They both watch as steam rises a few inches out of the mug then disappears into the air.

"He hired a new social media consultant. Perky little thing named Kendall Sage. She's going to get him on Twitter." She forces a smile but Drew doesn't respond. He continues to look sadly into his cup of coffee as though it held all the words she's left unspoken. Juliana lets the smile fade from her face. It isn't that funny.

"Do you have a lawyer?" he asks. Just like her brother to go straight into problem-solving mode.

"No," she says, embarrassed she hasn't thought that far ahead. But really, she hadn't known she was going to say that to Mahaz. But his reaction had doubled her conviction.

"Do you have your own money? Separate from his?"

"No," she says. "He never wanted that. I do have my retirement account from work and there is the household account. He doesn't check that very often."

"Well, let's start there," he says. "You need to start building up a savings account of your own, just in case. And you need to find a lawyer. I'll ask Cathy to recommend someone." Cathy, Drew's wife, works as a paralegal at a law firm specializing in estate planning.

Drew's cell phone erupts with an angry buzz. They both jump. He pulls it out of his pocket and looks at the screen.

"It's the control center," he says. "I have to take this."

She takes a sip of the coffee. It tastes bitter but she likes it.

Drew does more listening than talking on the call, getting up to pace from her kitchen to the family room and back again. He says okay a few times then ends the call.

"I've got to go," he says apologetically. "But I'm going to call Cathy once I'm in the car and ask her to start getting some referrals to attorneys for you. And we'll help you with money if you need us to."

He stands up and drains the coffee mug like it is a shot of whiskey. She presses her head into his chest again and wraps her arms around him. She whispers thank you as he hugs her tight.

"So what happened? What's the emergency?" she says.

"Water treatment systems aren't responding," he says. "We may have to ask for emergency rationing."

"In a neighborhood or something?" she asks, her mind still on the idea of divorce attorneys and banking accounts and passports.

"No, Julie. This is big. This would be for all of Los Angeles."

He leaves so quickly she forgets to slip him her passport for safekeeping.

Chapter 10

Mahaz's mother, Yalima, wears Western clothes and no *hijab* when she comes to Juliana's house to sit with Omar. She had grown up as a diplomat's daughter and married a wealthy Saudi who took her all over the world for his oil business. Yalima is more a citizen of the world than of any one country.

She still keeps a townhouse in Riyadh and travels back there twice a year, but she spends the rest of her time living in a three-bedroom apartment in Beverly Hills and entertaining friends. Mahaz is her only child.

Juliana puts her best face on, not wanting to let Yalima know there is trouble afoot in her marriage. There may be a time in the future when Yalima could be an ally to her, but she isn't ready to broach the topic today. Instead, she smiles and embraces Yalima, breathing in her Hermès perfume and taking care not to rub the rose pink lipstick she had just applied onto her mother-in-law's fine winter white blazer. She can tell by the cut and the stitching that Yalima did not pick it up from the Macy's sale rack, like the jersey dress Juliana has on.

"So Mahaz is keeping you busy with work?" Yalima asks with a wink of her almond-shaped brown eyes. "You know I am happy to come take care of Omar whenever you need. It is no imposition. Today, you rescued me from another lunch talking about plastic surgery with old ladies. Butt implants. These should be for the young, yes?"

Juliana smiles. Yalima is always outspoken and funny. She wishes Mahaz inherited more of her sense of humor. His dead seriousness makes for dull conversation sometimes, even though he is a very eloquent speaker.

"You can see I don't need them," Juliana says, jutting her hip out in an exaggerated pose. "I got mine by having two kids and no time to work out."

"Yes, much cheaper," Yalima says. She grasps Juliana's hand and leads her to the staircase. "And how is dear Omar?"

"Sleeping, less pain," she says.

"When will all this adjusting and readjusting be over for that poor boy? Do these doctors not know what they are doing? Or do they think he is a guinea pig for their experiments and not a teenage boy?"

"I don't know," Juliana says. "He said yesterday that it was his fifteenth time in the emergency room. My heart broke in pieces for him. He never complains, you know."

"Well, I brought his favorite honey cakes," Yalima says, shaking a brown paper bag in her hand. "And what time is pretty Leila home from school?"

"She should be here no later than four. One of the other mothers will drop her off. And please get her to at least start her homework. I should be back before six."

"My friend Rana is putting together a catalog for her clothing line," Yalima says. "She is looking for models and I told her about the beauty of my granddaughter. I told her I would take some pictures of her today to show her."

"Modeling?" Juliana says. "Well, I know Leila would love it but Mahaz?"

"You leave Mahaz to me," Yalima says. "Do you mind if I take the pictures to show Rana? I'll just take a few snaps with my phone to email her. If she picks Leila, then very well. If not, no harm done."

"I guess so," Juliana says. Leila has the long, thin frame that makes for a good clothing model, and a pretty face framed by long, straight black hair. "But no losing weight for it, she's skinny enough as it is."

"And no butt implants, I promise," Yalima says.

Chapter 11

Juliana walks into the meeting room at the DoubleTree Hotel in Culver City not sure what to expect. About twenty people mill about in the space, mostly casually dressed in T-shirts and jeans. Self-conscious of being dressed too much like a "corporate suit," she slips out of the black blazer and smooths her hands over the soft jersey of her dress. At least she wears flats instead of heels.

Everyone seems to know everyone else, and as she has come to expect at these techie gatherings, she is one of two women in a room of twenty men.

A good-looking, trim man with broad shoulders and a thick neck fringed in coarse black hair approaches her.

"You must be Juliana," he says, extending a hand. She shifts her laptop bag on her shoulder and offers her own.

"Ken Oakey?" She'd expected to see a pale, unshaven mess, the kind of guy who spends all his time drinking energy drinks and staring into the light of his computer monitors. But Ken has a healthy, fit appearance. His T-shirt, which reads "One Nation, Under Surveillance," fits him snugly. He clearly spends some time at the gym as well as in front of the computer. Often the two don't go together.

"I've met your husband a couple of times," he says. "He's brilliant."

"Yes, yes," she says, putting on her indulgent smile. Wasn't she so lucky to be married to such a brilliant, special man? "Tell me what it is you do?"

"This and that in security," he says. "Consulting for a couple of companies. And of course botnet fighting in my spare time. My office is in Westwood. Anyway, find a seat. We'll get started in a few minutes. We're going to have a bunch more people on the conference bridge though. Not everyone's in LA."

Ken hesitates a moment before returning to the front of the room. Juliana catches him giving her a backward glance as she sits down next to the other woman. She is grumpy-looking, probably in her early fifties, with long grey hair and big brown eyes. Bright blue reading glasses are perched on the end of her nose. She stares into her computer without acknowledging Juliana's presence. Her screen is covered in a pink and gold privacy shield that reflects light in her eyes and gives her complexion a rosy glow.

"This is why I want to live off the grid," the woman says to her computer screen, peering at it through half-glasses. Juliana pulls her laptop out of her bag and sets it up on the conference table.

"Do you know the wifi password?" she asks the woman. She doesn't seem to hear her, so after waiting a moment, Juliana touches her shoulder lightly. The other woman jumps as though bitten by a snake, and her chair teeters backwards. Alarmed, Juliana steadies the back of the chair with her hand and apologizes.

"I was only asking what the wifi password is. I'm sorry I startled you."

The woman turns in her chair to face Juliana, her hand on her heart as though checking her heart rate, then smiles, exposing crooked yellow teeth.

"You shouldn't use hotel wifi," she says. "Security risks. You never know who is listening in. Do you have a VPN?"

Juliana knows that her husband prefers her to use the virtual private network they have through UCLA. It provides a secure tunnel straight to UCLA servers so as to avoid anyone with bad intent intercepting her email or web browser activity.

She nods and the woman points to a white board in the corner of the room where someone has written the password in big block letters. As she copies it down, she notices Ken looking at her. Was he watching her? She stifles a smile. Was he attracted to her? God, the attention feels good. Not that she'd do anything. But what is the harm in enjoying a man's attraction?

"Did you hear about the water shutdown?" the woman next to her asks.

She remembers Drew's emergency phone call earlier that day. "What happened?" she asks.

"Just a few minutes ago, the City of LA asked everyone to stop using water. Some kind of emergency with the treatment systems."

"The whole city of LA?"

"That's about four million people," she says. "But here in Culver City, we're all right somehow. Like a little island of water in a dry sea."

"How can that be?" she says.

"Different cities have different water systems," she says with a shrug. "Anyway, shutdowns like that don't happen that often on such a large scale. Must be a big problem."

"Do they say how long it will last?" Juliana asks while she texts Yalima. Does she know about the water problem? Maybe she should ask her mother-in-law to fill the bathtub or go buy bottled water or something. She hates to bother Drew in the middle of the crisis, but she texts him, too, to ask for advice.

"They just say there will be an update in another hour. Glad I live on land with a water well," the woman says. "Best to live off the grid in these times."

Ken claps his hands together twice to get everyone's attention. He stands in the middle of the horseshoe of tables, and when everyone's eyes turn to him, he clears his throat.

"Thank you all for coming here today. The importance of what we are going to discuss is underscored by the city of LA's announcement that its water treatment system isn't operating correctly, because that is just the kind of thing that could be caused by the kind of botnet army someone out there is building."

There is a rumble in the room as the participants shift in their chairs and speak in low surprised tones to one another.

The woman next to Juliana speaks out loudly. "Is someone saying the water outage is connected to the worm?"

Ken holds his hands up, palms toward his audience, and shakes his head. "I'm not saying that. I haven't heard anything to connect the two, other than the little grey cells in my brain, which I'll admit, are operating on very little sleep. I just can't help but note that this is the kind of situation that could be caused by hackers, though this would definitely be on a larger scale than we've seen before."

"Could just be a broken water pump as well," says a beefy guy with a Santa Claus-style belly but none of the merriness. "Remember the KISS rule. Keep it simple, stupid."

"Yeah, sure. Could be a broken water pump," says a thin guy in a denim jacket and a camouflage cap. "But I could penetrate a SCADA system in two minutes. It isn't hard to get into these utility systems. And at the rate this worm is going, I bet you a hundred bucks that it slipped right past most utility firewalls."

"All right, all right," Ken says. His eyes flit to catch Juliana's. "Look, not everyone in here knows everyone else, so say your name and why you're here before you speak."

"Chances are all the worm's creator wants is money, anyway," the beefy guy says. "Oh, my name is Basil Rogan. I work for a little web search engine I think you've all heard of."

"Google," the woman next to Juliana whispers to her with a roll of her eyes, as though she hadn't guessed. "He works that into every conversation."

"You people in LA have run out of water again?" says a Portuguese-accented voice emanating from the black starfish-like speaker phone. "That's what you get for building a city in a desert."

"Introduce yourself, Henri," Ken says.

"Henri Braga, Universo Vivo, Brazil, where I might add, it is well past cocktail hour. Look, for all we know, the worm is stage one of an elaborate money-making scheme to become the world's biggest sender of spam. It just may be the most successful one we've seen in building a botnet. I think it raises the issue of whether or not PersonalPro should be pushing security updates out automatically to block its security holes rather than waiting on civilians to upgrade their machines. Which they never do."

A tall and slender man with blond hair fading into a shiny pink scalp leans forward, his jaw flexing. He is the only person, other than Juliana, in business attire. She thinks his white button-down shirt makes him look like the only adult in the room. He glares at the speaker phone. "Dan Kowalczyk, PersonalPro. Look, we're dealing with this and I didn't dial in to get free advice on how we should handle our customers."

Ken walks around the table to stand behind Dan, and rests a hand lightly on his shoulder.

Juliana reads a text from Yalima that says the water is still running at the house but they had been warned on the news not to drink it. She is waiting for Leila to come home then she will go to the grocery store to buy bottled water.

She and every other person in the San Fernando Valley, Juliana thinks, but she texts simply "thanks." Still no text from her brother.

Ken talks in a reassuring voice, trying to calm the waters. "We know you're doing your job, Dan. We're here to talk about the worm and how we can get ahead of it. At the rate it's spreading, we're clearly seeing the start of a multi-phased effort here. We just don't know what the endgame is. We do know it is going to wake up in five days. Beyond that, we've got the start of an idea of what it might do. Mo has been working on this nonstop, and I've asked him to share with you what he's found. I hope the rest of you will share what you've seen as well. It's going to take a concerted, joint effort to fight this thing."

A dark-skinned man with the rounded cheeks of a boy begins speaking from his chair. "I'm Mo Mansour. I work for Ken. The worm does some of the usual things at first. It disables antivirus software, it patches the PersonalPro security hole." A few people snicker here, but it makes sense to Juliana. Wouldn't a good burglar lock the door behind him?

He speaks in clipped phrases that seem to indicate he is trying to slow his brain down enough to get the words out of his mouth.

"Then it opens up a back door, I assume so it can communicate with its creator. Then it does something interesting."

Juliana types notes rapidly in her laptop, her eyes on Mo.

"Then it checks for an Arabic keyboard."

Juliana looks around the room, only to find Ken's eyes on hers. He seems to be looking at her every time she casts her eyes in his direction, and she wonders if he thinks she is staring at him. She quickly averts her eyes around the rest of the room, seeing a few others who look like they don't know what it means that the worm is seeking out Arabic keyboards.

Mo must have seen the blank stares among the nodding heads, because he clears his throat and begins to explain how the worm checks for location by going to a particular website to get geolocation data for the computer it has infected.

"If it sees an Arabic keyboard or the geolocation data shows the computer is in one of the seven Arab Persian Gulf states, the worm does not install itself."

The check for Arabic keyboards means only one thing, Juliana thinks. *Now everyone will start speculating Islamic terrorists are operating in cyberspace, particularly with extremists beheading journalists and aid workers for not converting to Islam.* She looks at Mo, who is trying to keep his face neutral even though he must know that suddenly he and everyone with Middle Eastern roots could be cast into a net of suspicion. Just like Mahaz has been, after 9/11.

Juliana types the information about the check for an Arabic keyboard into her notes with a sinking feeling. Mahaz really should be here, not her. He has much more to add to this discussion. He knows every internet security geek and player in the world but particularly in the subset based in the Middle East. It is not a large community. She texts him the bit about how the worm is targeting everywhere but the Persian Gulf region to see if he has any comments she should share with the group.

"Arletta Therault. Internet citizen," the woman next to her says by way of introducing herself. "So the worm is avoiding Arabic machines. That could be because the worm's creator is a citizen of one of those countries and doesn't want to break the law there by harming his fellows. They've got some pretty stiff penalties for crime there, you know. Eye for an eye stuff."

Her comment makes Juliana think about the lectures that Mahaz gave her on their first trip to Saudi Arabia before they were married. He had handed her a long dark blue cloak, called an *abaya*, and a lighter blue *hijab* to cover her hair.

"You'll put these on while we are still on the plane," he said. "You have to, it is the law. You have to be respectful of local customs, Juliana, for they are very serious about these things." But he had made it sound adventurous and fun, in the same tone as he might suggest she wear cowboy boots in Texas or eat lobster in Maine. *When in Rome*…she had thought.

The list had been long but Mahaz ticked through it fast. Don't drink on the plane, for alcohol consumption is forbidden. Don't photograph the palaces or anything remotely governmental. Don't photograph people on the street. Don't go out in public alone. If you go into a restaurant, enter through the back for the family area; do not sit with the men in the front. Women cannot drive in Saudi Arabia.

She had loved him so much she didn't complain or even make the expected high-minded comments to her Los Angeles friends about how restrictive these rules were to women, even though wearing the *abaya* on the immaculate streets of Riyadh was hot and stuffy and limiting. She had chalked every difference up to the cultural and religious variances between the Middle East and the United States and considered herself, like Mahaz, an ambassador between the two, ready to showcase the best of each. She had envisioned herself moving between them as smoothly as Mahaz's beautiful mother did.

It has not worked out that way. Despite her best intentions and her deep desire to be culturally sensitive, Juliana has never been able to shake the over-arching feeling that the Saudi culture fundamentally views her as "less-than" because she is a woman. Yalima, perhaps because she was born there, does not seem to struggle with this dichotomy. She is outspoken, independent and argumentative with her son and her friends, but easily slips into the anonymity of life as a covered woman in a way that Juliana never can.

She had returned to Riyadh after that visit with Mahaz twice but then no more. Has it been twelve years since she had last stepped foot there? It must be, as she remembers her fear at flying in the months after 9/11, holding Leila, who was a toddler, in her lap the whole way.

The thought of Mahaz taking Leila to the Kingdom, where she would be swallowed up by a floor-length robe, her black hair tucked underneath a scarf, and allowed to go out only if chaperoned by her brother or father, makes her want to cry.

"Introduce yourself," Arletta says in a low voice. "Say your name and what you do."

Juliana looks up and is startled to see everyone staring at her. She catches Ken's eye once again and he gives her a friendly smile. "I just mentioned that you've come from UCLA," he says.

"Juliana Al-Dossari. I do communications for UCLA's Center for Information Technology. You might know my husband, Mahaz Al-Dossari. He's sorry he couldn't make it today."

As if on cue, her phone beeps with a text from Mahaz. "Now watch the Americans blame it on jihadists," the message reads. "Maybe it's a ruse designed by Russian or Chinese hackers to divert suspicion."

Maybe, she thinks. *If so, it is an effective one.*

Chapter 12

Chrysalide's creator dials in to the task force meeting from a disposable, pay-as-you-go cell phone and identifies himself as Dan Jones, a data analyst from Sol Systems, a made-up name at a real world mid-size technology company. It is a fake identity that sounds just boring and true enough that no one would question it.

He tells himself that he needs to keep tabs on this loose band of white hat geeks but the reality is that they are so far behind him, it only increases his already firm confidence in the strength and resiliency of *Chrysalide*.

Most of them believe this is about money, and they are right to calculate that the kind of botnet army he is building could reap millions and millions of dollars just through sending spam emails and perpetrating credit card fraud. But that is not his interest.

G0d_of_Internet has much bigger ambitions, as do the people who fund his work. Money is good, but power is better.

Ken Oakey surprises him, though, opening the call by making a connection between the worm and the water utility outage. Isn't there a saying about even the paranoid being right sometimes? Well, let him howl in the wind.

As the call drones on, G0d_of_Internet realizes just how little information the group has assembled. He types a new TorChat message to his collaborator, Proxyw0rm, saying only "all quiet here."

Proxyw0rm replies: *Chrysalide* Phase A working beautifully.

Chapter 13

Juliana Al-Dossari is so beautiful his eyes keep seeking her out in the hotel conference room. Ken feels like he conducts the whole meeting to her intelligent blue eyes and soft smile.

Some guys have all the luck, he thinks, picturing her husband who is not only the smartest guy in most rooms, but also movie star handsome and charming. Of course he has a beautiful, smart wife. They probably have perfect children and a perfect home and a big yellow Labrador called Rex. And Ken is probably so attracted to her because she is unavailable. That's what his mother would say anyway. According to her as well as several ex-girlfriends, he is afraid of commitment, so wanting a woman who is unavailable wouldn't surprise any of them. He doesn't agree with them. He just hasn't found a woman he wants to share his life with, though one came close.

Arletta has Juliana cornered as she tries to pack her laptop bag to leave, probably lecturing her on the particulars of password hacking or the dangers of public wifi. Ken heads over to introduce himself.

"Thanks for coming, Juliana," he says, cutting Arletta off mid-sentence. "I know some of that was really technical, but we're glad to have you here."

She smiles at him, and he feels the room freeze as though they are the only two people in the world.

"It should have been Mahaz, but I'll fill him in," she says. The sound of her voice is musical. It makes him feel slow and soft. He rests a hand on the table for added support. Arletta stares at him, visibly amused.

She slides the zipper on her bag shut with a loud zzzzpff and puts her right hand out. "Nice to meet you, Ken," she says.

He takes her hand in his with a gentle squeeze, as though he is afraid he will break it. Her skin is cool and pliant.

When she walks away, he sees Arletta watching him watch her.

"That woman was like an emissary from an alien planet at this meeting," she says. "Now why would Mahaz send her to something like this?"

"Too busy, I guess," Ken says. He doesn't really care why and he isn't about to speculate. Geeks can be so gossipy.

Ken turns around at the sound of heavy footsteps behind him. A tall and skinny man in jeans and what look like handmade cowboy boots claps him on the shoulder with his enormous hand.

"Ken, we should talk," he says in a deep voice.

"Do I know you?" Ken asks, puzzled. He looks at Arletta but sees the same lack of recognition on her face.

"Let's step outside where I can have a smoke too," he says, pulling a cigarette out of a pack. "I'm with Homeland Security."

Arletta looks like she is going apoplectic. She hates authority, hates government surveillance, and she seems poised to give this man hell. Ever the peacemaker, Ken holds his hand up, suggesting wordlessly that Arletta cool it, and then follows the man out of the room.

They walk in silence to the courtyard, where the man lights the cigarette too close to the door. A black-suited female member of the hotel staff scurries over and tells them to move twenty feet away from the exit.

"Fucking California," the man says as they walk toward a bench at the courtyard center. The palm trees create long shadows in the late afternoon light.

"My daughter tells me I should try these e-cigarettes. All the nicotine but none of the carcinogens. These kids all think technology is the answer." He takes a puff and exhales, blowing the smoke straight up.

"Sorry, I didn't introduce myself in there. I'm Bryce Ballen. United States Department of Homeland Security. But I already mentioned that. And I know who you are because Jeff Dendrich told me to find you. Said you're one of the good guys."

Ken nearly sighs with relief. Jeff Dendrich is his college roommate and now has some top-secret job at the National Security Agency. Ken hasn't talked to him in at least six months, but he knows that Jeff won't steer anyone to him who isn't on the up-and-up. He lets some of his wariness drop away as the man takes another deep drag on his cigarette.

"So what can I do for you?"

"Possibly nothing. I thought I'd introduce myself. Ask you to keep me posted on what you find."

"You're welcome to join the calls, and participate, just like everyone else," Ken says, slightly annoyed. *Or just listen in like you do already*, he thinks.

Bryce blows more smoke out and gives him a very icy smile. "Yes, thank you. Have you ever considered that maybe the bad guys are monitoring your calls too? As a security guy, you should have those calls locked up."

"Yeah, the thought has crossed my mind," Ken says. "But open and transparent is how we roll on the inter-webs." He punctuates the last word with a sarcastic tone.

"Right," Bryce says. "Let's all hold hands and sing *kumbaya* later. So what made you say the stuff at the start of the meeting about how this virus could be used to attack the LA water system?"

"First, it's not a virus," Ken says, unable to resist schooling this arrogant lawman. "Viruses are spread by people clicking on attachments. Worms spread on their own."

The man looks completely unimpressed with his lesson, and Ken gets the sudden notion the agent is baiting him to get him to talk freely.

"Look, I'm a worst case scenario guy," Ken says. "And I've seen a lot of different kinds of worms, and this one is by far the most contagious I've ever seen. It's hard to imagine that someone would build such a thing without having really big ambitions for it."

Bryce's eyes glitter as the courtyard lights blinked on. "So, how would you hack into a water utility system?"

"All of them use supervisory control and data acquisition systems, or SCADA. These systems are not designed for security. Kind of like the internet. And like someone said in the meeting, most hackers can penetrate SCADA running on PersonalPro in a few minutes. But I think you know that."

"So, seriously, how would you do it?" Bryce takes a last drag and drops the burning cigarette on the cement, where he grinds it out with his boot.

"Aw, I don't know. Do it like they did with Stuxnet. Infected USB drives introduce the worm, let it spread across the network. Use a programmable logic controller rootkit and modify the codes so that you're giving commands while making sure the user only sees normal operations functions. You can type that into a search engine and learn all about it."

"Jeff told me that you built a worm in college to break into the

SCADA system for the dormitories."

"That was a hundred years ago," Ken says. "I was trying to impress a girl. But making it so she couldn't shower for two days wasn't the fast path to her heart."

"We think you're right about the connection between the worm and the water outage. The Department of Water and Power has a little problem you may have heard about, and we think it is part of this," Bryce says. "Jeff said you're the guy."

"You mean it's already active? Mo said it wasn't supposed to wake up for five days."

"Someone has shaken it awake," Bryce says.

Chapter 14

"Well, that was a lovely meal, Yalima," Juliana says. "And it's so nice to have everyone around the table." She reaches over and squeezes Omar's hand, figuring that is the most amount of affection he will allow her. *Having my teenage son annoyed with my shows of affection is a wonderful thing*, she thinks. He is feeling better.

"Yes, *amma*, you order food to be delivered like a professional," Mahaz says. Juliana is relieved to hear him joke with his mother. It means he is in a good mood today and maybe she can talk to him later, tell him she wasn't serious about the divorce. Anything to try to cool his thoughts about taking the children to Saudi Arabia until she can make her own plans.

"I am very good with the credit cards," Yalima says. She must sense Mahaz's good mood as well, for she gets up to find her phone.

"Look at these pictures I took of Leila, Mahaz," she says. Leila leaps out of her chair and stands behind them. At five feet ten inches, she looms large over tiny Yalima and her seated father.

"These are wonderful," Mahaz says. "Leila, your eyes are as big as the moon and just as beautiful." He tilts his neck up so he can see her face. "But you still need to study your math. You cannot rely on your looks alone, beautiful girl. You must constantly surprise them with your brains."

Juliana smiles to hear him say that. It sounds like the old Mahaz. The one she had married. The one who had wanted to live in the United States for its freedoms, for the way women are allowed to live. Since that night in the hospital, she has been building up the idea of him wanting to put Leila in a golden cage, but maybe she has overreacted.

"Who says that I will have a career where I need math?" Leila says.

"You need math in college," he says. "No matter which career you choose. And we don't want you to drop out of college like your mother, do we?"

Ouch, Juliana thinks. She fiddles with the knife resting beside her plate. There it is. The offhand diminishment. The sharp knife that slides in without you feeling it. He makes it sound like her worst decision ever when he had been completely supportive and happy when she had taken a semester off and never gone back. Instead, she had followed him to Palo Alto for his year as a research assistant at Stanford while he had finished his dissertation about security risks in something called a Remote Procedure Call, a service of PersonalPro software that allows computers to share data. She still doesn't understand two-thirds of it.

Leila is trembling with excitement, her eyes fixed on her grandmother, waiting for her to raise the issue of the modeling.

"Mahaz, you know my friend Rana?" Yalima begins. Mahaz nods as she walks back to her seat across the table and sits down to face him.

"Rana has a line of clothing she is selling to some boutiques and she wants to have Leila model the clothes for her catalog."

"Please, Dad! It will be so fun! And Mama Yalima will come with me to make sure nothing happens."

Mahaz sits back in his chair and looks at his mother.

"What kind of clothes are these?"

Yalima shrugs. "They are western-style, yes, but modest, of course."

Mahaz answers her in Arabic, and they speak for several minutes in the language that Juliana does not understand and Omar and Leila only know a few basics.

Leila watches their conversation like a ping-pong match, trying to read the tones and emotions they are conveying, if not the words. Omar asks to be excused and Juliana nods her assent. She begins clearing the dishes from the table, carefully stacking plates first then gathering utensils.

Yalima rises from the table.

"Mom, you're okay with this, aren't you?" Leila pleads.

"Your dad and I need to decide together," Juliana responds with more diplomacy than she feels. She looks at Mahaz who sips his muddy Arabic coffee calmly as though he doesn't hear a word they say. Juliana and Leila both know the decision rests with Mahaz. If things were better between them, Juliana might have tried to intervene quietly on Leila's behalf later. But to speak out against him now will only feed the flames.

"Look at this catalog, *habibi*. There are no swimsuits or low-cut dresses."

Yalima lays the glossy booklet in front of him and he glances at the cover. A beautiful dark-haired woman in loose fitting pants and a flowy cardigan that stretches to her ankles stares back at him.

"It is the principle, *amma*," he says. "Leila's beauty should not be exploited for commerce."

Tears brim in Leila's eyes.

"It's not fair!" she says. "I never get to do anything I want!" She runs from the dining room and the three of them listen as her feet pound up the stairs.

"Sleep on it, *habibi*. Look at the catalog. It would give Leila great confidence and she would have fun, too. What is so wrong with that?"

"Juliana, I suppose you would be happy to see her do this? It is the American girl's dream, to be a model."

She flexes her jaw, anger rising.

"American girls have lots of different dreams, Mahaz," she says. "I'm surprised you haven't figured that out by now."

With trembling hands, she picks up dinner plates and turns on her heel for the kitchen, not even curious to see his reaction.

Chapter 15

Ken sits in the passenger seat of Bryce's big American sedan, obviously a Homeland Security-issued vehicle, surprised that they are not headed to downtown Los Angeles. He knows the Department of Water & Power has its headquarters off of First Street, but Bryce has exited the freeway in Echo Park miles before the downtown core.

He pulls up in front of a nondescript building the color of dog vomit and parks in a red zone. He throws a placard on the dash that says Homeland Security that Ken assumes is enough to keep the police or the aggressive meter maids from giving him a ticket or towing the car off. Handy thing to have in a city like Los Angeles where people pray to the parking gods for good luck.

Bryce presses a button on a high-tech-looking black call box with a video camera affixed to the top. He says his name and Ken's, then flashes his badge and the door lock buzzes then clicks open. They enter a second room that is little more than a holding pen between two doors. After a few seconds, the second door buzzes open and they pass through into a spartan lobby where a security guard behind bulletproof glass pushes paperwork at them. "We need you to fill this out and give us a copy of your ID," she says.

Bryce takes the clipboard and hands it to Ken to fill out. Bryce doesn't seem to have to fill out the paperwork. He just flashes his badge again and she smiles at him like he's the highlight of her day.

"We're getting used to seeing your face around here," she says, clearly flirting with him.

"Is that a good thing?" he says, amping up the voltage in his smile. "Most people don't think so."

Ken scratches out his particulars on the form and hands it back to her with his driver's license. She studies both, then faces her computer, its bluish light tinting her face, and types something in.

"If only they had this level of security online," Bryce says in a low voice. "We wouldn't be here."

"I'm not surprised," Ken says. "Money, time and resources, the age-old excuses. 9/11 was a wake-up call, but there are so many of these systems and so much to do."

Bryce studies his phone. Ken stares at the white wall, unadorned with anything but scuff marks along the baseboard. A dust bunny has found a home in the corner. But his mind is on Juliana, whose presence at the meeting today feels like a riptide sucking him under. Even now, a few hours later, he feels disoriented and just slightly breathless, as though the waves that drew him under had deposited him on a strange beach. He can't remember a time when he's been struck with so much physical chemistry between himself and another woman. And of course, she is married. He knows he needs to cool it.

"Mr. Ballen, Mr. Oakey, here are your badges," the guard says, pushing white rectangles toward them. "Go through that door and they'll meet you in the cafeteria."

More buzzing and clicking from the door. Bryce pulls it open. A long and narrow hallway leads deep into the building, its corridors reminding him of the ones he wanders in his anxiety dreams.

The cafeteria is the first open door on the left. Fluorescent lights beam bluish, flickering light on the industrial-sized coffee maker resting on a peeling Formica countertop. It is remarkably clean for the end of a working day and empty. No one is seated at the lightweight chairs and tables scattered on a scarred and worn floor. A vending machine offers sodas for seventy-five cents, the cheapest Ken has seen in a long time.

A man with curly dark hair and a striped sweater walks at a fast clip toward them.

"We've disconnected from the internet," he says to Bryce, with a quick, nervous glance at Ken.

"Rashid Zeitun, this is Ken Oakey. He's the security guy I was telling you about."

Ken leans in to shake hands and sees beads of sweat ringing his hairline. Anxiety surges out of his brown eyes. This is a man in crisis. Is Ken the cavalry riding in to save the day? He hopes he isn't the only one.

They follow Rashid down another long hall and to another door where Rashid punches in a long code before the electronic locks grant them access.

Inside is a vast control room. Monitors cover one wall, showing live video feed of different water treatment and pumping facilities. About fifteen people sit at intervals along two rows of long desks facing the monitors. Three carpeted steps lead down to a pit where two men and a woman sit in front of a complicated control desk filled with more gauges, dials and buttons than the cockpit of a 747.

"Welcome to control," Rashid says. "Let me introduce you to Drew Wareham. He's head of treatment operations." He walks down into the pit and speaks quietly for a few moments to a man in a dark blue shirt. After a few moments of conversation, they come up together.

The first thing Ken notices about Drew is his nervous energy. The man seems about to explode with it. As soon as introductions are through, he puts his hands in his pockets and starts jingling some change or his keys. Something metallic.

"We think we've found one of the servers he's using," Drew says. "Same as the worm, just like you thought, Bryce. In Moldova."

"That's what they're seeing in Boston, too," Bryce says. "We think we might have one more incident in Dallas."

"Three hits on water systems today?" Ken says.

"Yeah," Bryce says. "News media is starting to link them but we haven't given them anything to go on. All the water utilities are saying it is a local problem with pumping malfunctions."

"Have you scanned your user logs yet? Looked for new accounts or any unusual permissions given?" Ken asks.

"That's what we're doing now," Rashid says. "We're working out options for cleaning this thing off our systems. Our antivirus software catches the usual stuff but this worm squeaked right in through our firewall undetected. Then it opened a backdoor for someone to come in and start messing around with the water treatment chemicals."

Drew chimes in. "I've got storage tanks full of contaminated water and no way to be sure that I can control the treatment process if we do turn the system back on."

"Reformatting the whole computer system isn't an option, I take it?" Ken asks.

"Are you kidding?" Rashid says. From down in the pit, a woman calls his name, pointing at her screen. Rashid pivots and leaves them without a word. He is a man at the center of a crisis. Ken knows the look well. He's worn it himself a few times in the past.

"Can I take a look at the system? Maybe look at the task manager, see what processes are running?"

Drew runs his fingers through his black hair. "Sure, Ken, we can take a look," he says. "But Rashid or someone on his team can give you more of a rundown than I can, though. I'm not the expert."

Bryce gives a curt nod. "You're available now, and they're not. Let's just take a look."

Ken and Bryce follow Drew to an empty terminal at the end of one of the long desks.

"Bad guys tend to name their applications and processes like normal systems files so they are hard to find," Ken says by way of explanation. He doesn't know either Bryce or Drew well enough to know if he is talking down to them or not giving them enough information. He pushes the worry aside. They are grown-ups. If they have questions, let them ask.

Ken has already formed his theory of what is happening. Some individual gained access to the DWP's SCADA system, either created a new administrative account or cracked the password on an existing one, and started issuing commands along the lines of "add more chlorine" and "override warnings." He probably set up another program that fed back "all systems normal" data to the real administrators sitting in this control room, so by the time they realized that the water wasn't being treated correctly, all they could do was shut down the pumps.

What most laypeople don't realize, Ken thinks, and what keeps him up at night is just how vulnerable these kind of systems are. And how many different kinds of utilities use them. Water treatment plants, electricity generators, oil and gas distribution networks, nuclear energy generators...all these operate on these same types of systems. All of them are maintained by a variety of different people with different skills and experience, creating the potential for lots of unlocked doors and windows for the bad guys to break in through. He guesses the bright side is that the sheer number of the systems gives the good guys an advantage. Their high numbers and decentralization mean that there are few really big, nationwide targets for the black hats to break through. But attacking three big cities in one day is definitely sending a message.

Ken starts scanning the list of processes running when Rashid comes running over to them waving his phone.

"CNN is reporting that a terrorist group calling itself the Islamic Crusade has attacked water systems in Boston, Dallas and Los Angeles," he says breathlessly.

"Shameless speculation," mutters Bryce. "Absolutely irresponsible to start a panic like that."

"No, no," Rashid says. "There's a video." He holds the phone in front of their faces and a man with his face wrapped in black fabric speaks.

"The war has moved from the deserts of Iraq and Afghanistan to the United States," the man says. Despite his words being muffled by his black head cover, it is easy to discern his low-pitched accent that substitutes "r" with a soft "d" sound.

"Americans, prepare to bleed economically now, as we target your economy and your sense of security in your own land. We will watch you stagger under massive efforts and expenses to increase your security that will never be enough. For there are thousands and thousands of targets in your country. These cyber attacks we have unleashed on your cities' water systems are only the beginning of our effort to keep you in a state of tension and anticipation. This is how we will wage war on your land—not by sending 'boots on the ground' as you have done in our countries, but by turning your systems and your innovations and your openness into weapons against you."

The video freezes and for a moment, the four men stare at the image of the masked man in black.

"There's thousands of water systems vulnerable," Rashid says.

"The potential has always been there," Ken says. "Like everything, the internet can be used for good or evil."

The phone's data stream spurts back to life and the man in the video continues his speech. "This is our warning shot. We wanted to get your attention, and now that we have it, we will cease sending commands to your water systems so that you may resume normal operations. But I hope that now that we have your attention, you have heard us clearly and that you will stop all military action in Muslim countries."

"Goddamn terrorists," Bryce says. "They've certainly upped their capabilities. If they're telling the truth, that is, and not trying to claim credit for something the Chinese or the Russians did."

"So, should we believe them that they're going to let operations go back to normal?" Drew says.

"I don't trust anyone, and this is way too easy," Ken says. "But still, let's test the system. Can you put it back online safely?"

Chapter 16

G0d_of_Internet watches the video Proxyw0rm sent of one of their brethren delivering the first part of the manifesto. He feels light, almost weightless, like nothing can hold him down to this chair, this building.

He thumbs through his well-worn Quran for the text that gives him great joy and motivation.

Those who have left their homes and striven with their wealth and their lives in Allah's way are of greatest worth to Allah. They are victorious.

Yes, today they are victorious. The battle is theirs! He is a latecomer to the cause, and even after two years he still feels like he is proving himself to the leaders. With his computer skills, he is a very high-value recruit and they treat him with awe and reverence. He's even received a phone call from Abdul al-Lahem, the man at the very top of the Islamic Crusade, thanking him for his service in praise of Allah. G0d_of_Internet knows that doesn't happen often and he appreciates the show of recognition.

G0d_of_Internet has lived in five countries in his life and traveled through more than thirty so far. He has seen great wealth and great poverty, sometimes next to one another. Scrawny West

African children picking through heaps of garbage for food, while millionaires sat in wine bars just steps away and averted their eyes. Hungry men in Latin America delivering packages for pennies on broken-back mules while businessmen zipped by them in expensive sleek sedans imported from Europe. Asian women who displayed and sold their bodies to thrill-seeking tourists, all to earn money to feed their children. Native Americans who lived on reservations with no running water or electricity, while fifty miles away a city built by others glitters in the night.

He's spent most of his life as a secular person, not practicing any form of religion or spirituality beyond that expected by his parents during his childhood. Trying to make sense of a world with such disparity without spiritual help was a confusing and random path, leading him to conclude that winning at life was to be wealthy and powerful enough to satisfy your every whim. Greed and lust and envy ruled him for a time. But, he learned, when you've amassed your wealth, when you've satisfied your lust and when you've overcome your envy by buying everything your heart desires, there is nothing else but more of the same. Then the purposelessness of this chase for money and pleasure becomes clear.

Islam today gives him great comfort, guidance and finally, his true life's purpose. To worship Allah, to surrender to him, and to fight His holy war. But, to do so on his own terms.

Chapter 17

Juliana raps her knuckles on Mahaz's office door only to be surprised as it opens nearly instantly. Kendall Sage stands on the other side, her hand on the doorknob as she looks over her shoulder at Mahaz, who must have said something funny because she is laughing.

Face-to-face with Juliana, her smile fades fast and is replaced by a flush in her cheeks. Her eyes drop to the floor. *Good for her*, Juliana thinks. *She should show some embarrassment in front of the wife of the man she is trying to seduce.* Without realizing she is doing it, Juliana plants her feet in a fighter's stance and feels her nails bite into her palms as her hands curl into fists.

"I have to be going," Kendall mutters, and lets her blonde hair cover her face as she ducks by and flees down the hall.

Mahaz sits behind his desk, and watches her over his dark-rimmed reading glasses. She crosses the carpet in five steps—it is a large office—and sits in the chair still warm from where Kendall had sat.

"Did you hear from Drew yet?" he says.

She unclenches her jaw and shakes her head. The other woman has left a trail of vanilla scent behind her. Mahaz's condescending tone from that night in the hospital room, when he told her she was merely jealous of Kendall, skips like a stone through her thoughts. Not trusting herself to take a deep breath for fear of crying, she tries to keep her voice on an even keel.

"I've texted him a couple of times. I guess saying he's busy is probably an understatement."

Mahaz leans back in his chair, as calm and remote from her as the clouds in the sky.

"I was going to head home. I just thought I'd see if you were going to make it for dinner tonight," she says. She wonders if he can tell that she wishes he wouldn't. The tension between them is unbearable, and she just wants to be alone with her children.

He looks at his watch, the handcrafted Swiss piece she'd had engraved for his fortieth birthday. Time flies, love stays, it reads.

"It's already 6:45," he says. "I'll be here another two hours at least."

Sweet relief. She even manages a smile. "What are you working on?"

"Kendall set up an interview for me in twenty-five minutes with CNN on this cyber attack. She's a wonder with the media. And after that I need to work on that presentation," he says. "You know, it turns out that Kendall has never been to an IUIA meeting before. Or Brussels for that matter. I think it will be good for her to go. She can live tweet my speech."

Juliana crosses her arms over her chest protectively. Kendall Sage is replacing her at work and in bed. *There is something wrong with him*, she thinks, *that he enjoys telling me this so much*. And something wrong with her that she puts up with it. She pretends she didn't hear him and changes the topic.

"I think you should be the one participating in that task force, not me," she says. "Everyone on it speaks fluent techie. Seems right up your alley."

He looks at one of the two computer screens on his desk for a moment, then back at her. "I don't have the time right now," he says. "And I'm sure the police or Homeland Security or whoever have it under control without needing a group of volunteers to play amateur detective."

Her mouth nearly drops open at his statement, because it directly opposes his usual point of view on such matters. She's heard him say multiple times that law enforcement and governments do not possess the knowledge or expertise to fight any kind of digital warfare. Over and over again in his speeches on the internet's fragility he has talked about the importance of this loose band of volunteers and true believers, and now he just tosses them aside like they are nothing.

"That doesn't sound like you, Mahaz," she ventures.

He takes off his glasses and pinches the thin bridge of his nose between his index finger and thumb.

"Just tired is all," he says. "Did you see this notebook that the Italian Minister for the Digital Economy sent me? It came with a note telling me how it was made by a little old man in Florence who does the binding himself. He learned how to do it from his father and his father's father and so on. Family business for five hundred years."

He slides the heavy brown book toward her and she runs her hand over the grooves and curves of the *fleur-di-lis* embossing on the smooth leather.

"It's beautiful," she says, irritated by his change of topic but recognizing she's just employed the same tactic.

"This craftsmanship, you don't see this often," he says. "We are losing this kind of skill in our digital world."

She lets an "mmm" sound emerge from the back of her throat. She hasn't come in here to talk about Italian leather.

"I guess I'll head home," she says. "I talked to Omar and he feels better. Says he wants to go to school tomorrow."

Mahaz is still looking at the notebook and nods with distraction.

"One other thing, Juliana," he says. "I've asked Kendall to look over the communications plan you did for this year and give us some feedback. I think she has some good ideas to improve it. You know, bring it up to the next level."

"For a social media consultant she sure has her hands in lots of pots," she says, spitting out the words like wine that has gone sour. He is clearly baiting her.

"She has a communications background," he says. "She used to work for one of the big video game companies. She knows about media and websites and all that." He waves a dismissive hand over the tools of communications as though they are child's toys.

Juliana swallows back tears. She worked so hard on that communications plan. Initially Mahaz said it was good and so did the instructor in the marketing class she took at UCLA Extension. Now some sleazy, husband-stealing consultant has it in her claws and is undoubtedly going to rip it to shreds.

He watches her fight back the tears from his seat, like she is an interesting animal in the zoo. She stands frozen in place.

"I'm sure there is room for improvement, Juliana, there always is. You have to be open to constructive criticism."

"She wants to sleep with you," she says, embarrassed how shaky her voice sounds, when what she wants to do is bellow the accusation in his face. "And now you are giving her a sweet contract so she can make lots of money. Do you know what that makes her? And what it makes you?"

His chair spins backwards as he crosses to her and takes her head in his hands. "You are imagining this," he says. "I am not going to sleep with this girl. She is more like a daughter to me. And she is an expert in her field, Juliana. She is helping us. She is a means to an end."

She looks into his eyes and there is the old Mahaz staring straight back at her and she wants to believe it so badly that she smiles at him and acquiesces.

"I'm so tired, too," she says. "I haven't slept well since the day before Omar went back into the hospital."

"Me neither," he says. Then he presses his lips to her forehead and she leans into him and then his mouth is over hers, his tongue working its way past her teeth. His hand slips behind the back of her neck and cradles her head. She responds to his kiss automatically, from nearly two decades of marital habit, for a split second before sliding her face away from his. She tucks an errant lock of hair behind her ear and backs away from him.

"I'm heading home," she says. "Good luck with CNN."

So, there is still part of me that loves Mahaz, she thinks. And that part of her refuses to believe he will really follow through on his threat to take their children to Saudi Arabia. That part of her also desperately wants to believe that there is nothing between Mahaz and Kendall. She feels torn in half. But couples grow apart all the time, and maybe that is what is happening to them. He has changed, grown more distant. How well does she know Mahaz today?

She knows who he has been and what they have been through together. They've overcome their families' lack of initial enthusiasm for their match, and their cultural differences, with the kind of brute force that only young love can bring. They built a life around his career and their children and she'd gladly placed her career aspirations in the cupboard and let them grow dusty.

She made sacrifices, and he has made some too. He turned down a prestigious post at Stanford because she wanted to be near her family. The bottom line is that they both made compromises to be together in those early days, and maybe, after all these years, those compromises have turned into debts to one another that are now due.

Chapter 18

"Gotcha!" Ken says. His excitement startles a grunt out of Bryce, who has nodded off in the chair next to him. It is their second afternoon at the Department of Water & Power's control center. Though the windowless room provides no evidence of daylight or moon light, the huge digital clock on the wall reads 17:30.

Bryce rubs his eyes and peers at the pixels Ken points to on the monitor.

"The bot accessed this website, trafficsales.tk, yesterday. This is how the hacker entered the network," he says. He is elated. They found a clue.

"Dot-tk? Is that a Turkish domain name?" Bryce says.

Ken shakes his head. "Tokelau," he says.

Bryce looks blank.

"It's an island-state in the South Pacific, near Samoa. They give the domain names away for free with very little verification. You just need a name and an email address to get one."

Dot-tk is a different kind of domain registry, one of nearly 225 known as country-code top-level domains. Each country in the world has one: for the United States it is dot-us, Australia is dot-au, and so on. Some are run by governments, others by non-profits.

"The dot-tk registry has a reputation for malware distribution," Ken says. "I'm not surprised to see one of their domains pop up as some kind of web shell or entry point for the hacker. They get away with it because their revenues account for nearly ten percent of the nation's gross domestic product."

"First the jihadists, now an island in the South Pacific," Bryce says. "We're bouncing all over the world."

"Internet is all about no boundaries," Ken says.

Ken's phone buzzes in his pocket.

"Mo," he says by way of greeting. "Perfect timing."

"I've got news," Mo says. "Where are you anyway? You just disappeared after the meeting. Either you are holed up with a woman or trying to solve the worm's riddle."

Ken smiles. "It's not a woman. It's my other obsession. Do you know anything about a domain name trafficsales.tk? I think it might be involved."

Mo pauses for a long time, then finally speaks. "Yup, there it is. Trafficsales.tk. It's on the list."

"What list?" Ken feels a tingling sensation in his spine, either because they are getting close to another clue, or he's been sitting too long in an uncomfortable chair. He misses the ergonomic features of his own office chair. The DWP's chairs are worn mid-century relics so old that they've come back into style.

"This is why I called you, Ken. The person who designed this worm, he or she is very clever indeed," Mo says. "I figured out what happens when the worm wakes up."

"Hang on," Ken says. "Let me put you on speaker phone. I'm working with a guy from Homeland Security and I want him to hear it too."

Ken waves Bryce over and they huddle over the phone's speaker.

"So on the day the worm wakes up," Mo says. "All the infected computers—and by now we're talking more than half a million—first check to see if they have an active internet connection, and if they do, they get a command to use it to contact the botmaster. Then the worm contacts the botmaster through one of a list of three hundred apparently random internet domain names that is generated every day. Basically, the infected computer works through the list of websites, going to each one to look for instructions. If one site offers no instructions, it moves on to the next one, and so on."

"So the botmaster just has to put his instructions on one of those domain name's websites," Ken says. "I take it the list of domain names is generated by an algorithm."

"Yup, and I'm working on cracking that too. I'm going to share it with the task force list already so we can work on it together."

"Let's keep it to ourselves for now," Bryce says. "The way you all operate has too much potential for leaks."

"That's the way we like it most of the time, Bryce. Open and free," Ken says.

Mo clears his throat. "Now the next thing to tackle is how to read the botmaster's code, and he's not making that easy. He's using three sets of code, and it's exactly what you'd expect. SHA-2, et cetera."

Of course. They may have figured out how the botmaster plans to give his instructions, but the trick now is to read those instructions once they are given. And those instructions are going to be embedded inside the highest level of public encryption there is. SHA-2 stands for Secure Hash Algorithm 2, a mathematical code generated by computers that allows two parties to verify independently that they are talking to one another and not imposters.

When Ken tried to explain cryptography to his mother one time, he used the terms he remembered from the 1960s *Get Smart* television series. "Remember when spy Maxwell Smart would say a prearranged code like "The geese fly high" and his counterpart would say "The frost is on the grass?" That code recognition is how they would know they could trust one another," he told her. "Computer cryptography worked something like that but at a much more complicated mathematical level."

Bryce looks at the domain name trafficsales.tk on the log. "Chances are that finding out who is behind it will be a dead-end, but we'll run it down," Bryce says.

"The hackers did their homework, huh? Look, Mo, I've got to get some sleep tonight and so do you. Let's send some emails out, and enlist help on the cryptography."

He tells Bryce he needs to head home. Tilly the dachshund has probably torn his mother's house to shreds with him away for two days. And he needs to sleep.

Chapter 19

When Juliana turns the car onto her street, she sees her parents' car parked in the driveway. Apparently Yalima and her parents orchestrated some changing of the guard without involving her. She wonders absently if she missed a text from them.

She was ready for Yalima's gossip and cheerful presence. Her parents' presence, on the other hand, brings comfort tempered with uncertainty. Has Drew talked to them about her and Mahaz? She doesn't know what kind of reaction to expect from them, other than their support. They will do anything for her.

Her father had parked their gold Toyota Camry crooked in the driveway, and Juliana doesn't feel steady enough to navigate around it into the garage. She leaves the car parked on the driveway behind her father's car, and walks to the front door. Funny, she never enters the house this way. Always she comes in through the kitchen. She feels like she's invading a stranger's house. Thin, curved tendrils of new growth on the night blooming jasmine bushes that line the walkway reach toward her like question marks. The papery fuchsia flowers of the bougainveilla flutter in the light breeze.

Inside, the house smells like beef simmering in tomato sauce, and she hears Omar's laugh echo from the kitchen into the foyer. She puts her purse down and takes a deep breath to get her bearings.

Her mom stands at the stove with a wooden spoon in her hand and Juliana's only apron, a Christmas one mimicking Santa's shirt and belt, wrapped around her thin torso. Her dad sits at the breakfast table with Omar and Leila, playing Uno.

She wraps her arms around her mother and inhales the tuberose and musk of her perfume. And the meat sauce. She realizes she is starving. She isn't sure when she last ate.

"Want us to deal you in?" Omar says. "We're starting a new hand."

She shakes her head. "I'll help Mom," she says, but what she really wants is a glass of wine. She takes the first bottle of pinot grigio she sees out of the wine refrigerator.

"I don't need help, Julie," her mother says. "Everything's under control. Yalima had to leave, so she called us and we came over."

"Is the water back on?" Juliana asks.

Her mother shakes her head. "Not yet, but Drew said it was a matter of hours now. I'm cooking with bottled water. So scary."

Juliana yanks the cork out of the bottle and then takes a wine glass from the cupboard. She offers her parents some but they both decline. The kitchen feels warm and safe against the darkness outside the window. She sits down at the table next to Leila.

Omar draws a card and slides it in his hand. "Your turn, Grandpa," he says.

The wine is tart like a green apple, just as she likes it. She sighs as she feels it hit the back of her throat and then warm her from the inside out. Her father carefully lays down a pair of tens, and she sees Leila, always competitive, mentally counting the cards left in his hand.

Leila picks up a two from the pile and lays it down with a matching card.

"Your mother is worried the terrorists are going to strike financial institutions next," her father says in a low voice. "She wants to take our money out of Guaranty National Bank and stuff it in the mattress like her grandmother used to."

"I can hear you," her mother calls from the stove. "Don't make fun of me. It is a very real threat. The head of Homeland Security said so on CNN."

"What does Mahaz think of all this?" her father asks.

The air in the kitchen grows warmer, thicker. Leila pulls a card from the deck and then tosses another in the discard pile with a heavy sigh.

"He's always talked about how fragile the internet is," she says. "So of course he is not surprised. Anything can be hacked." Then she remembers the CNN interview and looks at her watch.

She tells them that Mahaz has an interview lined up and maybe they could catch it, then she turns on the television mounted under the kitchen counter.

Omar smiles, his chipped front tooth in relief against his bottom lip. Juliana loves the sweetness in his smile. That it is still there after fifteen trips to the emergency room and at least six surgeries is as much a miracle as the smile itself.

"I wish they'd hack my school or something useful," he says. She reaches out to ruffle his brilliant black hair gently.

"Drew said that Homeland Security brought some security expert over to look at the water system. I thought it might have been Mahaz but it was some other fellow," her father says.

A commercial for quick and easy loans wraps up with five repeats of a toll-free phone number and the charming grey-haired host of CNN's nighttime program appears, his lips together in a serious but friendly expression. He balances a pen between his fingers.

She takes a drink of the wine and lets it roll around her tongue for a moment.

"Leila, quit looking at your phone and pay attention! Dad's coming on!" Omar says.

Mahaz's face is slightly pixellated and fuzzy around the edges. She realizes he is calling the station via one of the online calling services. For budget reasons or whatever, CNN has chosen not to send a camera crew. He sits forward, pressing the tips of his fingers together, eager to talk. Eager to explain things to people. He loves the spotlight. He literally loves the sound of his own voice. He told her once that he sometimes falls into a dreamlike zone when he speaks, and can't always remember what he said.

"He looks handsome," her mother says. She leaves the stove but still holds the wooden spoon in her hand.

"We have Mahaz Al-Dossari, cybersecurity expert, with us today to talk about the cyber attack on three U.S. water systems," the host says. "Thanks for joining us Dr. Al-Dossari."

Juliana holds her breath as her husband smiles neutrally into the camera without speaking. After one or two seconds of delay, Mahaz deepens his smile and nods. "Glad to be here," he says.

"As a security expert, you've been talking for years about how something like this could happen," the host says. He glances down at the tablet computer in front of him. "Now that it has, what should we expect next?"

The delay makes Juliana freeze and she lets out a tiny sigh when Mahaz speaks. "What we've seen over the past few days should scare us. But it should not cripple us. Instead it should remind us that vigilance and preparedness are important at every level, even down to the laptop you are issued by your employer. You see, when it comes to breaking into systems, each one of us is the weak link. We open email attachments we shouldn't, we click on links that take us to websites we didn't mean to go to, we enter our personal information or passwords in spoof sign-in pages. I wouldn't be surprised if the water systems were hacked in just that way. All it takes is a bored employee clicking on what we call a Trojan attachment sent by someone trying to break into the system. Once the Trojan attachment is open, it starts spreading malware throughout the network."

Her father clears his throat. "That's how Mahaz said I brought that ILOVEYOU virus on our old computer." Juliana smiles at him. The infection reinforced her father's suspicion of the computer and the internet as a whole. He basically only uses the computer to look at pictures of his grandchildren and to play Sudoku.

"In the past, malware and hacking attempts like this have been mainly for money-making purposes," the interviewer says. "With the video we received today from jihadists, it seems that we are in a new type of battle, one where power grids, transportation routes and food distribution networks can be compromised. What can be done to fight this?"

"The potential for this kind of attack has always been there. Most of us, even computer security experts like me who worry about these kinds of attacks every day, have learned to live with the risk because we like the benefits of our interdependent world. I don't think we're going to go backwards to a non-networked world. We just need to be more vigilant. And we need government and law enforcement to get more involved in fighting cyber attacks, particularly those from other countries. Right now, we're very challenged fighting these attacks when they come from other countries."

"So, are we at the cusp of a new 9/11?" the interviewer asks, his bright blue eyes burning a hole in the camera with his intensity. It is the question on everyone's mind.

Mahaz gives a tight smile. If it is meant to reassure it falls short, thinks Juliana. "I don't think the threat level has risen to the kind of loss of life we saw with 9/11. These kinds of disruptions may lead to deaths and may much more certainly lead to loss of money and productivity. But maybe that is the cost of our lifestyles."

The host thanks Mahaz and he bobs his head with a smile. Another interview completed beautifully. Juliana marvels as she usually does at what a natural he is before the camera. No sign of nerves or self-consciousness. She has never been on camera like that and feels like she'd freeze if she ever were.

"Will Uncle Drew be on the news too?" Omar asks, leaning back in his chair so it teeters on two legs. Juliana presses her lips together to keep from telling him to stop, and admonishing him that his balance can't always be trusted. She knows better than anyone that her boy doesn't need reminders of his sickness. "He should be. He runs the water system."

"I think he's too busy solving problems to do interviews," her mother says. "He's letting the public relations people handle that."

After dinner, Leila and Omar scatter to do their homework in their rooms, no doubt texting and watching television and listening to music all at the same time. Juliana remembers her parents making her and Drew sit at the kitchen table to do their homework all those years ago, with the sound of the evening news drifting in from the living room.

As soon as the kids are gone, Juliana pours her second glass of wine and sits at the table with her parents who both have steaming cups of decaffeinated black coffee in front of them, an after dinner ritual they have practiced for decades.

"Drew told us about you and Mahaz, Jules," her father says. Her mother places her hand over Juliana's. It feels cool and dry like paper.

"Do you need help?" Their eyes are identical pools of sympathy. She feels relieved and grateful for their support, not that she imagines them having any other reaction. Telling them has felt like one giant obstacle, as though every hesitation they had at the beginning was justified. But Drew told them, so the worst part is over, and she realizes she is in desperate need of their guidance.

She thinks of her passport in her purse, and the panic that day when she thought Mahaz might steal it from her. Does she want to give it to them for safekeeping? It feels silly now.

"Drew said he would ask Cathy for some names of attorneys," she says weakly.

"He said you might need money," her father says. He spent his career making loans to small businesses at the bank. He is most comfortable with financial transactions. "We will help you. I'm going to go down to the bank and set you up an account."

"You can do that online now," she says with a smile, forgetting for a moment her mother's comment about hiding money in the mattress and the fear pervading the country over terrorist cyber attacks.

"Having your own bank account is a good idea, Julie," her mother says. Juliana hears what her mother isn't saying as well. That she should have had an independent account the whole time. That maybe she should have been more realistic about the marriage from the start. It is a legacy of their old distrust of Mahaz. But Juliana knew how much she loved Mahaz and wanted to believe that their marriage would be different. She easily yielded to his wishes that they have only joint accounts.

"Thank goodness he never made you move to Saudi Arabia," her mother says, removing her hand from Juliana's and wrapping it around the coffee mug.

Raw anxiety rises from her belly to her chest. She washes it down with a large swallow of wine. Yes, thank goodness they aren't in Saudi Arabia where *Sharia* law gives the father all the power over where the children live and what they do. Now all Juliana has to do is keep them in the United States.

Chapter 20

Juliana thinks of it as her nightly visitations to her kids. Both of them ensconced in their rooms, headphones on, laptops up. Like she does every night she puzzles over whether they are really doing their homework now, since the computers make easy one-stop shopping for both education and entertainment.

She knocks on Leila's door first, and when there is no answer after a few beats, she knocks louder then pushes the door slowly open. It is important to make sure she gives Leila some notice even if the music blasting in her ears prevents her from hearing the knock. Juliana's own parents were of the school of "knock once then open the door." She always resented that intrusion, wondering why they couldn't wait for her to say come in. Now, reviewing her parents' behavior as a parent, she chalks it up to different generations' thinking. She knows her kids need some privacy and space in order to be independent, though she tries to balance it with knowing what they are doing.

"How can you tell if your laptop is being hacked?" Leila asks when she sees her in the doorway.

Juliana sits on the edge of the bed near Leila's feet, which are covered in bright green fuzzy socks.

"Usually people figure it out when their computer is running more slowly than it normally does, or if their friends get emails from them that they didn't send," she says. "But you can't always tell with some of the worms that are out there. Why?"

"I was just thinking about it. You know, how dishonest it is to use other people's computers to do bad stuff."

"Yeah," Juliana says, wanting to reach over and smooth out the thin line of worry forming on her beautiful daughter's forehead. "It sucks. Just don't share your passwords with people, baby, and don't open attachments from people you don't know."

Leila rolls her eyes with all the drama and magnificence of a teenage girl. "I know that," she says. Her voice has just the slightest ring of annoyance. "So, are you going to talk to Dad about the modeling?"

The modeling. She had let it go with the worries of the day. Pushing it on Mahaz is easily the worst idea in the world right now for her marriage, just because of the timing. She isn't sure she can convince him of anything. But then again, why is he so against it anyway?

"You know I've dreamed of doing modeling since forever," she says.

Juliana remembers Leila practicing her catwalk moves after every episode of that reality show about modeling. She is very excited about it and she has the height and the slim figure. But to be realistic, Leila has also gotten very excited about other careers too—being a dog trainer, an ambulance driver and a teacher. Those changing dreams are all a part of growing up, aren't they?

"Please, just talk to him," Leila says, pleading as tears fill her lower lids. "I just want to try this. It could be my big break."

It is her weakness, Juliana acknowledges, that she hates, absolutely hates, to disappoint her kids. They are good kids, they study, do their homework, are respectful to adults. Why can't she at least talk to Mahaz about the modeling job and see if she can convince him? It will mean so much to Leila. She can see that now. Plus, she told Yalima it was okay to show the photos to her friend, so in a way, Juliana started them down this path. She ought to at least finish the job.

"Yes, I'll talk to him," she says. "But no promises." Leila practically knocks her off the bed with the force of her hug, and Juliana holds on as long as she can, smelling her fruity shampoo. Her baby girl. Hugs don't come that often in the teen years.

In Omar's room, she finds her oldest staring intently at the computer, his face flushed as though he ran a mile.

"Some of my friends are idiots," he says. "Haskell posted this stupid cartoon about Muslims on Facebook and everybody's making jokes. I said something about how my dad is Muslim and Haskell was just like, well, you're different, you're like us."

She reaches out to smooth his hair back from his forehead and is surprised to find his hair damp and his skin hot. She places her full palm against his forehead and he jerks away.

"I'm fine, Mom, it is just a little stuffy in here," he says.

Her heart sinks. The room's temperature feels cool to her. She knows immediately that Omar is getting an infection, and he knows it too, based on how he pulls away from her.

"Any other symptoms? You dizzy? Tired?"

"No," he says. "I'm fine."

"Then let me get the thermometer and take your temperature for real," she says. "If you're normal, then fine."

He nods, but his eyes glint like a trapped animal who knows he is doomed. Kids with illnesses like his know when they are sick. He just doesn't want to admit it.

She walks into his bathroom, stepping over the wrinkled bath mat and grimacing at the dirty sink bowl ringed in facial hair and toothpaste. She opens the medicine cabinet and pulls out the electronic thermometer. She catches her image in the mirror and sees a tired woman, mascara smudged, lips pale with no trace of lipstick left, and her face tight with worry. She doesn't want Omar's temperature to be elevated either. She wants nothing more than a normal reading, for the simple excuse of the stuffy room to be the truth for once. For there to be no infection racing through his body that has already been through too much.

But her mother's instinct tells her otherwise. She shuts the medicine cabinet door and returns to her son to confirm her suspicions.

Chapter 21

G0d_of_Internet is tired but exhilarated. He knows he should go home and rest, but he loathes to leave the silence of this room for the noise and chatter awaiting him at home. He prefers to sit alone in this quiet place, reflecting on the work he did and the work still to do.

For the seventeenth time today, he checks the *Chrysalide* log to see the total number of machines infected. Over 750,000 so far. He delights at how fast the propagation rate has accelerated. It exceeds the results from the simulation modeling he did months before, when they began working on the idea.

He is most proud of the feature he created to highlight the highest-performing machines, the ones that infect the most other machines, indicating a strong connection to the internet.

Knowing which computers are the most widely connected is valuable information, like an insurance policy against the bot being dismantled. Should anyone be able to take the botnet down, G0d_of_Internet could rebuild using the most connected computers. No need to start all over again with random infections, as he did the first time. Now he possesses the data he needs to sustain the botnet after attacks.

Proxyw0rm has marginal hacking skills, and the leaders of their group have none. Sometimes G0d_of_Internet cannot shake the sense that he is the master teacher to slow pupils. He longs for a partner who can understand the full beauty and symmetry of what he built. This lack of a real peer is in large part why he dialed in to the task force call and why he indulges himself by monitoring the security chat channels and mailing lists. He wants to watch them unfold his beautiful castle of computer code and admire its battlements, its moats and its towers. Only other security experts and coders can truly understand the magnificence of his creation. Is he so wrong to want to receive their accolades? He is only human.

On launch day, with an expected nine million computers infected, the panic will override any appreciation for the beauty of his code. He feels the pain of bitter disappointment that he will be only the anonymous author of a footnote in history.

A prick of fear awakens in his stomach and spreads, oozing out of him. An oily slick on top of water. Has he done everything correct? Are there flaws he overlooked or was blind to? Has he been too prideful? So much is at stake now. He considers going through the code again, but thinks better of it. His eyes are too tired now, and his brain would be unlikely to find errors now. Another reason why having a real peer to work with would help.

He hears al-Lahem telling him that pride is a dangerous thing. That he has built this for the glory of Allah. As the Quran says, *He who has in his heart the weight of an atom of pride shall not enter Paradise.*

Though it has been weeks since he has prayed the five daily prayers, G0d_of_Internet takes his prayer rug out of the drawer and lays it carefully on the floor. He takes his shoes off and stands at the edge, facing east toward Mecca and slowing his mind down in order to set his intention for prayer. He then raises his hands to his ears and says *Allah Akbar*, or Allah is the greatest, then recites the first chapter of the Quran, letting the sacred words wash over him and cleanse him of pride.

Chapter 22

Tilly the dachshund lies curled in a ball on Ken's lap, and he crooks his arms around her sleeping form to type awkwardly on the laptop keyboard on his home office desk. She is a possessive, nervous and high-strung miniature dachshund, and after two days with Ken's mother and her ditzy Pekingese, she glues herself to him this morning.

In the background, CNN blares with some talking head that Ken only half hears. "Private and public networks in the United States have increasingly experienced cyber intrusions and attacks over the past twenty years. Even with firewalls and other steps to maintain security, these interconnected networks are fragile and vulnerable to attack. At the same time, the government, the military, businesses and individuals are completely dependent on the internet for a variety of everyday functions."

Yeah yeah, Ken thinks. It's easy to talk about it, but that is just hot air. He wants to do something about it, find a solution, not posture and pose on television.

The key, he thinks, is to sinkhole the three hundred domain names that the worm is generating daily. Mo cracked the domain-generating algorithm and is building a list of the domains it will generate for the next fifty days.

If the white hats have the domains pointing to a sinkhole instead of the web, then the hackers can't use them to send their commands.

The first one he wants to find out about is trafficsales.tk, but the WHOIS database shows it as registered to some shell company in the Cayman Islands. Only court orders will unlock the mystery of who owns that domain, so he leaves that sleuthing to Bryce with his deep resources at Homeland Security and turns back toward the problem of the three hundred domain names a day.

He places a phone call to the Los Angeles office of the IUIA but only gets tangled in voicemail boxes and automated answering systems. He needs to start at a higher entry point. Over the years, he's known many contacts who wound up part of the IUIA volunteer community, creating policies related to how the domain name system functions, so he scans the online list of its board of directors looking for familiar names.

When he sees the name of Dr. Mahaz Al-Dossari he stops.

He knows it is only an excuse to talk to Juliana again, but he can't stop himself from plucking her business card out of the stack on his desk and dialing her mobile phone. She is a married woman, he reminds himself. Probably happily married. But he listens to the phone ring and pictures her smile and her wide brown eyes.

"Hello?" she says.

"It's Ken Oakey, from the task force. Did I catch you at a bad time?"

She sighs. "I have time. I'm waiting on some test results on my son at the hospital. We just wait and wait."

He feels a sting of guilt that he called her on false pretenses. She sounds shattered and soft.

"I'll let you go," he stammers. "It was nothing too important."

"Don't do that," she says firmly. "I could really use the

distraction. I was just about to get the laptop out and start answering emails. You can only sit and worry for so long without driving yourself nuts. So you read your email and you make your grocery lists and the world spins around you."

Her words run together. She is on a sharp edge, he can tell. He doesn't want to waste her time with what his mother called "hemming and hawing" about whether or not he should get off the phone. He plunges forward, updating her on the lists of domain names and asking her if Mahaz could ask the IUIA to help set aside the ones for the next fifty days.

"What will you do with them all?" she asks.

"We'll park them on a server somewhere and then 'sinkhole' any requests to access those sites into a dead-end location. That will keep whoever's behind this from sending out commands via those websites."

"Smart," she says. "It's like cutting off the army's communication channels."

"Exactly."

"The water system attack," she says. "That's got to be related to this, don't you think?"

He isn't sure if his visit to the Department of Water & Power is secret or not, but decides off-the-cuff that he can trust her. And, though he hates to admit it, maybe he wants to show off, just a little, to this woman who dominated his thoughts for the past two days.

"I think so," he says, and he fills her in about his visit to the control facility the night before.

"I bet you met my brother," she says. "Drew Wareham. I've been trying to reach him today but he's harder to get ahold of than the President of the United States sometimes."

Ken breaks out into a smile. Her brother? He can recall a family resemblance now that he thinks about it.

"What a small world that you and Drew got paired up last night," she says. "So glad they got the water back on this morning. We were about out of bottled water and I wasn't relishing the idea of braving the stampedes at the grocery store."

"I live in Beverly Hills. We've got our own water system and some in-city storage so we were spared the water shut-off," Ken says. "But still, pretty scary stuff. People like your husband have been talking about how hackable those systems are for years, but it was like science fiction to most people. They think it will never happen."

"Count me among them," she says. "So you're looking for a contact at the IUIA, huh? Look, Mahaz and I are friendly with the CEO. Let me call her and set up an introduction so you can make the ask."

He hangs up, glad to have made progress on the domain name registration issue, and even more glad to make another connection to this extraordinary woman. He holds her business card between the pads of his thumb and middle finger, and taps it lightly on its end against the desk. Tilly lifts her head from his lap and looks to see the source of the sound, then, with a sigh upon realizing there are no treats involved, she rests her head again on his leg.

Chapter 23

Valley Presbyterian Hospital is a cluster of rounded structures topped with flags, and reminds Juliana of a fortress. The building and doctors and nurses within were both her son's saviors and her son's captors. An old Bible passage flicks across her mind: *the Lord giveth, and the Lord taketh away.* She isn't sure where she heard that before—one of those television preachers, maybe—since going to church has never been among her family's habits.

She sits in a chair between twin windows overlooking Vanowen Boulevard from their fifth floor perch. Omar lies in the hospital bed covered in a thin green blanket and crisp white sheets already damp with sweat.

Infections are yet another complication from hydrocephalus. Juliana knows that infection often requires removal of the shunt, but doctors are trying a dose of intensive antibiotic therapy to treat it, hoping to avoid another operation.

Last night, Omar's temperature shot above a hundred degrees, and the skin on his neck where the shunt is embedded glowed red. She saw tears in his eyes when she told him that they must return to the hospital. God, she would do anything for him to have one week as a normal teenager.

He is dozing now, woozy from the cocktail of high-dose antibiotics combined with anti-nausea and anti-diarrheal drugs to combat some of the side effects. Despite the dim light from the closed blinds, she can discern his features perfectly. He is clearly cut from the same genetic fabric as Mahaz: the high cheekbones, the full lips, the tawny skin. She wants to hold him in her arms and just make this hospital room, this sickness, go away forever. But she can do none of that. And what she said to Ken is the truth. The larger world keeps spinning around, even if your own personal world screeches to a halt because your child is ill. So you sit and you wait and you look at your emails and you smile at the orderlies and listen to the nurses and doctors. On the best days you feel optimistic and strong and on the worst days you offer your soul to the devil, asking him to let you suffer instead of your child.

She shakes her head as though to chase the despair out. She knows from much experience that this kind of thinking usually spirals into depression and she doesn't want that to happen. Not now. She picks up her phone and calls Deann England, CEO of IUIA, to make the connection for Ken, but has to leave a voicemail instead.

A wiry man with kind eyes and a backpack knocks on the open door. "I'm the hospital chaplain," he says, waiting a discreet distance for her invitation. She is well-versed with the etiquette of visiting chaplains in hospitals, though she hasn't met this particular one before on any of their visits.

"Come in," she says with a glance at Omar. His long eyelashes part like butterfly wings as his eyes flicker open. "Omar, it's the hospital chaplain."

Omar's eyes flutter shut, his face unmoving, and she wonders if he decided to play possum rather than talk to the man, or if he is deep in dreams and not even aware his eyes opened.

The chaplain stands in the center of the room, and shows no sign that he wants to sit down. Juliana notices how heavy she feels, like her body is weighted down with bricks. Even holding her head upright saps her strength. She forces herself to her feet and walks to the chaplain with her arm extended.

"I didn't mean for you to get up," he says. "My name is Joseph Freeman."

"Juliana," she says, too tired to give her last name. What does it matter anyway? He will probably forget it the minute he leaves, just like she has already forgotten his name.

"I hear your son is a frequent flyer around these parts," he says with a smile. His eyes exude kindness and patience, no doubt the result of years spent providing comfort to the troubled and the sick and their loved ones. *How draining that must be*, she thinks.

She decides to joke with him. Keep it light. "Are they offering free airline tickets or something? Because Omar has racked up a lot of nights here."

"They should work on that," Joseph says. "So, how are things going today for you?"

She starts talking about Omar, how the doctors want to beat the infection back with antibiotics, how they hope to avoid surgery. The chaplain is a sponge, absorbing the words and the feelings with a sympathetic expression and always those kind eyes fixed on hers.

"Valley Presbyterian has great doctors," he says. "I know they'll do the best for him. But how about you? How are you holding up?"

"Me?" Her throat expands then chokes out a sob. "I'm doing all right." The tears start flowing down her cheeks and she takes a slow breath. There is a chance Omar pretends to be asleep but instead listens to every word, so she points at the door and follows the chaplain into the bright antiseptic hall. An orderly in royal blue scrubs pushes a cart full of sheets and pillowcases and blankets into an adjacent room, and a few moments later, a woman in a bright pink pantsuit and a messy chignon steps out and leans against the wall.

"Are you okay, Juliana?" he asks. She starts when she hears him use her name. She was sure he had forgotten. She racks her brain for his name but draws a blank.

"Sorry for the crying," she says. "I do that a lot."

"I can understand why," he says.

The woman in the pink pantsuit fishes around in her purse, then takes out a hot pink flask adorned with tiny crystals. She unscrews the lid and takes a swig, then winks at Juliana.

"Do you want to pray together?" the chaplain says. Suddenly, Juliana wants to be done with him and talk to the woman in pink.

"Sure," she says, not certain when she prayed last but figures it can't hurt. The man grips her hands lightly and closes his eyes, his chin pointed at the ceiling. She closes her eyes and bows her head, grateful the tears dried up quickly. Sometimes she fears that when she begins crying, she might never stop.

"Holy God, things are difficult for Juliana and her son Omar and their family today. Thank you for being present with us now and helping us to walk through this day and this time. Remind us that when we are fearful You are with us every step of the way. We know that You will be there with us no matter what. Amen."

She opens her eyes to see his again. Up close, she can see short white hairs on his dark sweater, probably from a dog who sat in his lap before he left home. She considers for a moment how hard his job must be, walking in and out of hospital rooms all day. The smell of sickness and death and antiseptic, the crying relatives and their shell-shocked looks.

She squeezes his hand as though to acknowledge all this. "Thank you for the prayer," she says. He smiles and gives her hand one last squeeze, then turns away.

The woman in the pink pantsuit watches him enter the next room, then walks over to her.

"He doesn't come in my daughter's room any longer. I think he thinks I'm the devil because he saw me sneaking a drink from my little flask," she says. She smiles and raises her eyebrows like she thinks it might be true. "I don't hide it. I figure a little Johnny Walker is better than Valium."

"You took a swig out here for his benefit, then," Juliana says. She likes this straight-talking woman wearing a Barbie doll suit. Even wearing three-inch heels, she is nearly a head shorter than Juliana is. Her good humor makes everything seem just a little more bearable.

"Maybe," she says, the grin flashing across her face again. "Want a drink?"

"No, I shouldn't," Juliana says. "I'm so tired I think it would put me straight to sleep."

"And that's a bad thing?"

Juliana casts her eyes up and down the hallway. Only one nurse is in view at the station, her face trained on the computer screen in front of her.

"Okay," she says. The woman hands her the flask and she holds it between her fingers feeling as guilty as a teenager sneaking a smoke outside the cafeteria. She takes a swallow and grimaces at the burning sensation on her lips then down her throat.

"Are you a single mom too?" the woman asks. "Oh, by the way, my name is Clancy."

Juliana introduces herself then shakes her head. "No, I'm married still."

Clancy screws the lid back on the flask and tosses it into her purse as the chaplain reappears in the hallway. Clancy and the chaplain exchange curt nods and just as she predicted, he skips Clancy's daughter's room. He knocks lightly on the next door and is welcomed in.

"You say it like you mean to say 'married but not for long.' I know exactly where you are coming from," Clancy says.

The orderly rolls the linen cart out of the room where Clancy's daughter is. "All done, ma'am," she says.

"So what is your daughter in the hospital for, if you don't mind me asking," Juliana says.

"Oh, hell, I don't mind," Clancy says, hoisting her big tan purse to her shoulder. "What else is there to talk about in the hospital? She has leukemia."

"Mom!" a young girl's voice shouts from inside the room. "The stupid tablet froze."

Clancy winks again at Juliana. "I thought this generation was supposed to be fluent in all things technology," she says. "But somehow I'm chief technology fixer in this family of two. I'll catch you later, Juliana. Stop by anytime you need a break...or a drink."

In the hallway, the lights flicker twice and darken. All around her Juliana hears the machine hums and whirs wind down, and for two breaths, the hospital ward is completely dark and silent. Juliana feels her way along the wall to Omar's room.

In what seems like an orchestrated crescendo, the lights buzz back on and the machines and computers flare to life. The nurse at the station jumps up and runs toward the loud beeping that emanates from one of the rooms. Charged with adrenalin, Juliana goes to Omar's bed and takes his hand.

"I'm right here," she says.

"What happened?"

"I don't know."

Chapter 24

"What?"

Bryce does not sound like he is in any mood for chitchat so Ken jumps right into the reason for his call.

"Mo had an idea for…"

Bryce cuts him off. "The program analyst on your payroll?"

"Yeah," Ken says. "He has an idea for how to do some clean-up on the Department of Water & Power network."

"Well, good for him," Bryce says. "Because it's under attack again. This time the power side."

"Shit." Ken lifts Tilly off of his lap and plops her on the floor so he can stand. He needs to move. He needs to think.

"Yeah, shit is right. I thought you said this worm thing wasn't set to go off for days."

"It isn't. This is something else," he looks out of his window at the gleaming luxury cars passing by on Charleville Road. "I don't know what it is."

"Maybe it is a rehearsal. You ever think of that?"

"Tell me what's happening," Ken says.

"Three transformers on a key high voltage transmission line short circuited. Immediately lost seven thousand megawatts of power.

Systems interface actually showed everything functioning normally."

"They're probably using the same back door," Ken said. "That's what I was calling about. We have an idea for how to close it."

"Can you try it now?" Bryce says. "See if you can stop what's happening now?"

"Sure," Ken says. "I'll call Rashid."

Bryce isn't like most law enforcement types Ken knows. Most of them have one-way conversations with civilians for the most part. It is an ongoing annoyance in the security world. Some of these guys with the badges act like everything is top-secret, even when they are flying completely blind. Bryce is different because he is more willing to share information.

He calls Rashid, but gets dumped in voicemail. He leaves his message, then sits on the couch in front of the television and flicks it on. Tilly pads in behind him, jumps up and reclaims her spot lying alongside his thigh. A CNN reporter stands on Wilshire Boulevard where traffic is already jammed up behind her because the traffic lights are out.

"Chaos on the streets of Los Angeles with a massive power outage stranding thousands," the reporter says. "The Los Angeles Department of Water & Power has been unavailable for comment other than to say that they will have the power back on as soon as possible. Meanwhile, traffic has completely snarled on most major freeways as people left work early in a panic to be with family and loved ones. An estimated two thousand people are trapped in the Metro subway system and light rail."

The camera cuts to a grey-haired black man in a suit who speaks from behind the wheel of his SUV. "I'm going home right now so I can get my family out of the city now, before anything else happens," he says. "This is crazy. It's like LA has become some huge target and all I know is that I'm getting my family out of here."

CNN switches to aerial footage of the city's downtown interchange showing bumper-to-bumper traffic at a complete standstill.

When Ken's phone rings, he jumps and this makes Tilly bark angrily at him, whether because she is disturbed or because she is worried about Ken, he can only guess. He strokes her long back as he answers the phone.

"Ken Oakey? This is Deann England of IUIA. Juliana Al-Dossari gave me your number."

"Great," he says. He fills her in on how the worm is working, and how it will generate a list of three hundred domain names each day where the botmaster could hide in order to give his secret commands.

"There's a good chance the botmaster is behind one of them right now," Ken says. "This may be how they're doing the attack on the electricity supply."

"But the worm's still spreading, right?"

"Think of this as the first act," Ken says. "And right now the only way we have to stop the second act is by grabbing up these domain names before they do."

"You can count on us," she says.

Chapter 25

G0d_of_Internet reads the letter that Islamic Crusade leader Abdul al-Lahem had written in English for the American people on his secure email channel.

My message to you is simple. You live in a world of illusion. You imagine you are safe in your country but you will see disaster and catastrophe beyond the greatest imaginings of the Hollywood movie studios you love.

We offered your leaders a way out, and that was to remove your military forces from Muslim countries. They may take our threats seriously, but they do not act on them. Instead they say they do not negotiate with terrorists and that they are winning this war on terrorism.

Now we must continue our pledge to fight this war in your homes, through the internet that you have come to depend on for so much. Today we have struck electricity systems in several of your cities. Are you nervous now? You should be. The coming days will test every one of you.

Indeed they will, he thinks. The fear and humility he felt before has vanished in his supreme confidence. He reviewed his program twice today, and now feels more certain than ever that he produced nearly flawless work. He looks again at the code he wrote for Day Zero as they call it. Launch day. The day his *Chrysalide* will become a butterfly.

He programmed it in C++, used as the base of thousands of automated applications. Video games, search engines, medical systems, automated manufacturing processes, operating systems for mobile phones, and financial trading systems. To know C++ is to be able to unlock the functioning of thousands and thousands of automated applications.

It is the financial systems that G0d_of_Internet's contacts are most interested in. This water and power systems hacking is a sideshow, a flexing of muscles. Designed to strike fear and cause panic.

A chat message pops up on his screen, breaking him out of his memory and into real time.

Proxyw0rm: *Allah akbar.*

Indeed, he thinks, *God is great.*

Proxyw0rm: Soon you will be with your brothers in Yemen.

Don't count on it, G0d_of_Internet thinks. *I won't hide in the slums of Yemen long.* He thinks with satisfaction of the money he hid away for his use once he is on the run. There is nothing noble about poverty. No one chooses to live in third world conditions. You are there by fate or misfortune, not by self-selection.

When the United States financial systems go down in a few days, his money will be safely sitting in Switzerland, God willing.

Proxyw0rm: Do you have any new information from the security email lists?

G0d_of_Internet opens a new mailbox to look at the most recent emails from these internet do-gooders who publicly proclaim all their efforts to stop the advance of the worm. Volunteers, he scoffs. The United States spends so much money on its mighty military and leaves its critical communications system basically unguarded. Fools.

He scans through a few of the emails.

A woman named Arletta Therault loves to do recaps of their

progress. She is either trusting, or foolish. He doesn't much care which. From her emails, G0d_of_Internet learns they unpacked *Chrysalide* and know a few more things.

G0d_of_Internet: They know about Day Zero, as we wanted. And they know about the domain names algorithm.

Proxyw0rm: Time for Chrysalide 2.0?

G0d_of_Internet: Yes.

Proxyw0rm: We think you ought to reconsider using an untested encryption method, no matter how good it is.

G0d_of_Internet: It is not untested. I have tested it many times.

Proxyw0rm: It is an unnecessary risk.

G0d_of_Internet slams his fist on the desk. Who is this fool to tell him what was or wasn't a risk? They would be nowhere without him.

G0d_of_Internet: I do not agree. It goes out as it is.

Chapter 26

Four hours later, Juliana is relieved to see Mahaz walk into the hospital room with Leila on his heels. Despite her anger at him, she needs to lean on him for support. It is an old habit and a hard one to break during a time of crisis.

"I'm sorry it took us so long to get here," he says, setting down his laptop bag carefully in one corner. He eyes her like a boxer might size up an opponent in the ring. "Traffic is terrible. It took me an hour and a half to get to Leila's school from UCLA, then another forty minutes to get here. Stoplights are out everywhere, and I swear the traffic cops with their hand signals do not help the situation."

Leila slumps into the chair next to where Juliana sits and puts her head on her mother's shoulder. "I got carsick," she says.

Juliana strokes her long dark hair. "My poor baby," she says. "Do you want me to get you a soda?" Leila shakes her head.

"Hi Dad," Omar says. Mahaz places his hand on Omar's forehead gently.

"You're still fighting this infection they tell me," he says.

"I don't want another surgery," Omar says. "Because that just leads to another one and another one. Aren't they supposed to have all these super drugs that can kill anything?"

"How long until we know if the antibiotics are working?" Mahaz asks Juliana, his eyes softer now.

"They're real cagey about that. Twelve hours, the infectious disease specialist said, but then he also said it depends."

Mahaz flexes his jaw then sighs. If there is still one bond that Mahaz and Juliana share, it is the worry and frustration that accompanies a sick child.

"Did he say 'time will tell' too? And 'we'll see'?"

Juliana gives Mahaz a small smile in response. Lack of concrete answers is their most common vexation. Sometimes Juliana wonders if medicine is mainly educated guesswork.

"Have you been watching the news?" Mahaz asks. "People are streaming out of Los Angeles like they did during the riots in 1992."

"We had it on for a while, but they asked us to turn it off an hour or so ago to conserve power. I guess they're running power off of a back-up diesel generator. It's pretty scary to have the water go down one day and the power the next."

"Maybe it will come back on quickly like the water," Mahaz says. "Maybe they are just sending a message and don't mean serious harm from this."

She shoots him a look of disbelief. "Don't mean serious harm? They've shut off the power to an entire city and its hospitals, its fire systems, its police dispatch system, mobile phone networks…it's chaos. People are getting into fights over bottled water at the grocery stores."

Omar pushs the controls to raise the head of the bed so he can see them better. The bed whirs as a woman's voice floats out of the public address system, announcing evening services in the chapel.

"What if I have to have my surgery and something goes wrong with the power?" Omar says. Juliana aches for him. He is trying so hard not to cry in front of his father. But he is scared.

Mahaz stretches his arm over the bed rails to touch one of the few parts of Omar's arm not covered in tape or IVs or the blood pressure cuff. His eyes soften as he looks at their son.

"You must not worry too much, *habibi*. Do you know that surgeons and doctors operate in worse conditions than this and save lives still? Think about those surgeons in war zones, mortar shells blasting around them, operating with flashlights held by nurses. We humans were not always dependent on electricity you know. Thousands of years we lived without it."

This is the old Mahaz, Juliana thinks, *comforting and reassuring our son.* It feels good to be in a familiar pattern for once, after months of moodiness and disappearing acts. Mahaz is a good father. He loves his children and she is glad for that. He doesn't really intend to take them to Saudi Arabia, does he? Surely it is just a threat, spoken out of anger. For he knows as well as she does that the opportunities for both, but especially for Leila, are so limited in Riyadh. While here in the United States, the possibilities for them are nearly limitless. That freedom was Mahaz's primary reason for moving here, after all. He wasn't faking that desire years ago. He followed through by living here for more than two decades. They share these same values still. Don't they?

She almost convinces herself that his earlier threat is just that, an empty threat spoken in anger, when she remembers the children's passports are missing, that he hid them somewhere out of her reach. The horrible anxiety returns, nearly choking her.

A nurse comes in to check the IV drip that is feeding antibiotics from a clear bag into Omar's veins. Juliana studies her as she traces her gloved hand down the tubing to his arm and then back to the skinny arms of beige medical equipment, nods, and walks to the computer to enter something into the terminal. She presses the mouse, then lets out a small snort of frustration when nothing happens. No power, of course. Because the hospital lights are on and some of the systems are working off of electrical generators, it is easy to forget that not everything is powered, Juliana thinks. Her head feels heavy, and her eyelids start to close as she watches the nurse take the paper file from the holder in front of the door and make a manual note.

Juliana wants to surrender to this deep tiredness within her and fall asleep. Sleeping also means escape from these worries that plague her. But maternal instinct—on a high alert since Mahaz's terrible warning—keeps her nerves jangling just enough to forestall rest.

In a dreamlike state, she watches as Mahaz leaves the room and returns shortly with a folding chair he found somewhere. He sets it up to the right of Omar's bed and brings out his laptop and looks around for a plug.

"Power's out, Dad," Omar says. "See, you are just as dependent on it as we are."

Mahaz laughs. "It is true. It is so automatic that I plug in that I forgot the power wasn't working," he says. "Fine. What can we do that does not use electricity?"

"We could play gin rummy," Leila says. "Does anyone have cards? Mom?"

Jolted to life, Juliana scrounges in her purse to check but comes up empty. Sometimes she remembers to throw a deck in for these hospital stays and sometimes not. She's so tired her brain was practically scrambled when they left last night for the emergency room.

"We could tell stories," Juliana offers instead. Both Leila and Omar groan.

"We've heard all of your stories, Mom," Leila says. "I've got another idea. I could sing the song we're learning for Showstoppers." Showstoppers is the name of the choral group she is a member of at school.

"That sounds good," Mahaz says. Juliana tilts her head back and closes her eyes as Leila begins to sing in a breathy, soft voice the words to "Day by Day" from Godspell.

The room goes still as they listen to Leila's voice float above the beeps and the voices and phones ringing. Her voice grows more confident with each line. The blood pressure monitor inhales air then lets it out in hiccups that somehow fall into rhythm with the song.

My children have an endless capacity to surprise me, Juliana thinks, glancing at Omar who shuts his eyes. Leila in particular is full of surprises, late to develop her speech but then once she decided to talk, you couldn't keep her quiet. She constantly pushed the boundaries as a child. She was hungry to know the answer to every question. Why was the sky blue? Why can't humans fly? Why don't dogs speak English?

It breaks Juliana's heart to think of Leila in a society that keeps women as second-class citizens. Juliana remembers how her own confidence was shaken on those early trips to Saudi Arabia. Just wearing the *abaya* did things to her modern, independent mind. It made her slouch and slink around corners, not wanting to be noticed. It made her ashamed of her body. And the rules forbidding women from driving, from riding bicycles, from getting into cars with men who were not family—those rules made her dependent on Mahaz in ways she hated.

She will fight to her last breath to keep these children here. Her mind returns like a broken record to the missing passports. *But he's a good man*, she tells herself. *I'm sure there is a good explanation. And this is absolutely not the time to talk about it.*

Chapter 27

The jewel-box home where Ken grew up smells like fried onions and Ken's stomach grumbles in response. He unhooks Tilly's leash from her collar and the dachshund bounds into the kitchen then bursts back out of the doorway at full speed, with his mother's dog, Maxie, on her tail.

Ken's mother lives in Culver City, a city that prides itself on its small-town feel despite its presence in the epicenter of Los Angeles. It bridges the gap between the tony homes and world-class shopping of Beverly Hills and the working class neighborhoods and the old horse-racing track of Inglewood.

His mother maintains the house as a time capsule of furnishings and knick-knacks from forty years of living, the last ten alone after his father died of stomach cancer. In the garage, he knows he can still find artifacts from his childhood: the TRS-80 I microcomputer from Radio Shack, the Sears Video Arcade console, and the Hobie skateboard. Inside the house, the brown shag carpeting is worn flat, the wallpaper is faded and the couch sags. But it is spotlessly clean.

The kitchen is flooded with afternoon light from the west-facing window over the sink. Ken sees she set a place for him at the square kitchen table. He kisses her on the cheek as the dogs skid around the kitchen linoleum and then dash back out. He can hear their paws thud on the carpet.

"So, you're working on this Crusader worm?" she asks.

"Crusader worm? Who's calling it that?"

"It's all over the television, honey. They've named it after the terrorist group that turned the water off. On the local news they've created this graphic with black lettering and a green worm. I think it is supposed to be scary but they made the worm look like a caterpillar."

Ken sits in one of the stiff-backed chairs and lays his phone on the vinyl placemat.

"Yeah, I'm working on it. Even got contacted by Homeland Security," he says, not too ashamed to brag, just a little bit, to his own mother. "We've figured out how they're going to send commands, and I'm working to stop that."

She comes up behind him and spoons hot noodles with onions and chopped up sausage onto the plate.

"Have you been eating well? And sleeping? You're getting too old for all-nighters," she says. She sits in the chair to his right, making a small grunt with the effort.

"You're not going to eat?" he says.

She shakes her head. "I had a late lunch."

He pierces the slippery noodles with his fork and shoves them in his mouth, realizing again how hungry he is. He makes it halfway through the meal when his cell phone rings.

"Solstice Networks is on board with helping to register the domain names," Mo says. Solstice is a clearinghouse for internet services that manages the directories for top-level internet domains like dot-us and dot-com, and is the global face of some of the country-code top-level domains like China's dot-cn and Russia's dot-ru.

"That's good," Ken says. "The algorithm is only producing domain names in five extensions. Dot-com, dot-cn, dot-net, dot-info, dot-me. So if we bring Certi-check on board with helping us register the domain names and waiving their fees, we're in good shape."

"About that," Mo says. "I have other news."

Ken braces himself for the load of bricks he thinks Mo is about to drop on his head.

"Tell me," he says.

"There's a new version of the worm. Crusader 2.0," Mo says. "The honeynet started catching it about four hours ago."

The rush of adrenalin Ken feels is quickly followed by a competitive urge, the kind he experiences after a particularly challenging volley in tennis. The hackers are trying to show him that they could up their game. Well, so could he, Ken thinks.

"I think they're watching our moves," Mo says. "We just figured out how to kill their communications via the domain name algorithm, and this new version takes that to the next level."

"What do you mean?"

Tilly jumps up to put her paws on his knee, her classic begging position. He picks up a noodle and drops it into her waiting mouth.

"Don't feed that dog table food in my house," his mother says. He raises his eyebrows at her and tries to look innocent, not that it ever works on her.

"They added more top-level domains to the mix," Mo says. "A hundred more, and they upped the number of domain names generated per day to five hundred."

Ken thinks about the hundreds of other top-level domains that are now available since IUIA's launch of its new generic top-level domain program two years prior.

Before that program, there were only twenty-two top-level

domains, like the familiar dot-com and dot-net, and another two hundred or so country-code top-level domains. But now, hundreds of organizations are running domain name extensions like dot-baby, dot-guru and dot-games. And on top of that, domain name extensions are now also in other scripts, like Arabic, Chinese and Hebrew.

"So this could just keep growing and growing," he says. "They're toying with us. So now, in addition to Certi-check, we pretty much have to get every registrar in the world on board."

It is a good thing that IUIA is on board to help, he thinks. As the coordinator of domain name registries around the world, they are pretty much the only ones who can make such a concerted effort happen.

"We also may have a lead, though," Mo says. "They're using a different encryption method this time. An experimental one."

"Seriously? Why would they use an unproven encryption method?" Ken says, shaking his head. "There are probably less than a thousand people in the world who would know how to use something like that. Who's the author of it?"

"Mahaz Al-Dossari," Mo says.

Ken's lips curve into a smile without his conscious intent. Just hearing his name conjures up for Ken the image of his wife.

"There can't be that many ways to get your hands on a paper like that," Ken says. "Is it even published online?"

He hears Mo's fingers flying over the keyboard with tiny clicks.

"It's posted on his website at UCLA."

Another excuse to call Juliana, Ken thinks selfishly. His mother will scold him royally if she knows that he is making excuses to chat up a married woman. She wants him to find someone to share his life with, and if that union also brings grandchildren, so much the better. She is probably on to something. Isn't part of Juliana's appeal to him her unavailability? Is he so selfish that he subconsciously avoids real relationships in favor of fantasies?

He hangs up with Mo after agreeing to contact one of the Al-Dossaris about the web traffic logs to the site where the paper is posted online. They can scan the list of visitors, which cannot be a long list, given that digital encryption is strictly the realm of the uber-geek. If Ken can convince Bryce to take it seriously, then maybe they can use the resources of a big agency like Homeland Security to run down the individuals who downloaded the paper in the months since it was published.

He finishes eating his meal as his mother washes pots and whistles quietly. It is a habit of hers that always makes him smile.

"Am I going to see you on the news tonight?" She grins at him. "My bunco club is coming over tonight and I'd love to be able to brag to the ladies about how you're solving the war on terrorism from your computer."

"I leave that to the other guys," he says, smiling back at her. "The ones with the big egos."

"Last time I checked, you were no shrinking violet," she says. "Be safe out there."

She hugs him tightly. Sensing movement in the kitchen, Tilly and Maxie swerve into the kitchen again and stand on their hind legs trying to get in on the action. Ken picks Tilly up and kisses her on top of the head.

"Thanks for taking Tilly, Mom. I'll see you later," he says.

Chapter 28

Footsteps on the tiled hallway echo in the room as Juliana watches Dr. Theressa Duva shuffle through a series of papers in a folder.

"The infection is not getting better," Omar's doctor says. Dr. Duva is a straight-shooter with a big heart and the height to match, and Juliana is so glad they found her after Omar's diagnosis. She is kind, compassionate and funny. Case in point: A pin on her white lab coat reads "I listen to the voices in my stethoscope."

"I know you don't want another surgery, Omar, but it's the only way."

Omar's eyes cloud briefly, and Juliana wonders if he might cry. She certainly feels like crying. He must be so frustrated, she thinks. And she hates to see him helpless like this.

"What about the power situation?" Mahaz asks.

Dr. Duva shakes her head. "We know about as much as you do on that. I'd like to put in transfer paperwork for Omar to be taken to Providence St. Joseph in Burbank or Glendale Adventist. Those cities aren't on the same grid as Los Angeles. I think we can get him on an ambulance transport in two hours."

"Can't we wait? Maybe the power will come back on, like the water did," Omar says.

Dr. Duva closes her folder of papers and slings them under her arm. "I don't think we can, kiddo. You've got one hell of an infection," she says.

"Traffic is gridlocked," Mahaz says. "I don't think that even an ambulance's lights and sirens are going to make much of a difference out there."

"I still think this is the best shot," Dr. Duva says.

Juliana lets the words wash over her. She never gets used to making these life and death decisions. Her eyes meet Mahaz's and she can see his pain matches hers. For the moment, they are a united front in their trust of Dr. Duva, and belief that she does not recommend the transfer and surgery lightly. Juliana nods and Mahaz tells Dr. Duva okay to start the transport request.

After the doctor leaves, they agree that Mahaz will take Leila to Yalima's place in Beverly Hills for the night and Mahaz will meet them at whichever hospital they end up at. At least school is cancelled, Juliana thinks. The power outage means that for once Omar won't be met with a total avalanche of make-up work to do after another extended stay in the hospital.

Her phone vibrates in her purse. Ken Oakey again, this time asking her for another favor. He wants the visitor logs to the Center's website.

"I don't have any way to access them from here," Juliana says. "Mahaz has his laptop with him, maybe he can send you the logs when he gets to his mother's house."

"How long will that take?" Ken says.

"I don't know. An hour or two? Traffic's terrible."

"Is there anyone else? Maybe someone who's in the office?"

Kendall Sage, Juliana thinks. Her mouth twists, as does her gut, at the idea of calling her for help with anything. But she does have access to all the web traffic data, for her analysis of their online communications efforts. Let Ken call her directly, she decides. She isn't about to wade through the fake friendliness of small talk and expressions of concern about Omar with her husband's latest mistress.

"We have this consultant, Kendall Sage," she says. She feels like she spits the woman's name out and wonders if Ken or Mahaz notice the animosity in her voice. "You can call her to ask for the website logs. Tell her you talked to me and Mahaz and we said it was all right."

After she ends the call, she turns to Mahaz to tell him what Ken wants, as she figures Kendall's first act will be to check with him that it is okay. Mahaz shrugs as though it is nothing to him, and she turns back to her son who lies perfectly still under the thin green blanket, waiting for yet another surgery.

Chapter 29

From the high perch of his Jeep Wrangler, Ken can see that Overland Avenue is backed up all the way to the Mormon Temple near Santa Monica Boulevard. Where do people think they are going anyway? Some idyllic countryside where they can live off the land? Ken is so pumped with adrenalin he wants to mow them down to get to the office.

He slides out of the going-nowhere lane and turns onto a side street into one of the Westside's neighborhoods of multimillion-dollar mansions built to the edges of their tiny lots. People call them McMansions for how fast these cookie-cutter homes spring up, gobbling up lots once home to post-World War II starter homes with big lawns. He notices a black SUV hop out of the traffic as well and follow him onto the street. So, he thinks, I'm not the only guy with a good idea in this town.

Relieved to be moving again, Ken uses the voice command system built into the Jeep to dial the number of Kendall Sage that Juliana gave him. At a stop sign, he makes a left and sees the black SUV behind him do the same. Did Homeland Security send someone to follow him?

She picks up on the second ring and is all business. She tells him she pulled the list of internet protocol addresses that accessed the cryptography proposal. Internet protocol addresses, or IP addresses, are strings of numbers given to every device that connects to the internet. Kind of like street addresses or telephone numbers for gadgets. The IP address identifies the network interface attached to the internet connection. Cell phones, laptops, tablets, game consoles…all possess their own IP addresses. They say in today's electronics-obsessed world, the average person has something like seven IP addresses.

Anyway, from the IP addresses Ken knows he should be able to get a general location for each, as well as the name of the company that provides internet connectivity to that address. From there, with a little help from Bryce, he may able to drill down to names. These may lead to one or more of the hackers. Certainly this Islamic Crusade group has more than a few people working on hacks of this size and complexity.

He gives Kendall his email so she can send him the list and thanks her. A glance in the rearview mirror and he realizes that the black SUV with a tinted windshield is still behind him. And kind of close. Like bumper-kissing close.

Irritated, he bangs on the brakes and shoots his middle finger in the air behind him. He can't see any reaction from the driver behind the tinted windows, but the SUV stays behind him through another right turn. Though it does give him slightly more room.

Why is someone following him? Maybe Bryce sent some of his Homeland buddies to keep an eye on him, but the more Ken thinks about it, the less sense that idea makes. Wouldn't Bryce have told him?

Is it possible that the Islamic Crusade has people on the ground in Los Angeles? It isn't hard to imagine, since they targeted two of the city's utilities in the same number of days. The DWP hack is good enough to make Ken think that whoever did it has some inside knowledge of the system or has done a lot of homework.

Ken is about five blocks from his Westwood office. He considers making a U-turn, doubling back through the gas station on the corner and heading in the opposite direction, just to give them some trouble. But all that will accomplish is wasting his time. He is sure that if they are following him, they have already figured out that he is heading to his office. And it isn't like the address is a secret or anything. It is posted on his website.

So this tailgating must have another purpose, then. To send him a message that they are watching. Though they are bumper to bumper, he can read and commit to memory a few letters "XRP" from the license plate number.

Ken rubs the back of his neck, his fingers biting into muscles in a futile attempt to ease the tension accumulating there. Even though his office is just blocks away, he figures it will be another ten minutes at least before he is there. He inches the Jeep forward, then spins through his music collection on his phone and selects hardcore electronic music with its beeps and snares and bangs. As he cranks the volume on his custom sound system, he hears a pop that sounds impossibly close, followed by a clunk on the Jeep's metal body.

He looks in the side mirror and he sees a man's hand pulling a gun back inside. Whoever they are, they are now shooting at him. His shoulders cave over the steering wheel waiting for the hit from behind. His mind empties out, but for a fleeting image of his mother and Tilly, but it slips away from him as he waits for the next shot to be fired.

But none comes. The line of cars in front of him glides forward a few feet. Did no one hear the shot or realize what happened? Was it real? Then he watches in the rearview mirror as the black SUV does a three-point turn and peels off in the opposite direction, tires squealing. He slumps against the back of the seat, relieved.

Ken takes his foot off of the brake and lets the Jeep roll forward until he is at the stop sign. Getting shot at in real life is way more intense than it is in *Halo* or any of the other video games he played. He feels claustrophobic in the Jeep now and wants to jump out and run a mile. The surplus energy goes to his hands, which are slick and shaking like crazy on the steering wheel. Catch your breath, he tells himself. So he sits for a few moments, and takes two deep breaths until the motorists behind him lean on their horns. Someone flips him the bird. Los Angeles drivers, only concerned about getting where they want to go. He doesn't care. His stomach churns into a wave of nausea. He unscrews the lid on one of the ever-present water bottles rattling around in his cup-holders, and takes a long drink.

He calls Bryce and leaves a message, something along the lines of they're fucking shooting at me. Then he drives the few blocks to his office—traffic is mercifully lighter—and pulls into the subterranean parking garage. The right taillight is shot to splinters all collected in the little wire mesh cage that Jeep so thoughtfully put around it. They probably did that to protect the plastic from bouncing rocks, not bouncing bullets, but welcome to the jungle, Ken thinks. The chess game he is playing, matching intellect for intellect in the cerebral world of computer programming, is now something real.

Chapter 30

Juliana sits in the front seat of the transport ambulance with her head craned backwards so she can watch the back of Omar's head. Dr. Duva sits in the jump seat, white-knuckling the metal grab handle as the ambulance jerks through traffic.

The traffic is worse than she imagined. Cars were stopped for so long that the drivers shut the engines off. A few stand on the freeway's concrete and lean on the door frames of their automobiles, smoking and staring into the distance.

"We're gonna need lights and sirens to get some attention, ma'am," the driver says. He looks ex-military to Juliana, with his blond hair cropped so short it resembles peach fuzz. His eyes are hidden by wrap-around black sunglasses. He is careful to keep his face neutral, but Juliana detects the slightest quiver of excitement in the way his lips curl. He flicks a few switches and the sirens scream as he noses the ambulance into traffic and weaves through three lanes of traffic. Most people respond, either backing up or pulling forward enough in the stalled traffic to let the ambulance make its way to the northbound side of Sepulveda.

The sun is setting, leaving pink-tinged clouds in the west. They pick up speed on Sepulveda, driving down the middle lane designated for left turns as though it is their own private bypass. Strip malls and gas stations and car washes whiz by. Juliana watches the blur of typical San Fernando Valley scenery broken by the occasional stucco apartment building or church.

Blandness on a grid, Juliana thinks, but still her home. She grew up in these Valley flats, far from the twisting canyons and the big movie star houses that are south of Ventura Boulevard. Living in "the valley" is as much a Los Angeles insult today as it was thirty years ago, but she doesn't mind. It is home.

From Sepulveda, the driver skims onto Sherman Way and drives up the entrance to the 405 Freeway on the shoulder, bypassing another snarl of cars waiting to get on.

"Looks like we're going to have to drive the shoulder all the way," the driver says to her, reminding her of a cowboy with his half-hidden smile at the joy of driving fast. She looks back at Omar.

"I wish you could be up here," she says to him, making her voice as bright and carefree as she can. As though they take ambulance rides through mobs of fleeing citizens all the time. "We're driving past six lanes of stopped traffic. It's something to see."

No answer from Omar, not even a nod of his head. She catches Dr. Duva's eyes and mouthes, "Is he okay?"

"Eyes shut," she mouthes back. She puts her stethoscope on his chest and listens, rocking back and forth with the motion of the ambulance.

"Sounds okay," she says. She pumps up the blood pressure cuff and counts off. "130 over 80."

A Toyota Camry pushes its black nose onto the shoulder, like the driver is trying to peer into the distance to see how far the line-up of cars extended. Juliana wonders for a split second how the Camry's driver doesn't see their flashing lights. "Stop!," she yells, but the Camry driver can't hear her and the ambulance driver already knows what he needs to do. The ambulance driver swerves to the right and hits the brakes hard. The ambulance began to tilt, the driver's side going up slightly. Juliana wonders frantically if they are driving on two wheels. Out of nowhere, she remembers Omar showing her videos of cars being driven on two wheels—he'd called it sidewall skiing. Omar. She wants to turn around to see her son, but her eyes are glued on the road ahead, the pending impact into the side of the black Camry. She is shaking so hard she can feel her earrings flick against her neck. Then there's the sound of tires screeching and the siren starts up, impossibly loud. She can smell the pads burning as they lock onto the tires. Juliana's body snaps forward against the safety belt then ricochets back.

The ambulance crunches into the tan sound wall with a sickening thud. Blood streams from the driver's nose and his sunglasses hang crookedly off of one ear. Juliana unsnaps the seat belt and scrambles out of her seat to the back, where Dr. Duva is bent over Omar protectively.

The two paramedics, a man and woman, open the back doors wide and jump out. Through the front window, Juliana sees the black Toyota, mangled and smashed into white truck. Brown smoke rises from its ruined hood. Its windshield is shattered, a spiderweb of broken glass, reflecting back the ambulance's flashing red and yellow lights. The passenger door on the right side hangs open and she sees the profile of a woman sitting still, her head back and her arm twitching.

"Omar, talk to me," Dr. Duva says.

"Did something hit him?" Juliana says. Breathing hurts, so she tries to take shallow breaths so her ribs will quit screaming in protest. A metallic taste coats her tongue and the back of her throat, but her mouth is too dry to swallow it away.

Dr. Duva shakes her head, but she looks unsure.

Omar is still strapped into the gurney and it is still locked. But he is unresponsive.

Dr. Duva fishes in her pocket and brings out a miniature flashlight and holds one of his eyelids open, then the other. She places two fingers on his jugular vein.

"Omar, Omar, it's Mom," she says. "Can you hear me, baby?"

Nothing. This isn't happening. Can't be happening. Juliana feels the heat rise in her throat. Hot tears fall onto her cheeks.

"Omar, you wake up right now," she says.

"Maria," Dr. Duva shouts. "Eddie! The kid's in defib!"

The doctor reaches for the defibrillator while the driver tries to climb past Juliana to the back to help. Juliana cups Omar's beautiful head, that strong chin, in her hands. "Baby, stay with us," she says.

It is not his time, God. You can't say this is his time. He's barely done anything. He may have kissed a girl or two but he hasn't even been in real love yet. He's barely old enough to drive a car. He barely needs to shave. He's a baby. He's my baby. He hasn't voted. He hasn't made enough mistakes yet. He hasn't made ANY real mistakes yet. He's hardly lived, between the headaches and the hospital stays and my overprotectiveness. If anyone should die today, it should be me instead of him. Not him.

"Clear!"

His body ripples against the restraints and thumps back against the gurney's padding.

Dr. Duva listens through her stethoscope to his chest, shakes her head and the driver turns toward the machine again.

"Clear!"

The electroshock pulses through his body and Juliana holds her breath. *I'll breathe when he does*, she thinks.

Dr. Duva listens again to his chest, then smiles. "We have a normal rhythm now," she says.

Juliana expels the breath in her lungs with force and a relieved smile. She breathes deeply in and watches Omar's chest rise and fall with his own breath.

"Is the ambulance still driveable?" Dr. Duva asks. "We really need to get this boy to the hospital."

"Let me check," the driver says. He hops out the back and circles around until he reappears in front of the windshield.

The female EMT appears at the back hatch. "Doctor? Woman out here having trouble breathing," she says. "California Highway Patrol just arrived. They're calling for another transport for her."

Juliana hears the ambulance engine cough then turn over.

"It's running," the driver shouts from the front seat. "We're banged up bad but looks like the wheels aren't obstructed. I think we can drive it."

"Let's do it," Dr. Duva says.

Chapter 31

Ken finds Mo hunched over his laptop in the office's tiny break room, a cup of steaming hot Earl Grey tea with lemon next to him.

"I think I'm getting a cold," Mo sniffles. He speaks through dry, cracked lips and his nose flares as red as the stripes on his flannel shirt.

"I think you've got a cold already. You're way beyond the getting phase. You should go home," Ken says.

Mo nods, but any words he intends to speak are overtaken by a series of sneezes. Ken backs away from him like he has the plague. Mo looks so pathetic, he questions whether he should tell him about getting shot at. He quickly decides he must, though. Mo needs to know what is going on. He might be in danger too.

"Maybe it's not related," Mo says. "Could have just been crime. A car jacking, maybe?"

"It felt more like a warning shot," Ken says. He grabs a can of beer from the refrigerator and pops the top. He doesn't usually drink in the afternoon but he also doesn't usually get shot at on his commute. "You should definitely go home, Mo," he says, as the other man blows his nose loudly. Mo nods, and Ken flees the room, holding his breath. He cannot afford to get sick.

Ken sits in his desk chair, beer can sweating in his hand, and looks out over the cemetery with its plain white headstones, uniform in size and color, creating a horizon of patterns that he usually finds relaxing to look at. But now, all he can think about is death. Whoever that was in the black SUV, they could have easily killed him today if they had wanted. They could have shot out his tires and forced him to crash. They could have aimed for his head or chest and shot him behind the wheel. But instead, they chose to shoot out his taillight after following him on a route he'd taken for years—his mother's house to his office.

His mother. Did this mean that these guys, whoever they are, know where his mother lives? Is she in danger? He is relieved when Bryce finally calls him back and interrupts his train of thought. He takes a long drink of the beer and lets it wash through him, dulling the sharp edges.

"I'm at UCLA," Bryce says. "Why don't I drive over there and we can talk in person?"

Ken gives him directions on how to access the parking garage. No point in ruminating, he thinks, and opens his email to look for the message from Kendall with the IP addresses of the machines used to download Mahaz's paper.

The list isn't long, as he expects. He takes another swig of beer. Only about fifty different IP addresses. Using cryptography is more in the realm of the computer security profession than the typical computer user. Most people aren't too concerned about sending their cat videos, emails or even pictures of their most private body parts in code. Among those people like Ken who do take the time to use encryption, a version named Pretty Good Privacy is popular. It uses a two-key method to protect corporate and government email messages, credit card information and passwords. One key is given to the person sending the message, and the other key is held by the recipient and used to decrypt the message.

What Mahaz created in this paper is so far above the standard of Pretty Good Privacy as to be nearly unbreakable. Not that there is such a thing as unbreakable code anymore. The most powerful computers in the world, like ones held by the National Security Agency or the Defense Department, may be able to crack the encryption, but even for computer security professionals, the task will take so long that it may as well be impossible.

The beer is working its magic and it is a relief to have a task to think about. Ken decides his first step with the list is to make a chart of the geographic region of each and the name of the internet service provider. This is the easiest information to find online and it may help him see if any patterns evolve.

He is about halfway through the list when his cell phone rings. He buzzes Bryce into the building.

The cowboy boots are obviously a staple in his wardrobe, Ken thinks, though today he wears a dark blazer over his shirt. Bryce casts his eyes around the grey and white reception area with its vintage Ms. PacMan arcade console in one corner and framed Star Wars posters on the wall.

"Nice office," he says. He pinches the bridge of his nose and takes a deep breath.

"Benefits of being the boss," Ken says. "You get to decorate how you want. You want a beer?"

Bryce shakes his head. "Being the boss sounds pretty good to me on days like today. You wouldn't believe the politics bullshit we put up with," he says. He opens his mouth as if to say more, then pauses for a moment before changing the topic.

"Who was the guy who just left?"

"Must have been Mo Mansour. He's my program analyst. I mentioned him before. He's the only other person in here today."

"How long have you known him?"

"Since college," Ken says. "Why?"

Bryce doesn't answer. "Anyway, I saw your Jeep in the garage. It looks like someone was trying to get your attention, maybe scare you a little."

"They've definitely got my attention," Ken says. "But that's not going to make me stop working on this."

"Good for you," Bryce says, pulling a small leather book from his pocket. "You see the shooter? Get a license plate number?" Ken gives him the information and watches while the other man scribbles the letters "XRP" down using one of those stubby golf pencils.

"Let me call this in to one of the desk jockeys," he says. "At least for once we've got a pretty clear-cut crime. I've got a bad feeling about these guys."

Ken tries to bring him up to speed on the work he is doing with the IP addresses. But Bryce is more interested in talking about who knows what Ken is doing.

"Lots of people know about the second version of the worm," Bryce says. "It's flooding into systems everywhere. But your idea for killing the communications via the domain names, what did you call that?"

"Sinkholing," Ken says. "That's where we direct requests to those sites into a dead end instead of resolving. That effort is going to give us a good list of infected machines too, if you want to scan it to see what government systems are infected."

Bryce nods. "Yeah, sinkholing. Who knows about that?"

"I think Arletta put it out on the email list of volunteers," Ken says. "And really, it's the obvious move anyway. Anyone who knows anything about this would figure that is what we would do as a defensive move."

There is a moment of silence as Ken realizes that he may have insulted Bryce by implying that he doesn't know something as basic as what sinkholing is. But if Bryce noticed, he just let it roll off his back without comment.

"Did you talk to anyone else today?"

"My mom," Ken says. "Oh, and I called this woman, Juliana Al-Dossari. She's on the task force. She's married to Mahaz Al-Dossari. Remember how I mentioned that the new version uses this crazy high level of cryptography? Well, he's the guy who wrote that proposal. Works at UCLA. I asked her if we could get a list of who accessed the web page where that paper was posted."

Bryce straightens in his seat. "What time did you do that?"

"Before I left my mother's house to come here."

Bryce shakes his head slowly.

Now it is Ken's turn to sit up straight. "You think that Al-Dossari's having something to do with this?"

"He has a lot of ties to Saudi Arabia," Bryce says. "Including some who are known supporters of Islamic jihadist fighters."

"That could just mean he grew up there," Ken says. "It's not fair. You can't just assume…"

Bryce cuts him off. "Save the liberal let's-give-him-the-benefit-of-the-doubt bullshit for your girlfriend. I live in the real world. And I don't assume anything," he says. "I just don't believe in coincidences."

Chapter 32

Three white-coated people wait on the ambulance bay as the damaged transport pulls into Glendale Adventist, a massive hospital complex north of downtown Los Angeles.

The smell of exhaust and burning diesel from the ambulance give way to the disinfectant and alcohol smell of the emergency room. Juliana catches a whiff of microwave popcorn cooking and is surprised it doesn't bring a hunger response. She hasn't eaten in hours. *Worry will do that to you*, she thinks.

Emergency rooms are noisy, fast-moving places. The people who work in such a place must thrive on the action, and she takes comfort in bustling efficiency. She watches as they swarm around Omar, their voices loud and their sentences broken bits of medical jargon. Machines beep and chime and jingle in the background.

A red-haired woman in pink scrubs approaches her with a clipboard. "Admissions paperwork," she says, and Juliana is relieved to have something to do, even if it is the most tedious of tasks. Doctor's names, medical histories, on and on. She's filled out forms like this a million times.

"Where are they taking him?"

"Prep for surgery," the woman says. "Come with me, fill this out and then I'll take you up to the surgical floor."

She follows the woman into the emergency waiting area, where she can feel the anxious eyes of a dozen people on her, all hoping, like she is, for relief or answers. Their eyes fall back to their phones and tablets and magazines when they see the nurse had not come out for them.

She settles into an empty chair near the admissions desk, where the head of the receptionist is barely visible through the window. Her ribs on the right side are still screaming in pain with every breath, and her neck is so stiff she can't rotate it to see her right shoulder.

She takes out a mirror to see if she has blood or bruises on her face, grateful there is none. She catches one glimpse of her own eyes, full of fear and anxiety, and snaps the compact shut.

She calls Mahaz to tell him they arrived at Glendale Adventist worse for wear, delivering the news of the accident and Omar's worsening condition as factually as she can.

"Juliana, are you all right?"

Her eyes fill with tears.

"I'm fine. Maybe a little banged up but fine. Our baby…"

"Omar will be fine, *inshallah*."

She hasn't heard Mahaz use the Arabic word for "God willing" in a long time, maybe years. Has he had a return to his religion? *A sick child will do that to you*, she thinks, remembering her own prayers in the hospital hallway before the lights went out. And among all this crisis, who minds a little extra prayer?

"I'll be there as soon as I can," Mahaz says. "We're just in Beverly Hills now, a few blocks from my mother's."

"Maybe you should bring Leila here," she says. She wants her daughter here so she can hold her close.

"Let us stick with our plan," he says. "Leila can stay with my mother and do her homework. Let us not have both children sitting in a hospital today."

She sighs. "All right, yes," she says before hanging up. Maybe she is being selfish anyway. Leila doesn't need to spend more time in hospitals than she already does. Let her be away from this place so full of worry and anxiety you can taste it on the air.

The woman with the pink scrubs pushes through the door and makes a direct line for Juliana.

"Come on," she says. "Bring the paperwork and we'll finish it upstairs. Your son is having a rough day today."

Juliana swings her purse on her shoulder and clutches the clipboard with the admissions paperwork to her chest like a shield.

"The accident?"

"Somehow he sustained a chest trauma in that accident." The woman takes unnaturally long strides for someone so short, Juliana thinks, struggling to keep up with her as she rushes through the long corridor toward a bank of elevators.

"That's what caused the cardiac arrest," she says. "They're waiting to see if he's stable enough for the operation to take the shunt out for the infection."

By the time they reach the elevator, Juliana is out of breath. She clutches the right side of her rib cage as though providing support will stop the pain, and the nurse gives her the once over.

"Did you get hurt in that accident too? Are you having trouble breathing?"

"It's just this pain, when I breathe. I'm okay."

The nurse grabs her arm and steers her back down the hallway they just traversed.

"You probably have broken ribs," she says. "And we need to make sure there isn't more damage."

"No, not now," Juliana says, trying to shake her hand off of her arm. "I want to be with my son."

"You're no good to him if you're not well," she says. "We need to get an X-ray at least."

Juliana stops dead in her tracks. "I'm not going. I need to be with my son."

"They have him sedated," the nurse says. "He's resting and I bet we can get this done before he even wakes up. Certainly before he goes into surgery. Please, come with me. You need to be looked at."

Juliana pauses for a moment, letting the words sink in. She feels torn and broken. The nurse, sensing her hesitation, decides to up the ante.

"You might have punctured your lung or had some other internal damage. You might be bleeding. You could feel okay now but later you'll collapse."

Juliana lets her shoulders slump. She doesn't have the energy to fight. She follows the nurse back into the ER.

Chapter 33

Niels Jansen's broad face pops up on Ken's online calling service while Bryce speaks in one-word sentences to his office.

"Did you hear that PersonalPro has put up a reward of $500,000 for identifying the people behind the worm?"

Ken hasn't. "That's a nice chunk of change."

"I guess they wanted to make it large enough to get some attention."

"The money might change things, get more people involved," Ken says.

"That's what I'm worried about," Niels says. "You know, some of the guys on the working group aren't participating for the pure research aspect. I think some of them are hoping to cash in down the line. All this data we're going to collect about the botnet has real and increasing commercial value, you know. Long lists of infected computers could translate into customer lists for some of the big anti-virus companies."

Ken knows this. He is in the true believer camp. He does what he does because he believes in the idea of the internet as good for the world. It is certainly exciting to work on the project, and yes, it won't hurt his reputation.

But people have made money off of domain names and the internet nearly since it began. The great American way. To think they won't is to seriously have your head in the sand. He knows firsthand that not everyone in the world is so idealistically motivated.

"Shayne contacted the Chinese and told them about the domain name generation and our sinkholing operation," Niels says in his trademark monotone style.

Shayne Pyther is brilliant, but—putting it politely—is as entrepreneurial as they came. He made his fortune snapping up domain names before anyone realized their value back in the early 1990s. Rumor has it he sold pornography-dot-com for two million dollars. He was at the task force meeting a few days ago at the DoubleTree boasting how he could penetrate a SCADA system in minutes. Typical braggadocio from one of the security community's most money-hungry members.

Ken's nostrils flare as they do when he is angry. "What's his angle? Did he ask them for money or do it out of the goodness of his heart?" That would be just like him to capitalize on the hard work of volunteers. Already one of Shayne's colleagues is marketing a "worm cleaning software package" aimed at taking advantage of the growing news coverage around the worm and the hacking of the water system. Ken checked it out. It offers nothing but protection against standard viruses and worms that have been known about for years. At best, Shayne is mislabeling the product.

"He said that he thought he should when he saw dot-cn appear on the list of domain names being generated. He said that was the best way to get CCN on board with helping to sinkhole the domains."

CCN, or the China Central Network, registers all websites ending in dot-cn. It also operates as an arm of the Chinese Information Administration, a sister agency to the one that operates the Golden Shield. Most people in the internet community refer to the Golden Shield as "the great firewall" for its country-wide website blocking and surveillance.

"Bullshit," Ken says. "Why wouldn't he talk to us first? I've already got the IUIA on board to help, and they were going to coordinate with CCN. And what if China's involved somehow? Homeland Security says our little group might be compromised."

Bryce, hearing the name of his agency, looks at Ken with his eyebrows raised while still holding the phone to his ear.

"So, that's why I'm calling you," Niels says. "Look, we've found an error in part of the code in the new strain. It creates the potential for us to insert our own code and hijack the entire botnet. You're the only one I'm telling about it because I think it is our opportunity to take down the worm before it does any more harm."

Ken goes completely still. It is the first beacon of hope he's heard that they can actually attack the botnet rather than just kill its communications network.

"Where is it?"

"The error sits in the encryption algorithm," Niels says, leaning in with a smile flickering around his lips. "Buffer overflow."

Bryce ends his call and walks to the monitor. "What's that?"

Niels pauses for a few moments before speaking. "And who are you?" Niels asks, not unkindly.

"Bryce Ballen, Homeland Security," he says, like he expects bowing and flagellation. If he does, Niels isn't about to give him any.

"Ah, you mean United States Homeland Security," Niels says. "Not my homeland security."

"Niels' in Sweden," Ken says. "Buffer overflow is a well-known hacker's trick. It's a vulnerability in pretty much every bit of software written in C or C++."

"Which is nearly everything you use on a daily basis, Bryce,"

Niels says. "It allows a hacker to interrupt whatever program or subroutine a computer is running and create a distraction. Then it points it in a new direction that the hacker chooses."

Bryce squints at Niels' tiny face on the screen. Before he can ask another question, Ken jumps in with an analogy he likes to use in the class he teaches. "Think of a computer as a person translating a letter that was written in a language he doesn't understand very well. Every time the person whose job it is to translate the letter comes to a word he doesn't know, he marks his place in the document and then turns away to look up the word in a dictionary. When he comes back to the letter, he looks for his place and starts again."

"Okay," Bryce says. "Got it."

"That's how a computer reads programs. Say there is a hacker who doesn't want the person translating the letter to read the real letter, because it says not to give credit card information to anyone. Instead, the hacker wants them to read a different letter, one that says to give the hacker the credit card number and expiration date.

"So the hacker sends a bunch of letters to the translator all at once, so that the translator gets confused and has to stop translating the first letter to handle all the incoming requests. Without getting into too much detail, all these incoming requests erase the marker the translator left on his original letter. So when he tries to go back to find his place in the original letter, he has to rely on the information the hacker sent instead. Which sends him to the new letter that tells him to give the hacker his credit card information. So he never sees what the original letter said. He sees only what the hacker wants him to see."

Bryce clears his throat. "So we need to hack the hacker then. If we're successful, we could take over the botnet."

"Potentially," says Niels.

"Is this something you two could do?"

Ken laughs while Niels shakes his head. "We might need some help," Ken says. "It's been a long time since I tried to exploit a buffer overflow. And even if we're able to exploit this one, it is only in the encryption implementation. It's not in the worm's actual payload."

"I might know someone who could help, but I'm going to have to pull in a lot of favors to get access to him," Bryce says. "Ever heard of AcidTwin?"

"The guy who hacked the Air Force looking for proof of UFOs a couple of years ago?"

"Yeah, him. We kept the FBI from pressing charges and use him for some special, covert projects. But here's the thing. None of this to the list."

"Do you think we ought to at least inform Dr. Al-Dossari? As a professional courtesy?" Niels asks.

Both Ken and Bryce shake their heads.

Chapter 34

Left by herself in one of the emergency examination areas after a series of tests, Juliana spends a minute noting mentally all the places she hurts, now that the doctor has pointed them out. Her arm, her right side, her lungs. Outside the privacy curtains, she can hear the chatter of the staff and the low multilingual murmurs of the patients and their families in for chest pains and stomach aches and sprained ankles. The emergency room at Glendale Adventist is packed, a well-lit oasis in a region largely without electrical light to fight off twilight.

A hand grabs the curtain and pulls it slowly to the side. An elfin looking man with a smattering of freckles on his young face and a blue net cap covering his hair peers at her. "Excuse me," he says.

"Yes?" She welcomes the visit and hopes it meant they are done with the tests and she can go find Omar. He steps in and the first thing she notices is his bare feet and calves. But then she nearly falls off of the hospital bed when she sees that underneath his dark blue Nirvana T-shirt, he wears nothing except for a worn green bath towel. She catches a glimpse of his very white upper thigh before deciding to keep her eyes trained exclusively on his.

"I'm Dr. Fitzsimmons," he says. "I understand you were in an accident." He holds his empty hands in front of him as though he is holding a clipboard. And he seems to be reading from that imaginary clipboard.

Juliana casts her eyes around wildly. Where is the nurse who brought her here? Is she on one of those hidden camera shows?

"Yes, I was in an accident," she says, calculating her steps to the hallway and what she hopes will be safety beyond. She has to find her son. She's been wasting time in the emergency room long enough with the X-rays and the CT scan and the endless waiting. She is not about to sit still for an examination from a man in a bath towel who wants to play doctor.

"But I'm fine. I was just going to take off and go find my son. He's being taken into surgery," she says.

She hops off the bed and tries to ignore the dizziness that clouds her head when her weight hits her legs. She leans back against the bed for support. The man moves toward her, exposing more leg. He smells pleasant, like cinnamon, she thinks.

She hears the clatter of curtains yanked open and the nurse in the pink scrubs appears like an angel from heaven.

"Mr. Fitzsimmons," she says. "We've been looking for you."

"I'm Dr. Fitzsimmons," he says, giving the nurse a scathing look.

Her face dissolves into an apologetic smile. "Yes, of course, Dr. Fitzsimmons," she says. "We need your, er, consultation on another patient." She wraps an arm around his shoulders and escorts him out of the room.

He turns his head so his profile faces her. "I have it on the best authority that your son will be fine," the man says, giving her a reassuring smile. "He has God on his side. They told me so."

Juliana can't help but smile. Maybe the man really has information from his invisible sources. Anyway, who is she not to believe it?

She watches him pad on bare feet across the tile floor, hitching up his towel that is slowly edging further down his hips.

After a few moments, the nurse returns. "Sorry about that," she says. "You must have thought we have a very relaxed dress code for our doctors."

Juliana smiles. "I was just afraid he was going to give me an unwanted anatomy lesson."

A thin black man in a white coat enters as well, extending his hand. "I'm Dr. Karatu," he says in a proper British accent.

"He's the real deal," the nurse says. "Medical license, pants…" Juliana appreciates that the nurse is trying to make her laugh, even if she is still just a bit disturbed by the intrusion.

"Mrs. Al-Dossari, the CT shows that your ribs are cracked, not broken. Doesn't look like there is any internal damage," the doctor says. "The most we can do for you is some pain relief."

"I'm fine," she says.

"You're still in shock," the doctor says. "You're not feeling the full range of pain yet. I suggest you take something, just so you can be comfortable and present for your son."

"Take me to him, please," she says. The nurse holds out a paper cup with a couple of pills in it, and Juliana chases them down with a drink of cold water. She needs to be with Omar. How long had she been down here? Where is Mahaz?

Chapter 35

The surgical waiting area faces a bank of windows looking out on the curving walkways between the buildings, now lit in an orangey glow from the small lights dotting the sidewalk at regular intervals. Juliana has the space to herself. No one else is waiting.

Mahaz arrives in a rush, skirting past three nurses in scrubs behind the desk who are chatting about what to serve at somebody's wedding reception. He gives her a perfunctory kiss on the cheek and drops into the chair next to hers, his expensive Italian loafers out of place in the hospital where it seems everyone from the doctors to the orderlies wear sneakers.

"They said on the news that the power was back on for LA," he says. "Hasn't helped much with traffic though."

She senses his presence like a heavy magnetic force, almost hypnotic. She was so ready to turn over control to the ER nurse hours earlier, and now to him. Must be the painkillers, she thinks, shifting position just enough to reignite the throb of pain in her side and make her feel more awake.

The surgeon strides in, his head covered in a green bandanna that matches his eyes. Juliana has seen enough surgeons over the course of Omar's illness that she knows instantly that the surgery went well.

She smiles before he even gets the words out.

"Mr. and Mrs. Al-Dossari?" he says.

They nod. "I'm Dr. Mantenga," he says. "The surgery went fine, as good as we could expect. He's stable and resting now in recovery. You should be able to go see him in about thirty minutes."

Mahaz stands up. He is taller than the surgeon by at least a foot, and he steps into the man's space like she has seen him do so many times. The surgeon holds his ground and shakes his hand, his neck craning at an uncomfortable angle to meet Mahaz's eyes.

He pumps the surgeon's arm. "Thank you, thank you," he says, then puts his arm on Juliana's shoulder and though his touch is light, she winces from the bruise forming on her upper arm. "We are so grateful," he says.

When the surgeon leaves, Mahaz settles back in the chair and brings out his laptop.

"So," he says. "What have you heard from your friends about these hackers that are using my encryption method?"

She blinks, thrown by the change in topic. "Nothing so far," she says. "I don't even know if Kendall and Ken got in touch yet. I dozed off for a while."

Blue light from the computer screen reflects off of his reading glasses. "They have," he says.

Of course, she thinks. Kendall Sage doesn't make a move without telling him.

"Log on to your email," he says. "See if there are any developments."

She fishes in her purse for her smart phone and brings up her email.

"These guys send about twenty emails a day to this list," she says. "I can see why you didn't want to be on it. They're more gossipy than Leila and her friends."

"I just heard there was a second version of the worm floating around now," Mahaz says.

"You know more than me," she says, her eyes scanning subject lines. "Oh, here. Here's one from that woman I sat next to at the meeting. Arletta Therault. It's about worm 2.0. She's asking if anyone else saw the hole she found in the code."

Mahaz straightens up and takes the phone from her. "Let me see that," he says. She reads over his shoulder but can't make sense of much of it.

"What's a buffer overflow?" she asks.

"It is a mistake," he says.

"That's a good thing, right?" she says. "The hackers made a mistake?"

Voices and footsteps sound in the hallway outside, breaking up the quiet little universe of the surgery waiting room. Mahaz rises to his feet and crosses to the window. Juliana stares at the grid of lights spreading away from the hospital complex to the mountains.

"Yes, the hackers made a mistake."

Chapter 36

"You have got to be kidding me!" Ken erupts as he reads Arletta's email to the task force email chain about the buffer overflow.

Bryce hits the brakes a few feet short of the stop sign and Ken's head snaps back against the headrest.

"What the hell happened now?" He takes a puff of his cigarette and blows the smoke out through the half-open driver's side window. Ken fills him in.

"This is the problem with civilians and volunteers," Bryce says, easing his foot off the brake so the car inches forward to the stop sign and makes a proper stop. "No sense of secrecy."

Ken glares at Bryce. As much as he wants to play for the good guys, his deep distrust of government stems from the National Security Agency's surveillance activities so well publicized in 2013. The internet was crowd-sourced and built from the bottom-up by people trying to make a difference, not by bureaucrats and law enforcement types eager to impose secrecy and borders and power structures.

"As I've said before, welcome to the internet, Bryce. Task forces and volunteers are how we roll," Ken says.

"So, how come our friend we're about to see doesn't play nice with you white hats?"

Ken thinks about AcidTwin, or Dylan Brody. "About ten years ago I heard him speak at a hacker's conference in Menlo Park. He'd presented a point-by-point proof why the United States government was denying the existence of UFOs and alien life on this planet that almost made sense."

Bryce raises his eyebrows as Ken continues. "Like a lot of people there that day, I just figured his brilliant mind was ruined by his well-known penchant for transvestite prostitutes, crack cocaine, and UFO conspiracy theories, not necessarily in that order. He went into a self-imposed exile after that. Dropped off the forums, didn't show up at the conferences."

Bryce parallel parks into a tight space in front of a two-story stucco apartment building plastered with hand made signs demanding owners "curb their dogs." The signs are completely ineffective, Ken thinks, picking his way through a minefield of dog poop to the metal gate leading to the apartment's courtyard.

A filthy pool glitters in security lights installed in each corner. Television laugh tracks and the smell of broiling meat wafts out from screen doors.

North Hollywood is a tumble down Los Angeles neighborhood, trying to remake itself as an arts district. But this apartment building where AcidTwin chooses to live is a throwback to its old reputation as a gang-infested neighborhood filled with cheap housing. Its claim to fame? That 1997 shootout where two bank robbers in body armor outgunned the LAPD for thirty minutes before getting shot in the head.

Bryce bangs on the metal edge of the screen door. The wooden door behind it creaks open to reveal the face of the hacker, now older of course, who Ken recognizes from the conference years ago. Behind him, a disco ball throws shards of white light on the walls and floor. Electronica pulses from two huge speakers flanking a fifty-inch screen television.

Bryce flashes his badge. "I'm the one who called you," he says.

AcidTwin focuses his eyes like lasers on Ken. "Where's your badge?"

"He's with me. Dylan, this is Ken. Ken, Dylan."

Bryce pulls the screen door open and Ken extends his hand out in greeting. AcidTwin backs up and flattens himself against the wall so they can enter.

Inside, the darkness is absolute. Thick curtains cover the windows. Only the disco ball and the three computer monitors on the kitchen table emanate any light. It smells faintly of marijuana smoke.

"We're here on business, not for a rave," Bryce says. "You could turn on a few lights in here so we can see."

AcidTwin shuts the front door, extinguishing the shard of light coming in from outside as effectively as someone sealing a tomb. Bryce, not one to wait, snaps up a light switch that fills the kitchen with dark red light. It makes Ken think of a crime scene with body parts stacked in the freezer and blood smears and drips on the carpet, and television reporters interviewing neighbors who say only that "he kept to himself."

"Don't you have any normal lights around here?" Bryce flicks the red light off and this time reaches for a metal work light by the monitors. Seeing normal white light glow, he nods with satisfaction and turns back to AcidTwin.

"I looked at the file you sent," AcidTwin says. "What you want is not easy."

Bryce lights a cigarette without asking and throws the match in a trashcan overflowing with beer cans and take-out food cartons. He points at the beer cans. "Don't you believe in recycling?"

AcidTwin shrugs. "Doesn't matter, really, does it?" The couch creaks as he plops down on the middle cushion and stretches his arms out to either side. "They just keep us busy with little 'good citizen' tasks like recycling so we don't notice the bigger, awful things that are going on all around us."

"Like UFOs, right?" Ken can't resist baiting him.

AcidTwin snorts and rolls his eyes. "You're obviously brainwashed, tagging along with Homeland Security like a puppy dog."

"Watch it, Dylan," Bryce says. "No need to get personal. And we're not here to talk about UFOs, right, Ken? We're here to talk about worms and buffer overflows."

AcidTwin springs off the couch like a nervous rabbit and goes to the table with the monitors.

"Do you know that your hacker named the worm?"

Ken shakes his head.

"It's here, embedded in this bit of code. He calls it *chrysalide.* French word for chrysalis."

"The caterpillar before it becomes a butterfly? I think I read my little girl a story about that," Bryce says.

"You have a little girl?" AcidTwin says. "I would have guessed bachelor for life, frozen dinners on the hot plate."

"How about married for thirty years, Dylan?" Bryce says. He drops his cigarette butt in a mug of forgotten coffee. "Anyway, so now we know the hacker is a poet. We're still in the same place."

"No, Bryce," AcidTwin hisses his name like a snake. "We are in a very good place. I know how we can inject poison into this chrysalis so the butterfly never flies."

"That," Ken says, "is a horrible analogy."

"But a winning strategy," Bryce says.

"Are you up for a hackathon, Ken?"

"Sure," Ken says. "I'll sleep when I'm dead, right?"

Chapter 37

He made a mistake. The worst kind, too. One of hubris. He became too arrogant and too prideful, admiring his code like a peacock preening and making a script kiddie mistake.

He'd forgotten to patch the buffer overflow.

Shame rises like a bubble in his throat, choking him with his own pride. He gave the enemy a foothold, a critical mistake in his fight for the glory of Allah.

Will he be exposed before he can leave the United States? Before he can execute the worm's grand finale? He feels his plans sliding through his fingers, grains of sand returning to the desert.

He shakes his head. Nonsense. There is no way they can actually figure out how to exploit the error before the launch date in two days.

Or is that thought further evidence of his pride? At this point, he has to assume they are trying to exploit the error. Instead of dismissing their capabilities, he would do well to assume that they have a good chance of being successful. It is foolish to think otherwise.

He should inform Proxyw0rm but he hesitates to do so until he ascertains a fix for the problem. He doesn't want Proxyw0rm to take control of what is quite a large Achilles heel in his beautiful botnet. *Chrysalide* has infected close to 1.5 million computers last time he checked and most of those were marred by the version 2.0 upgrade containing the error.

He knows Proxyw0rm and the Islamic Crusade employ other programmers, even though they've kept him isolated from any other team members. After all, the Crusade executed their hack into the water and power systems in several American cities without him, so safe to say they have some expertise they can lend. But he doesn't want anyone else touching his creation, which was to be the grand finale of the Crusade's terrorist campaign.

Chapter 38

Juliana looks at Mahaz hunched over his laptop, his tawny skin and dark eyes and perfectly straight nose, and starts a conversation with him in her head. She isn't brave enough yet to say the words out loud, here in another dim hospital room with Omar grogged out on a million drugs to keep him still and let him heal.

You didn't really mean you would take our children to Saudi Arabia, did you, Mahaz? You were mad, you were frustrated at me, and you said the first thing that came into your head.

The words bounce around in her skull, forming faster and faster. *Why do you even stay with me? It has been months and months since we've had sex, so long I don't even care to count anymore. Is it that you love the idea of your perfect American family more than the actual family itself? So that you're prepared to shatter us in half and move eight thousand miles away? To uproot our children, wreck their lives and keep them from me? To strip Leila of personal power, and make her little more than a possession?*

She watches him typing, his lips moving slightly as he concentrates on lines of machine language the way he did when he was a graduate student. Back then, they talked all the time, eating Thai food on the couch they found in an alleyway near their apartment up north. Then, Mahaz wanted to know all about her American childhood, like he wanted to soak it into his bones and make it his own.

"That is the life I want for my children," he said, and she tingled with love and excitement because when he said "my children" he gazed at her with deep longing in his dark eyes. She knew with great certainty that he wanted to have children with her. And she wanted the same. So she told him more stories about Fourth of July fireworks and bonfires at the beach and dollar movies on summer mornings and he listened and smiled and insisted they grill hot dogs even though it was the middle of winter.

When did you stop listening, exactly? Was it after that first trip to the Kingdom, surrounded by your cousins and your uncles who had expected you to marry a Saudi Muslim girl and return home after your American adventure?

Juliana rises and crosses to Omar. Her movement doesn't cause Mahaz to look up from his laptop screen. She sits on the edge of the hospital bed and his eyes flutter open. His long fingers lie flat on the blanket. Piano player fingers, her mother always said, not that Omar ever showed much interest in playing the upright at his grandparents' home despite six months of lessons. His long fingers fly over laptop keyboards and smart phones instead.

"Where are we?" Omar says, his cracked and dry voice the only thing that draws Mahaz's attention briefly. She pours a glass of water from the pitcher and holds the cup to her son's mouth. He takes such a small swallow that it barely wets his lips.

"You are in the hospital, after your surgery," she says.

"No," he says. "I meant what hospital."

"Oh, Glendale Adventist. Do you remember the ambulance ride?"

He shakes his head. *A story for another day*, she thinks, catching

Mahaz's eye as he moves to stand next to the bed with her.

"You need to rest more, Zoom," she says. He smiles at the use of his baby name, shortened over the years from Zoom Zoom because of how fast he crawled on the hardwood floors of their two-bedroom bungalow in Palms.

"I'm not a baby," he says, but he closes his eyes just like one and drifts back into that dreamless, druggy sleep.

Waves of relief continue to break over her that he survived, and she can see the same thoughts in Mahaz's face. Instinctively she seeks his hand out and squeezes, desperate for some comfort and connection with the only other person who can truly understand her pain and worry about Omar. They both love him fiercely. Isn't that almost enough to make them love one another still?

"Did Leila bring up the modeling again?" she asks, by way of introducing the topic. She knows her daughter. Leila will never bring the idea up again to her father. That's why Leila asked her to talk to him about it. Mom as the great convincer.

"No," he says, their hands coming apart without her knowing for sure who let go first.

"She talked to me about it afterwards," Juliana says, bracing mentally for an angry reaction. "She'd really like to do it, and I told her I would talk about it with you some more."

"It's not something I am going to change my mind about." His voice is low and flat. "Modeling objectifies women. It reduces them to glorified hangers for clothing. I'm surprised you're in favor of this."

"This just seems harmless, though, Mahaz. A friend of your mother's wants our daughter to pose in her clothes for pictures. Leila wants to do it. I don't think she's going to wind up in a lingerie catalog as a natural next step."

"Are you listening to me?" he says. "I'm not going to change my mind."

Yes, she thinks, *I'm listening to you. And I'm trying to figure out where the man I married went to, and how long he's been gone.*

"You say that like I don't get a vote in this decision. We're partners, remember?" she says. They'd written their own vows when they got married. To love and cherish one another as equal partners and helpmates. Anger flashes in his eyes, and she welcomes it. *Let's say these things that have needed to be said for years.*

"You are far too lax with her," he says. "You let her do whatever she wants."

"That is not true." She plants her feet, her arms resting on her hips, ready to take him on. She may lack confidence about her social media skills or not having a college degree, but she is completely sure of herself as a mother.

"And you're going to do a better job with her by wrapping her in an *abaya* and sending her to live with your cousins in Riyadh?" she says, anger hardening into conviction. "Over my dead body."

His eyelids drop to half-mast. "Over your dead body. So dramatic, aren't you, Juliana?" Her name is a curse word hissed through tight lips.

Her hand darts toward his cheek before she consciously makes a choice to slap him. Her palm hits his cheek and leaves a red mark along his jawline. His hand touches the place where she made contact, and then in one fluid motion he back-hands her and she stumbles into the armchair. The metallic taste of blood fills her mouth and tears flood her eyes.

"Something has happened to you, Mahaz. You've changed," she says. And now she understands without a doubt that he will take her children to Saudi Arabia, given the chance. And she is not going to let that happen.

"Dad, Mom!" Omar says, his forehead crinkled with worry and lack of comprehension. He grabs for her hand. "Mom, are you okay?"

"I'm fine," she says. "I'm fine."

"I have work to do," Mahaz says. He snaps the laptop shut and shoves it into his bag, and, without looking at either one of them, walks out of the hospital room and into the hallway. Omar and Juliana listen to his footsteps recede.

"What were you fighting about?" Omar says.

"Leila and that modeling job your grandmother got for her," she says.

"Did Dad say he was going to take us to Riyadh? Like to live?"

"He said something like that." Juliana doesn't want to lie to Omar but she hates to upset him. So she tries to find a middle road. "He is just mad. People say things when they're mad that they don't always mean."

"I don't want to live in Saudi Arabia, and Leila doesn't either," he says.

She looks at his thin face, his pointy chin jutting toward the ceiling. Mahaz must have looked just like this when he was seventeen, a boy in Riyadh dreaming of living in the United States, who wanted to eat hot dogs and apple pie, to explore the world beyond the family compound and *Sharia* law, and raise American children. But Mahaz, with his perfect health, never was as introspective and patient as Omar must be, living through long bouts of ill health and reduced activity. Mahaz lives in a world of capability and action that Omar only experiences on his best days.

She kisses him on the forehead, pressing her lips on his smooth skin and breathing in the smell of the Betadine mixed with his sweat. She won't let Mahaz take her children.

Chapter 39

Seven hours have passed since Bryce left them to get the work done, and Ken has spent most of that time trying to find a comfortable position on AcidTwin's broken-down couch as he works.

I'm too old for this, Ken thinks, pulling himself from the jaws of the couch in AcidTwin's dim apartment and noting all the different places and ways his back hurt. He draws the heavy curtain back a few inches and observes a mother in hospital scrubs walking with her young son across the courtyard in the early dawn light.

He stretches his back with a couple of forward bends, his lower spine cracking satisfactorily and reducing some of the pressure he feels.

AcidTwin's bookshelf is full of books: science fiction, UFO scholarship, astronomy and, oddly, cheese making. Ken plucks one titled *The Science of Cheese* but gets bored quickly flipping through its pages of line drawings and lengthy paragraphs about turning milk into curds and whey.

"I've got a nice *chevre* in the refrigerator. Tastes good on toast," AcidTwin says, a disembodied voice seeming to emerge from the three computer monitors in front of him.

Ken is hungry. He hasn't eaten since he was at his mother's house and that was twelve hours ago.

"Maybe just toast with peanut butter," he says.

"Try the cheese, don't be scared of it. It's good," AcidTwin says. "I sell out at the farmer's market every Saturday." He opens the refrigerator and takes out a yellow plastic container to the counter.

Ken walks the few steps to the edge of the kitchen and leans against the counter. "Cheese making, huh?"

"Hobbies, man. That's what keeps your mind fresh," he says. "Don't you do anything other than work?"

"I have a dog," Ken says, feeling a little defensive. "And I love what I do, so it's not work in the traditional sense."

AcidTwin pulls a serrated knife from a wooden block and saws into a loaf of French bread. "So, what got you into playing town sheriff with our friend from Homeland Security?"

Ken thinks about it for a moment, watching AcidTwin arrange thin slices of bread on the toaster oven tray with methodical precision.

"When the worms and viruses turned into money-making ventures instead of techies showing off, I felt like I had to take sides," Ken says. "You know, good versus evil. And you know as well as I do that law enforcement, all those government agencies that are supposed to protect us, they can't even see the cyber threats half the time. Let alone stop them."

AcidTwin punches some buttons on the black toaster oven and turns around to face Ken, his arms crossed on his chest.

"You've got a hero complex," he says. "The world resting on your shoulders."

"I don't see myself as Andy Griffith or Superman, Dylan," he says, sneering the man's given name. "What's your story, then? What makes you pound out code for a suit from Homeland Security? Patriotism? A sense of duty?"

AcidTwin yanks open a drawer and fishes noisily around for a spoon before answering.

"Trying to stay out of federal prison," he says. "Simple as that."

Prison. Yes, Ken agrees, even this dismal apartment is better than prison. Dylan can leave when he wants, watch goat's milk separate into curds, scan the night skies for amorphous globs of light and ghostly shapes hurling through the atmosphere, and speculate if they are vessels containing extra-terrestrial visitors or tourists from some future Earth where time travel is possible.

"The Air Force hack," Ken says.

"Among others," AcidTwin says. "You ever consider that glimpses and reports of things like UFOs might point to the next breakthroughs in technology innovation? And that that is why the United States keeps these sightings and studies relegated to the fringes and the crazies?"

Ken raises his eyebrows as the toaster oven beeps loudly four times. Grabbing a dishcloth to use as a potholder, AcidTwin tugs the metal tray out and dollops heaps of soft white cheese on the toast slices. Ken steps closer to the counter as though to take one, but the other man waves him away. He grasps a bottle of olive oil and drizzles the light yellow oil over the cheese, followed by shakes of freshly ground salt and pepper.

"Okay, now," he says, offering the tray to Ken.

Ken takes a bite. The cheese is creamy and cold, with a bright, lemony taste that pairs perfectly with the warm crunch of the bread. He chews happily and shoots AcidTwin an approving smile.

"You're right, that's good stuff," he says.

"I get the milk from a goat farm run by two gay guys in Oxnard," AcidTwin says. "I drive out there every couple of weeks to pick up a couple of gallons. The trick, though, is in how much salt you use. Some people try to limit the salt because they don't want to corrupt the flavor, but I've learned salt is more critical to the texture."

"Um," Ken says, finishing the second bite of the crostini. "Can I have another one?"

AcidTwin holds the tray out. "My point is some of the biggest technological advances were foreseen in the past, like Thomas Edison predicting in 1911 that all books would be so small and lightweight that you could hold a forty thousand page volume in your hands and it would only be two inches thick. So who are we to say that science fiction ideas like anti-gravity technology, time travel and teleportation are not possible?"

Ken chews thoughtfully. "But who's to say that the government's covering up any of those technologies? First, couldn't aliens elude the authorities pretty easily if they are so advanced? And second, while it's likely that some of the intelligence agencies have looked into the whole UFO phenomenon, it doesn't have to mean they found anything and then covered it up."

"The point is how would we know," AcidTwin says. "Look at all the declassified documents from the FBI and CIA, even from other governments. Clearly they were looking into the flying saucer stories."

Ken shakes his head. What is he doing talking science fiction with this guy when they have work to do? He's finished his portion of the code to exploit the buffer overflow, but he is sure that AcidTwin must still have work to do on the second, harder part of taking over the botnet.

"I think it is the stories of the little green men and the abductions that send people running," Ken says, finding himself compelled to keep digging into AcidTwin's UFO fascination. "I mean, seriously, an alien race is so advanced that they can travel great distances through space, yet they need to conduct tests on humans?"

"Jeez, everyone puts UFO stories in the same silly clown suit.

You know, most ufologists think that the visitors are actually humans from a future or past time? Perhaps a future in which technology has become so advanced it would be inconceivable to our puny present-day brains."

AcidTwin offers Ken the last crostini, and he takes it gratefully.

"We should get back to work," Ken says.

"What do you have left to do?" AcidTwin asks.

"I'm done," Ken says.

"So am I," AcidTwin says. "Show me yours and I'll show you mine."

Chapter 40

The footsteps in the hall are a quiet swish-swish that Juliana expects to pass on by the room where she sits, half-heartedly doing work, while Omar plays video games. More social than it appears, his game playing allows him to transport out of the hospital bed and into the sights and sounds and shadows of another virtual world. She knows he regularly plays against online competitors in far-flung cities like Kuala Lumpur and Rome as well as against his in-person friends from high school in Studio City and Sherman Oaks. The internet strikes down a little of the loneliness and isolation of the chronically sick.

The owner of the soft-soled shoes stops outside the door that the last nurse left half-shut after taking Omar's vitals. It opens as slowly as a door in a haunted house, but with no creaking. Juliana shuts down the list of media clippings from the Center she is compiling and puts the darkened phone in her lap.

"Come in," she calls out in a loud voice, sure now that it is not a member of the hospital staff. They never hesitate. *Maybe it is one of Omar's friends*, she thinks, but the timing isn't right. They would be on their way to school at this time of the morning.

First she sees thick black hair, then the bright blue eyes of Ken

Oakey, the man from the task force. He pokes his head in but leaves the rest of his body on the other side of the door, looking as uneasy as she probably did at that task force meeting.

"Come in," she says again. "Welcome. Omar, this is Ken Oakey. He works with me and your dad."

Ken walks in, his backpack slung over one shoulder. He carries a stuffed teddy bear and behind him trails a thin ribbon with a mylar balloon attached, reading Get Well Soon in purple and green and blue. Omar glances up from the tablet, sees the bear and rolls his eyes.

Ken looks at the bear and then back at Omar and finally at Juliana. "Guess I got the age range wrong, huh?"

"It's a lovely thought," she says, rising to take the balloon and bear from him. "I guess I never mentioned that my son was seventeen."

"You must have been a child bride," Ken says with a big goofy smile that inspires more eye-rolling from Omar. "Is Mahaz here?"

She has no idea where Mahaz is. She hasn't seen him since he walked out after hitting her. Remembering it, she touches her jaw lightly and presses the bruised skin to feel the bite of pain. She will never forget this.

"Are you okay?" he asks, taking in her face and the bruises mottling her right arm.

"The ambulance transport had an accident on the way here," she says, her shoulders tightening. "I was riding in the front seat. But I'm fine."

"Maybe the bear should be for you then," he says.

She turns the bear in her hand so that it faces her, and examines its glass brown eyes, plastic nose and the pink velveteen in its ears. She recalls either Leila or Omar having had a bear like this when they were small. But then, they had so many plush toys. Every year after Christmas and their birthdays she'd make them go through their old toys to make room for the new ones. For every new one, they had to donate another to charity. Mahaz always watched, amused at her effort to teach the children charity in the face of overwhelming abundance.

"They have so much they don't even remember what they give away," he said. She knew it was true but she still made them do it anyway.

She sets the bear down on her purse, then ties the balloon to a metal bar above Omar's bed. "Sure," she says. "I might just keep the little bear."

Ken pauses, looking around the room as though he isn't sure if he should leave or sit down. She feels herself flush. She senses Ken's attraction to her coming off of him in waves, a nice reminder she still looks good even at forty-two. But Ken knows she is married. So what is he doing here?

She starts moving toward the door. "Ken, why don't we go look for Mahaz? He might be in one of the waiting areas, trying to find the best mobile connection. This room is hit or miss."

"Sure," he says, following her out. "Nice to meet you, Omar. I hope you feel better."

Omar mumbles something that includes the words thank you so Juliana doesn't press him to articulate it further. In the hallway she blinks fast while her eyes adjust to the intense brightness. She pulls her cardigan sweater around her tight, feeling Ken's eyes on her as she leads him to the nearest waiting room.

A woman in her thirties lies across four of the chairs, her dark hair flowing like a curtain to the dark blue carpet. She's thrown her arm over her eyes to block out the light and sleep. *Somebody's wife,* Juliana thinks. *Or somebody's daughter or granddaughter.* She's slept enough nights in waiting room chairs to know better than to disturb the woman. Sleep can be very hard to come by in these places.

"I should just call Mahaz," she says. "Save us some time wandering the halls."

Ken shakes his head. "I didn't mean to be a pest," he says. "I just thought I'd come by."

"It's ringing," she mouthes at him. But after one ring, it slips into the automated female voice of Mahaz's voice mailbox. He had never bothered to create a personal message.

She leaves the message that she is with Ken and if he is still at the hospital to call her back. Maybe he left and went back to the office. Or maybe he is in a part of the hospital with bad reception. But when a mobile phone rings once and then goes to voicemail, doesn't that usually mean that someone pressed the button that says "ignore this call" in big letters? So he is ignoring her call now. She hopes it is because he is ashamed of striking her with his hand, although she certainly possesses no high moral ground to stand on, since she hit him first. With that one move, he inducted her into a whole new club of women, and it isn't one she wants to be a member of.

"I don't know where he is," she says. "We had a fight."

The words escape without her conscious intent, and they drift like thunderclouds in the air between her and this man she scarcely knows. And she sees something shift in his eyes, like he can see those thundercloud words crackling with her frustration, threatening their tenuous friendship with an intimacy born too quickly. Embarrassed, she plasters a smile on her face and retreats behind the most common blanket excuse.

"I'm so tired," she says. "I'm sorry I said that. We're fine." She takes a few steps further into the waiting room, as though to physically show she has moved on from the comment.

Ken follows, eyes on his sneakers. After a few beats, he clears his throat. "Having a child in the hospital must be very stressful. I mean,

I can't even imagine what you and Mahaz must be going through."

No, you don't know, she thinks, her eyes on the floor as they keep moving down the hall. *You don't know me and you probably don't know Mahaz very well and yet here you are, bringing our son a teddy bear and trying to solve what could be the world's newest cyberwar. Who are you?*

"Omar is a strong young man. He has made it through more in his short life than Mahaz and I have together. I have faith we will all get through this, too," she says as though on auto-pilot.

The hospital loudspeaker erupts with static and then a female voice saying something about a tamale sale by the volunteer council. Juliana wonders with some irritation what exactly has brought Ken to the hospital this morning.

Ken shoves his hands in the pockets of his cargo pants and jangles the keys and change he finds there. He seems to sense she is ready for a change in topic. Time to reveal the reason, or excuse, for this visit.

"Did Mahaz see that email from Arletta Therault?"

She pauses for a moment, wondering if this is the real reason behind Ken's visit. She remembers Mahaz's reaction to the email and nods. Resignation settles into the shallow wrinkles curving around Ken's eyes.

"He said the hackers made a mistake," she says. "That's true, right?"

Ken presses his lips together before nodding. "Yes, but we were just hoping to keep it off the mailing list for a while. But Arletta sent her email before we got that message to her."

A surgeon in dark purple scrubs and his face mask hanging loosely around his neck skirts by them and touches the shoulder of the woman sleeping on the chairs. She wakes with a start, and seeing the surgeon, swings her legs so her feet touch the floor. He speaks to her in a low voice as her perfect posture collapses and her smooth face melts into deep sadness.

Give the woman some privacy, Juliana tells herself, and she steps into the hallway so she is out of her line of sight. Today is a good day for Omar, but the worst possible day for that woman. Every floor, every room in this hospital is full of as many triumphs as defeats. *That's what keeps you grounded*, she thinks.

"I guess if they can hack the Department of Water & Power, they can hack the mailing list," she says.

"The mailing list is open," he says. "We make it easy for them to listen in. Maybe too easy. Who knows, maybe the hacker is one of us."

"Ken, I don't think you're the hacker," she says. "And I know I'm not the hacker because I'd have no idea what I was doing."

"No one suspects you," he says quickly. "Now, as for me, well, I'm sure people have their suspicions…"

She stares blankly at him for a moment until he smiles and shakes his head. "That was a bad joke. I was trying to lighten things up," he says. "It was stupid."

"I guess I couldn't think why on earth anyone would suspect you," she says. "Although if you were the hacker, then setting up the task force would probably be a smart move."

"Back in the day, I used to have a reputation for hacking the phone company. Kid stuff, but high tech enough to get law enforcement to take notice. Got in all sorts of trouble with Pacific Bell and the college provosts. I was joking because some people still think I'm nothing more than that."

She smiles. "Mahaz says that a lot of the security guys now were once amateur hackers playing a lot of pranks."

"I'm sure he did his share too," Ken says.

"Mahaz?" she says with a laugh. "He's as straight arrow as they come. I met him in college. He was always as serious as a heart attack about computer stuff. He saw it as his ticket out of Saudi Arabia. He would never have jeopardized that by hacking into the phone company."

"Right." Ken scrapes his hand through his black hair and focuses his eyes at some distant point on the wall. "He had more to lose."

She plucks at an imaginary piece of lint on her sweater, and realizes she is waiting for Ken to reassure her that Mahaz is above reproach and not on the list of suspects. That the Mahaz she knew would never do such a thing. But Ken maintains his distant stare a little longer than he should before muttering, "I don't know."

Fury takes over her mind and boils her blood. Ken came here because he thinks Mahaz is involved in the worm, and that with a little bit of flirting and compassion, she will help him implicate her husband.

"You think Mahaz is the hacker, because he's Saudi," she says, bouncing away from Ken like he is a magnetic field, her hands raised to signal him to keep his distance.

He moves toward her but she backs away. "We're all suspects, Juliana. It could be anyone. I'm sure people think it could be me, or it could be Mo, who works for me. He's from Qatar."

"You should leave now," she says, her palms still facing him like a stop sign. She backs down the hallway toward Omar and the sanctuary of his dark room.

Her husband is not a hacker. She sits in the chair next to Omar's bed as he sleeps and concentrates on her breath. He's Middle Eastern, so he must be a jihadist. Isn't that what everyone thinks?

She remembers the day he received his United States citizenship, his hand over his heart in that room of hundreds of immigrants, all reciting the pledges and promises in every accent imaginable. She made an apple pie to celebrate and they ate it out of the pie tin, not even bothering to cut slices. Then, he led her into the bedroom and kissed her so tenderly, whispering that now he had everything he wanted, meaning her, his United States citizenship. She was just twenty-three weeks pregnant with Omar then. He made love to her so gently and she was happier than she'd ever been in her life.

After a few breaths, her mind clicks through the events of the past few days like a slide show. The threat to take the children to Saudi Arabia. The missing passports. His fist on her jaw. His stress levels rising like mercury in a thermometer after hearing about the buffer overflow thing. "The hackers made a mistake," he said.

But he can just as easily have been talking about himself. He is not a man who takes mistakes lightly. He sees any error or oversight as a very personal reflection on his intelligence. And now he has disappeared.

She wants to believe her husband is innocent, but a heavy kernel of doubt now sits deep within her.

She fumbles for her phone and punches in Leila's cell phone number. She suddenly wants to hear Leila's voice, to know that she is okay.

Chapter 41

The message made G0d_of_Internet want to punch the wall, even though he should have known that his partners listened to the same channels of internet chatter he did.

Proxyw0rm: I understand we have a problem.

The programmer grits his teeth and types a quick response.

G0d_of_Internet: But I am working on a solution.

Proxyw0rm: Yes. Some of the brothers told me that there is a flaw in the new version of *Chrysalide*. In the encryption implementation.

G0d_of_Internet: It is a simple fix.

Proxyw0rm: Yes, I am sure you can fix it easily but my question is whether there is enough time. You should have told us as soon as you knew.

G0d_of_Internet: I wanted to find a solution first.

The programmer watches the cursor blink for several minutes. His stomach churns. He's torn between his need to stay on Proxyw0rm's good side for the time being, and his growing sense of urgency that he must finish the patch for *Chrysalide*. He knows his loyalty and duty to the Islamic Crusade can be called into question because he didn't tell them about the problem. Their reaction will depend on how this exchange with Proxyw0rm goes.

But he knows his own pattern of self-destructive behavior with authority figures. This isn't the first time his actions provoked the powers that be into pulling the carpet out from under him. The truth is that he hates working with others, and especially working for others. But as he often reminds himself throughout this project, one has to work through and with others to achieve great things sometimes. Patience and perseverance in all things.

Proxyw0rm: Abdul al-Lahem wishes to speak with you. Do you have the same mobile number?

The great man wishes to come off his throne to scold me and remind me that they are always watching, the programmer thinks as he types an affirmative answer back to Proxyw0rm. *I will reassure him as best I can, but then he must understand that I have work to do.*

The phone rings and G0d_of_Internet hears the hiss and clicks of an international connection, followed by a deep breath.

"My son," Abdul says. "Peace be upon you in these exciting times."

G0d_of_Internet responds in the traditional way with "Upon you be peace."

"Tell me what is going on," Abdul says, apparently choosing a neutral approach. "Will our plan still work?"

"A problem was discovered, and I am solving it."

"Why did you not ask us for help?"

G0d_of_Internet decides Abdul will value honesty more than an excuse. "I didn't think I needed help."

"One hand does not clap, *habibi*. Cooperation is necessary to accomplish anything, and unity is power. You are very smart, but sometimes you are not wise," Abdul says. "We've talked before about your pride and how it holds you back from Paradise. But this is a conversation for another day, when you are here with us. Today, I need to know that we will be ready come the launch day."

Al-Lahem's gentle chastisement only shows how dependent they still are on him. A satisfied smile flits across his lips. He will soon show them just how much. Until then, he must bow and scrape and work within their system, no matter how much he hates it.

"We will be ready, *inshallah*," G0d_of_Internet says.

"Very good, then."

The line goes dead in his hands, and he looks at the phone screen for a long time. This last piece, this finale, if it works properly, will destroy the financial records of the largest American bank, wiping clean the retirement accounts, checking accounts, mortgages, credit card bills. They designed this final salvo to shake the confidence of the Americans at their core. Just like on 9/11, the jihadists will use the Americans' own systems and openness against them.

But everything must work perfectly, and he must ensure that no one can control the botnet except himself that day. So now, having eaten the humble pie served gently by his sponsor, he resumes work on his ultimate vindication.

Chapter 42

Damn Bryce for saying anything, Ken thinks. If the other man hadn't enjoined him to bypass Mahaz, then he wouldn't have frozen like that in front of Juliana. Ken sinks into one of the waiting room chairs and lets his backpack drop to the floor. How has he not thought of a better response to her question about people suspecting Mahaz? Two of his ex-girlfriends and his mother told him he had a sensitive side, but he sees no evidence of it in use today. Just now with Juliana, he was as callous and blunt as a kick to the curb.

"You think Mahaz is the hacker," she said, probably never doubting her husband's innocence. But Ken had turned as dumb and mute as a statue, his mind blank while her eyes darkened with disappointment. No doubt she drew only one conclusion from his reaction, that he thought Mahaz was a suspect.

To be honest, he isn't even sure he does. But Bryce said not to tell him about the buffer overflow, and that was enough to plant the seed of doubt that sprouted up with her plea for reassurance. *Imagine if you were married to someone*, he thinks. *You had kids with them. And then you find out that people consider them a suspect in a computer hack that shut the city's water supply down for a day. Wouldn't you rally to your husband's defense? Of course you would.*

The closest Ken has been to marriage was a girlfriend four years ago who worked as a rock band promoter. Carly was the first woman he ever said those three words "I love you" to, and he thought at the time he'd taken a huge step. But she considered those three words the start of something bigger, a lot bigger, and pushed him to move in with her so aggressively that he split like a scared rabbit. Score one for fear of commitment, zero for love.

Juliana seems like a very different kind of woman than Carly or the other women he dated. He admires the resilient way she takes care of her sick son and the way she talks about life going on. She's developed what he thinks is a healthy way to cope with unquestionable sadness and worry, and that is to not let it control her any more than is necessary. A lot of people, he thinks, would be imprinted with bitterness or paralyzed by suffering, but he had seen no traces of that in his limited interactions with her.

She is also beautiful.

Enough, he tells himself. *Married is married and you just told her that you thought her husband was a cyber terrorist. Move on already.*

He gets to his feet, knees crackling from too many hours sitting without exercise, and hoists the backpack over his shoulder.

"Ken!" He turns to see Juliana walking to him, veering around an orderly sliding a long dust mop over the floor like a dance partner.

"I'd hoped you hadn't left yet," she says. She runs a hand through her hair, and he is struck with nerves like a pimply teenage boy on a first date. His throat dries up with his desire to say the right things to her.

"Do you have a few minutes to talk?" she says. "Maybe we could go to the cafeteria to get something to eat?"

They walk silently through the corridors to the cafeteria. "All hospitals are the same," she says. "You come into these cafeterias and you can't tell if you're at Glendale Adventist or Valley Presbyterian or Cedars-Sinai." Ken looks at the glass displays and meager salad bar, smelling steam from the hot food bar. They arrived at a quiet time, with no one in line and only two tables occupied. A dark woman in a hairnet scoops eggs and bacon onto plates for them and pushes them across the glass countertop.

They settle at a corner table with a view of the entrance and exit. She eyes him with some nervousness and what he thinks might be resignation. Not sure what to expect from this sudden invitation to a heart-to-heart conversation, Ken flushes and waits for her to speak.

Juliana points to the arrangement of pink roses and white-tipped peonies in a round clear vase on the table. "Fresh flowers in the cafeteria are a sign the hospital has a lot of money," she says with a grim smile. "I think their Assistance League does the arrangements."

She turns her attention to her tray of food and flattens the scoop of yellow powdered eggs with the back of her fork. Ken bites the corner of his plain wheat toast and chews it slowly. It tastes like cardboard.

Suddenly, she sets her fork down. Her eyes burn into his. "Do you know what things were like for Mahaz after 9/11? For everyone with an Arabic surname? The airport security people kept him for six hours when he was trying to fly to New York for a conference. Six hours, asking the same questions over and over again, questioning his loyalty and his patriotism. He missed his flight and he missed the conference but no one apologized.

"All that language everyone was using made it worse. Crusade against terrorism. Holy war. They were putting a stigma on people just because of where they were from and what religion they practiced. It made me so mad. But Mahaz wouldn't get angry. He just said that America was a great country, and that he was so glad to be here. That he had dreamed of it since he was a boy. He tried to close his eyes to that discrimination. He wouldn't see people's mistrust. He refused to. He loved this country."

Her lower lip trembles. Ken feels a tingling start in his arms and rise to his heart.

"I'm sure." Ken fumbles to open a plastic packet of grape jelly for his toast. He remembers going out for a drink with Mo a few nights after 9/11 when a drunk came up behind them and spat on the floor near Mo's feet.

"We should kill you all!" the drunk shouted at Mo, who stood there holding his glass of sparkling water with a shaking hand. Ken stepped into the drunk's space, nose to nose, telling him in a low voice that Mo had lived in Los Angeles for twenty years. That Mo was a better American than he was. He remembers this injustice and endeavors to find sympathy for Mahaz. Can he simply be a victim of racial suspicion? For that matter, does Bryce also suspect Mo?

Juliana picks up a piece of bacon and nibbles one end.

"He's changed," she says. "He threatened to take my children to Saudi Arabia during one of our fights. He even went so far as to hide their passports from me."

Ken isn't sure what to say. Taken in light of Bryce's suspicions, Mahaz's act of hiding the passports sounds dubious. Still, Ken feels the stirrings of hope. No matter what he does, he simply cannot seem to turn off his romantic interest in her.

"You're in a rough patch," he says, more than a little uncomfortable with the story as well as his emotions. Is he a bad person because he draws hope for his own heart that this beautiful woman is having marital difficulties? Isn't there a German word for this idea of taking pleasure at the tragedies of others? *Schadenfreude*, he recalls. Joy at another's misfortune. Although his feelings aren't born out of wanting bad things for her or Mahaz. His feelings stem from this attraction to her he can't control.

"His reaction to the news about the buffer overflow was to go straight to his laptop, and he spent three focused hours staring and typing," she says.

Ken's ears prickle and he shifts in his seat. *She knows something*, he thinks. "Did you see what he was working on?"

She shakes her head. "Not really. Looked like coding, but then he also had some news websites up. The usual chat screens in Arabic and email. I didn't really pay attention."

He thinks about the plan to hack the hacker. AcidTwin is deploying their hastily written code as he sits in this sunny cafeteria. Will it work? Still probably too soon to know, but he extracts his phone from his pocket to see if he has any new text messages. There are none.

"Probably the best thing you can do is just keep your eyes open," Ken says. "Does this Islamic Crusade seem like a group he might be involved with?"

"I have no idea," she says. "I feel like I hardly know him lately."

Ken reaches over and touches her wrist without thinking. Her skin feels cool under his fingers. "It's going to be okay," he says. Her smile is slow and sad and sweet. He wants to take her in his arms and tell her that over and over, but he settles for this simple, friendly gesture.

Chapter 43

"I brought you a chocolate chip cookie from the cafeteria," Juliana tells Omar. He takes the treat, wrapped in a paper napkin, and bites into it, crumbs falling on the pale blue fabric of the hospital gown.

She warily scans the room for signs of Mahaz. "Did your father come back?" She attempts to make her tone neutral. The effort of doing so without betraying the fear and worry and, yes, even anger, in her voice provides her a new respect for her divorced friends who maintain a beautiful civility about their lying, cheating spouses in front of their children.

"No, and I don't care if he ever does," Omar says. *Me either*, she thinks.

But out loud, she says, "Don't talk that way. Your father loves you."

"Yeah. He loves me so much he wants to make me leave all my friends and live in Riyadh."

Being a mother means you must be a warrior for your kids, Juliana thinks. And she is ready for this battle.

"I'm not going to let him take you to there, Omar, I promise." As she says the words, her resolve straightens her spine. "Did you talk to Leila?"

"Yeah." Omar stares at the white and tan bed sheets and blankets covering his long legs, obviously weighing just how much information he should give his mother. Juliana gives an impatient sigh.

"When? I called her about an hour ago and she hasn't called me back. I thought she would have called on her break after first period."

Omar shifts on the bed and chews the cookie slowly. "Um, I talked to her before then, I guess," he says. His eyes dart around the room like a frog trying to catch a fly. She knows with a mother's intuition that he is hiding something.

"What is it? You told her about Dad saying he wanted to take you both to Riyadh and she got upset, right?"

"Something like that."

Her patience snaps in pieces. Despite his fragile appearance and the fact he is in the hospital after suffering major trauma, she wants to shake him.

"Omar. Tell me now."

He crosses his arms over his chest and looks just beyond her, a mixture of relief and guilt all over his face. "She was going to skip class and go to that modeling thing Grandma told her about. The photo shoot is today."

Juliana lets out a deep exhale. She didn't realize the photo shoot was today. Another example of Leila's strong independent streak, something she usually takes pride and satisfaction in but today, she knows it will only make everything worse.

"Does Grandma know?"

His eyes return to hers. "No, she wasn't going to tell her. She was just going to use one of those ride-sharing services to the store in Beverly Hills."

Juliana considers her options. Mahaz will be furious if he finds out. He may even suspect her of colluding with Leila so she could participate. Would he take his rage out on Leila? She doesn't want to chance it. What she wants to do is find Leila and keep her close. She can sit at the hospital today with her and Omar.

She kisses Omar on top of the head absently, then calls Leila's mobile, only to get her voice mail. "Leila, I know you're going to that photography shoot today. This is not a good idea. Call me so we can talk," she says in her message.

Her next call is to Yalima, who picks up on the second ring. Juliana quickly fills her in on her conversation with Mahaz and Leila's plans. She omits the physical details of the fight with Mahaz. No need to encourage Yalima to take sides, as undoubtedly she will take Mahaz's.

"I'll drive to the store right now and get her," Yalima says. "Let me call my friend and tell her what is happening."

Juliana thanks her and hangs up.

Omar crumples the napkin from the cookie and shoots it at the wastebasket a few feet away, missing by inches. Juliana bends over to pick it up and tosses it in the trash.

"You know, she did it partly because of what Dad said, about moving us to Riyadh. She wanted to make him mad," Omar says.

"I get that," Juliana says. "But your father is under a lot of pressure right now, and I'm afraid his reaction will be stronger than any of us expect."

"Like he might hit her?"

Juliana comes back to his bedside and brushes the fringe of black hair from his forehead. "I don't think he would do that. Your father hitting me wasn't right, but in fairness, I hit him first. I provoked him."

"Mom, you're just making excuses for him," Omar says. "Next you're going to say it is part of the culture he grew up in, which is

184

stupid because he chose to live here in California. He's always said he dreamed of living in America."

"It wasn't right, Omar. But marriage is hard, and…"

Omar interrupts her, his right palm raised like a stop sign. "I don't want to hear it. I know what I saw."

Her phone rings with the classical music ringtone she'd assigned to Yalima's number.

"Hello?"

"Juliana, my friend Rana said that Mahaz showed up about fifteen minutes ago and took Leila. I tried calling him but he didn't pick up."

"Who told Mahaz she was there? Did Rana call him?"

"No," Yalima says. "She doesn't even have his number. And I'm sure it wasn't Leila. Rana said the color drained out of her face when she heard his voice shouting for her. Rana said he was so angry."

"Did you call him, Yalima?" Juliana grits her teeth. Yalima shares a tight bond with Mahaz and the values of the old country have a way of popping up unexpectedly even with such a Westernized individual as Yalima. "It's okay if you did. I understand why you would."

But Yalima laughs, though it is more shrill than full of mirth. "Juliana, I am not a crazy woman. I knew very well how he felt about the modeling idea and if I knew that Leila decided to go on her own, I would have either retrieved her myself, or called you, not him."

"Maybe the school called him when she wasn't in class," Juliana says, though it seems much more likely that they would have called her first. She is usually the first one they dial when the kids are sick. And if Mahaz is with Leila, why hasn't one of them called her to let her know what is going on?

"Let me know if they come to your home, or if you hear from them," she tells Yalima.

Chapter 44

Ken speeds along the 134 freeway past Griffith Park enjoying the sweet spot of Los Angeles morning traffic when the congested roads clear temporarily. The commuters have parked their cars and then their butts at their jobs and the little old ladies are just getting ready to drive to their doctors' appointments. He guns the Jeep past seventy miles per hour, his fingers sliding over the satellite radio stations to find the down tempo electronica station.

Juliana. She is too smart to be a damsel in distress but she certainly needs help. Is it just a custody battle? Or is Mahaz planning on fleeing the country and leaving Juliana behind? To save her children, she may be willing to help them get control of his laptop. Or at least get close enough to either insert a USB drive programmed with an Auto-Run Trojan. With that kind of access, they may be able to stop the worm very quickly.

But the missing passports bug him. If Mahaz is the hacker, he's not working alone, even if he is the mastermind of the worm. Ken wonders what would draw someone like Mahaz to the cause of the Islamic Crusade. Is it possible that he took the job for money, or is there a deeper ideological reason behind his defection?

Ken knows several people in the hacking world who take black hat jobs like this for money, but he doesn't know Mahaz well enough to determine if he shares characteristics with those people. They are more motivated by greed, people who follow the smell of money like Tilly the dachshund follows him when he holds a plate of food.

He exits the freeway at Lankershim. At the light is a huge Toyota dealership, three stories tall, with mannequins placed on each floor waving at passing drivers. The mannequins in their sun-faded clothes and hats never fail to get his attention, which he assumes is the intent of the ploy, unless the owner just likes to play dress-up with life-size dolls.

Within minutes, he parks the car on a side street by a freshly mowed vacant lot and heads for AcidTwin's apartment. Daylight does not improve the building's aesthetic, but at least he can avoid the minefields of dog poop surrounding the entrance with ease.

Two young men, lithe and graceful, pass by him on their way to a dance studio across from the vacant lot. One wears a purple T-shirt with slim jeans and big white headphones holding down long blond hair; the other wears a loose black top over silver pants with unlaced combat boots. The shorter one stops, then springs into a graceful somersault in the middle of the street.

Bryce stands outside the apartment door, cigarette smoke streaming out of his mouth. He shakes his head slowly at Ken's approach.

"He says the code didn't work, along with a bunch of other techie gobbledygook I couldn't understand. I need you to go in there and figure out if he's lying." This last part he delivers in a voice so low Ken has to lean in to hear him over the sound of other people's televisions, and a man's loud, one-sided conversation about what someone named Marianne did yesterday.

Ken's eyes drift to the cracked sidewalk. He kicks a pinecone the size of an egg and it skips under the rusted iron fence and into the dirty water of the pool. When exactly did he become such a part of the establishment that a federal agent asked him to determine if a hacker was lying?

"Why would he lie?"

Bryce's shoulders lift slightly, as though some higher power pulled them upward with puppet string.

"I don't know. Why wouldn't he?"

"Isn't it in his best interests to cooperate? You know, to stay out of prison?"

"I am a member of the 'trust but verify' school of thought," Bryce says. "Interesting fact: People always attribute that to Ronald Reagan, but it was really Teddy Roosevelt who said it first."

Bryce turns to exhale a thin stream of smoke toward the courtyard, but a sudden gust of wind pushes it right at Ken. He coughs and waves his hand in front of his face.

"You really ought to try those e-cigarettes," Ken says.

"You sound like my daughter," Bryce says. "Where have you been anyway?"

"I went to visit Juliana Al-Dossari at the hospital. Her son just had surgery."

Bryce draws on the cigarette but keeps his eyes on Ken.

"Juliana Al-Dossari, huh? That good-looking brunette from the task force meeting who just happens to be married to a person of interest? What on earth were you doing there?" Bryce's eyes narrow before he turns his head to blow the smoke toward the apartment door.

"You're going to be more interested in what I found out," Ken says, dismissing the other questions. He gives him a quick rundown of their conversation, including the missing passports.

Bryce pulls out his phone. "He probably has a U.S. and a Saudi passport, but I'll put a warning out on both. At least we can try to keep him from leaving. If he's the hacker, then he knows we're on to him. Dylan told me that even if he somehow missed the emails in the listserv, he would have likely noticed the attempt to exploit the buffer overflow."

Ken opens the screen door and steps into the dark apartment. It smells of fermented milk. AcidTwin sits in front of his monitors, light reflecting off of thick reading glasses.

"Game over, my friend," AcidTwin says. "The people who built *Chrysalide* are geniuses, and they know how to use our own weaknesses against us."

He points to his middle computer screen. "Meet *Chrysalide* 3.0. No more weakness in the cryptography implementation, plus now the worm jumps onto any USB drive that gets inserted into an infected computer," he says. "Our code didn't work. *Chrysalide* spat it out like a bad shrimp. All the infected computers are dutifully doing their upgrades as we speak."

"Show me," Ken says. AcidTwin pulls up different files and windows, and after examining them, Ken sees what he means. They haven't even been able to establish a toehold in the worm's network. He closes his eyes briefly and takes a deep breath. AcidTwin is right. The worm exploits all the weaknesses that people like him have been warning about for years. Don't use simple passwords like "admin" or "000." Pay attention to data going out of your network as well as what is coming in. Install security updates for software.

Now the worm is a parasite, living and feeding off of this giant global network, spreading on its own. Ken can almost imagine it blinking into consciousness, ready to wreak havoc at the bidding of a group prepared to launch a cyber holy war.

Chapter 45

Noon creeps into the hospital wing with the rattle of food carts, the smell of steamed broccoli and the opening theme song of a soap opera that Juliana hasn't watched in years. Not since she was nursing Leila, she remembers. Has it been that long really? The violin and percussion strains remind her of Leila's soft weight in her arms, the fine hair on top of her head, the tingling in her breasts. The soap stars are the same, only a little bit worse for wear for being fifteen years older.

Then her baby Leila walks in the hospital room door, Mahaz at her heels. Her normally creamy skin is blotchy from tears, her eyes puffed up and globs of black mascara smeared under her eyes. Her hair is still perfect though, in a shellacked ponytail that snakes down her back. Without making eye contact with her, Leila flattens herself into the chair near Omar's bed. He reaches out to her, whether to grab her hand or give her a hug, but Leila stays out of reach, a tiny rounded figure of misery.

Juliana stares at Mahaz, trying to read his mood. His face is a dark cloud of anger and something else she can't identify. Something that flickered and then vanished. Again her mind fills with questions that she isn't sure she should ask now. The air in the room ices over, freezing the words on her tongue and closing all of their throats so they can't speak. On the television, a blonde actress points a perfectly manicured finger at another blond woman's face. "I'll never forgive you for what you have done to my life, my child, my husband…"

Dr. Duva knocks on the open door and walks in, shattering the silence and returning the focus, at least temporarily, to Omar's health. She carries a tablet computer in one hand. The other hand is out of commission in a pale pink sling.

"From the accident?" Juliana says, pointing to the sling.

"Yes," Dr. Duva says. "A sprain, nothing more, but I'm supposed to rest it."

If Dr. Duva picked up a weird vibe from them, she was determined to barrel right through it regardless. Juliana admires the woman's pluck.

"So, young man, I think they might release you tomorrow if all goes well," she says.

"That's great news," Juliana says.

"Awesome," Omar says.

"But you'll still need to rest. We won't quite want you at a normal activity level for a while."

"I shouldn't travel on an airplane, though, should I?" Omar's face hardens. He keeps his tone flat and even, but Juliana can hear the anger that punches the words out of his mouth.

"What have you got planned, Omar? A trip to Cabo San Lucas with some pretty girl from school?" Dr. Duva casts her warm friendly smile at Juliana then Mahaz. "You folks got a family trip planned?"

Juliana watches as Mahaz mentally separates from the three of them and Dr. Duva. He watches a commercial for life insurance as though it shows the Saudi National Team playing in the World Cup. Time for her to defuse the situation.

"No, not really," Juliana says. Her eyes slide to the floor.

The tension in the room finally penetrates Dr. Duva's cheerful countenance. She straightens up and looks at the television for a moment, then finally back at Omar.

"I'd say no airplane trips for a few weeks," she says. "An abundance of caution about keeping you in consistent air pressure after your recent surgery." Mahaz acts like he doesn't hear her, still razor-focused on the television. Omar and Leila exchange smiles, but on Omar's drawn, pale face and Leila's tear-stained one, the smiles are more pathetic than strong. Dr. Duva backs up a few steps, as though the ice Juliana imagined a few moments earlier is driving her out of the room.

Juliana crosses to Dr. Duva and puts her arms around her thin shoulders. "Thank you for all you did for Omar," she says. "You saved his life."

But Dr. Duva is already pulling away. "That's my job," she says, still walking backwards with her eyes flickering everywhere but Juliana's tearful face.

Juliana wraps her arms around herself. The room seems cold and heartless, and Mahaz's presence in the room is a black hole of anger, pulling each of them into its gravity field. She longs to be out of that room and somewhere warm, like the kitchen of her home or better, her mother's kitchen table.

"I took her phone away." Mahaz's deep voice cuts the air and jolts three sets of eyes to his face. He crosses his arms over his chest. Does he feel outnumbered in this room? Or is he so convinced of the righteousness of his stance that he does not care?

"I don't want it back," Leila says. Her face, turned to Juliana, is a mask of anger and fear and betrayal so strong it mimics the soap stars on the television screen. "He used it to find me."

"What do you mean?" Juliana's eyes flit from Mahaz to Leila.

"He put some tracking software on it and found me that way. He probably has it on your phone, too, Omar," Leila says.

Omar snatches his phone from the bedside tray and studies it, his index finger swiping and tapping its tiny screen. Juliana thinks about her own phone and how she always asks Mahaz to set them up for her. She supposes she can understand his instinct behind keeping tabs on the kids, although she doesn't agree with it at all. But did he use her phone to track her, too? Or is he beyond caring where she is? Either answer makes her feel tired and sad.

"Leila," she says. "You shouldn't have skipped school to go to that photography shoot. I was so worried about you." She folds her arms around Leila's neck and kisses her cheek. The young woman smells of hairspray and tastes like salt from her tears. Juliana wants to scoop her in her arms like she did when Leila was a little girl and hold her until all the tears pass. But she also wants to shake her for doing such a stupid thing.

"Is this an act for my benefit?" Mahaz sneers at her. "Did you tell her to go to get around my wishes?"

She unclasps her hands from Leila and stands up straight. "Mahaz, you are not thinking straight. Of course I didn't tell her to go."

Mahaz's anger seeps from his rigid shoulders and his eyes lock on Juliana.

"These children are growing up without any values other than commercialism and self-promotion. It shames me that my daughter wants to bare her body for men to see."

"Mahaz," she says. "Let's step outside then and talk."

"No. We'll talk right here."

She hates fighting in front of the kids. How many arguments has she swallowed down because she doesn't want them raised in an antagonistic atmosphere? She wants Omar and Leila to feel like they live in a stable, happy home, but Mahaz chooses to make it too hard. She can control her own reactions, but not his.

"What do you want to tell me, Mahaz? I'm ready to hear it."

His voice lowers dangerously. "What is your problem, Juliana? I have given up so much for you, my country, my life. All I ask is that you support me as a wife should, particularly a wife who has gotten everything she wanted."

"We've both made sacrifices, Mahaz. Let's not rehash old arguments here." *Married couples knew all the right buttons to push when they argued*, she thinks. After so many years neither one can claim a moral high ground. But still, here they stand, traveling such old roads with familiar terrain. She knows the litany of injustices inside and out. She didn't let him take the position at Stanford. She complained too much about the Riyadh heat and the *abaya* and embarrassed him in front of his uncles. And her responses were always that he didn't encourage her to finish college. He didn't want her to work outside the home.

"I want Leila to learn respect and modesty, and I have found that I must teach her this myself."

Leila jumps to her feet, her eyes blazing with rage. "You mean I should wear the *hijab* and live in some dusty compound in Riyadh where I can't even ride a bicycle or go shopping alone," she shouts.

Juliana instinctively wraps her arms around Leila, only to find her daughter leaning into her as though drawing on her mother's strength. Leila's body shakes, and she feels the girl take a deep breath as though the intensity of her feelings has sucked the oxygen out of her.

"It's easy to win hearts when you give children whatever they want," Mahaz says, his eyes on Juliana. "But I am trying to give them what they need. Discipline. Respect. Honor."

His fury and his self-righteousness vibrate off of him and provoke a visceral hatred in her. Juliana opens her mouth to tell him he is full of shit, but the words freeze when she sees him take Leila's phone out of his pocket, strip off the protective Hello Kitty cover and throw it on the floor.

"What in the hell are you doing, Mahaz?" she says.

He grinds the heel of his shoe into the screen, and strides out, reminding Juliana of Omar and his toddler temper tantrums. Except Mahaz doesn't seem harmless, and this doesn't seem like the end of the argument. She hugs Leila tightly.

Chapter 46

He fixed the programming error. Such a simple matter it took him only hours to do so. He must be more careful in the future, though, especially with the small details. To have power as he does is a burden one must carry with great gravity and responsibility, and he let his desire for revenge cloud his thinking.

He's heard the story many times about Imam Ali, the cousin and brother-in-law of the Prophet Mohammed, who, as a warrior for Allah, found himself straddling his enemy, his sword raised to deliver the final blow. The enemy, realizing his end is near, spits into the Imam Ali's face. Imam Ali brought the sword down quickly, but not into the man's heart. Instead, he slides it back into its sheath, then rises to walk away and lets the man live.

"Why did you spare me?" the man asked.

"When you spit in my face, anger rose inside me, and I realized that were I to kill you, it would be from revenge and not for justice," the warrior said. "And that was something I could not do."

G0d_of_Internet accepts that it isn't right to seek revenge. He should wait for Allah to deliver justice. Allah, who knows all and sees all. Abdul al-Lahem would tell him the same. But really, do Abdul al-Lahem and the others need to know if the final hack also happens to settle a few scores for him personally? This work he did, for Allah, has taken its toll on his family and his life. He made so many sacrifices, and the next few weeks and months will be further tests of his willingness and supplication. Yes, he is a warrior for Allah in the holy war, but he's never pretended to be a holy man like Imam Ali. Surely he, a mere mortal trying to live right, deserves the opportunity to teach a lesson or two to a deserving *kafir*. After all, Allah gave him this power and it follows logically that he is supposed to use it judiciously.

Chapter 47

Ken drops onto AcidTwin's sofa like a bag of flour, sinking deep into its frame thanks to worn-out springs. He is exhausted and is pretty sure he lost track of the time and date. Being in AcidTwin's dark, cheesy-smelling apartment has the same disorienting effect on him as those windowless Las Vegas casinos.

"Do you have anything to drink?"

AcidTwin looks up from a pot of heated milk on the stove.

"I've got a nice *kefir*," he says.

"Tell me that has alcohol in it," Ken says.

"Well, it is fermented," AcidTwin says. "But not intoxicating, unless you get high off of probiotics and vitamin K."

"I was thinking more along the lines of beer if you have it."

AcidTwin waves a wooden spoon at the refrigerator. "Have at it, man."

Ken's phone rings while he heaves himself out of the sofa's sag. "Mo, what's up?"

"*Chrysalide* three is a serious upgrade. More stable, and way more defenses against debugging or reverse-engineering. Most of what they're using has been out there for a while, but it just shows they're building in more layers of defense."

"Armoring the gates of the castle," Ken says. He takes a beer from amid multiple unmarked jars and plastic containers cluttering the innards of AcidTwin's refrigerator. "You think it's the same guy doing all the versions?"

"It's conceivable," Mo says. "And if it is one guy, then he's feeling good about himself. He thinks he's the shit. He's got it built so that his little upgrades are being digitally signed. More ability to spread faster, more protection, everywhere you look."

"I'm going to put you on speaker, Mo," Ken says. "I'm here with AcidTwin, and I want him to hear this."

"Sure, right, fine. Hey, AcidTwin," Mo says. "We met at DefCon a few years back."

"Mo is my right-hand. Brilliant analyst. He's been unpacking *Chrysalide*."

AcidTwin lays a cheesecloth over a tall bowl, then shuts off the stove burner. "Hey," he says.

Mo doesn't hesitate to get to the point. "So *Chrysalide* is generating fifty thousand domains now."

Ken lets out a low whistle.

"And it gets better. It's randomly selecting five hundred from that list. It's using something like a hundred and ten top-level domains now. I mean, this dude is using everything he can think of to keep his lines of communication to his botnet going."

Ken takes a swig of the beer, its cold bitterness jarring but welcome.

"Does this strike either of you as a really bad boxing match?" AcidTwin says. "I feel like he's ducking and feinting and we can't find our footing."

"He's had a lot more time than us to put this strike together. My guess is he's been working on this for a long, long time," Ken says. "We need to remember that."

AcidTwin pours the hot milk into the cheesecloth, then clatters the pan into the sink.

"Anyway, isn't that the fun of it?" Mo's voice rumbles out of the phone followed by three sneezes.

"You're still sick." Guilt hits him like a wave. Ken realizes he hasn't even checked in to see how Mo was doing.

"Yes, I'm at home, Ken, don't worry. I'm not in the office infecting the ficus tree. But really, isn't matching wits like this fun? I mean, this programmer, whoever he is, I bet he's having some fun. He's clearly watching our moves and countering."

"Yeah," AcidTwin says as he fusses with the cheesecloth. "Those Islamic Crusade guys really know how to party it up."

"I like a challenge as much as you, Mo, but I don't know how fun it is, with so much at stake," Ken says. "I don't know if we can keep up the domain name registration at this rate. I mean, fifty thousand a day? It's not going to be easy. So far, the algorithm has been generating nonsense domains like yazblubfor8.com but when the growth rate skyrockets like that, you're going to get some domains that match real ones, and then you've got a real problem. Are we going to get AliBaba in China to sinkhole some of its webpages? Or Amazon?"

"Isn't that what your friends in law enforcement are for?" AcidTwin says.

"What if we could get control of his command and control server?" Ken says.

Dead silence except for the slow drip of whey from the cheesecloth.

"You know who he is?" Mo says.

"And you're implying he's near enough where the three of us could actually get our hands on his computer?" AcidTwin says. "That's a pretty amazing coincidence."

Ken remembers Bryce saying he didn't believe in coincidences. "Think about it. Los Angeles got hit in both attacks so far. The water system attacks were in LA, Dallas and Boston. The power system attacks were in Phoenix and LA. LA is the common denominator."

"LA is also a big target. Eight million people, home to the movie industry and reality television shows, which I assume the Islamic Crusade is no fan of. Our city is symbolic of Western culture poison, man," AcidTwin says.

"He probably has a couple different custom-built machines," Mo says. "And you know he's ready to destroy them at a moment's notice. I don't think that's the way."

"Keystroke logging could work," Ken says.

"Seriously, that's a long shot," AcidTwin says. "More like a Hail Mary pass."

"I'm brainstorming here," Ken says. "Ever hear of it? No idea is a bad idea."

AcidTwin gives Ken a look usually reserved for slow, tech-challenged civilians. Ken recognizes it because he's given people that look himself.

"Ken, think about it. He's got to have anti-logging detection on his C2. So the only way would be doing it through a piece of hardware so it happens outside the computer. But that's risky. You've got to physically install it, and then physically remove it after you catch the guy. And I'm sure our guy isn't letting anyone he doesn't know get close enough. So unless you had an insider, like one of his Islamic Crusade buddies that you just happen to play soccer with, and who just happens to want to betray his buddy and his cause, I don't think it's going to work."

Ken shakes his head, barely able to wait for AcidTwin to finish speaking. "But what if we had that insider?"

AcidTwin lets out an exasperated sigh and lifts the cheesecloth so he can peer in the container. "Just spill it, already, Ken," he says. "We don't need the cliffhangers. What do you know?"

Mo's voice rings out the phone. "You think Mahaz Al-Dossari is the hacker. And you want to enlist his wife to help us."

"The crypto guy at UCLA?" AcidTwin says.

Ken nods. "I'm not the only one who thinks so. Homeland Security is looking at him too. He's got connections to the Saudi royal family, he's one of the most brilliant security guys in the field, and his wife said he's been talking about going back to Saudi Arabia and taking their kids."

AcidTwin makes a buzzing sound, the kind you hear on game shows when someone gets the answer wrong. "Circumstantial, and probably racist, because the dude is from the Middle East."

"Version two did use his cryptography, with the buffer overflow vulnerability," Mo says.

"Yeah, and look how fast the hacker fixed that," Ken says. "Don't you think that shows he was seriously familiar with how that algorithm worked?"

AcidTwin raises his eyebrows and shrugs.

"Probably worth a try," Mo says.

"The Ghost model is the easiest to install," AcidTwin says. "Let's do it."

Chapter 48

"Your phone's dead, Leila," Omar says. "It won't even power up." He thrusts the useless phone aside onto the tray table by his bed, its screen an elaborate cobweb of cracks.

Leila flops into the high-backed armchair with a sigh. "Can I get a new one, Mom?"

Impatience and irritation pump through Juliana's core and up into her head. She pivots from the hospital room window, irritated. "Not right now, Leila! Can't you think of anybody but yourself for a minute?"

Both kids stare at her with their mouths open, reminding her of gasping fish, and she regrets losing control in front of them immediately. She crosses to Leila and puts her hand on her shoulder.

"I'm sorry. I need to think about it, Leila. Just give me some time."

"It's not fair," Leila says, tilting her face up to Juliana's. "Dad broke my phone."

"You're not using mine. Don't even think about it," Omar says. He grips his phone tightly in his right hand and brings it to his chest, prompting eye-rolling from Leila.

"What? Are you afraid I'll see your sexy photos with Alicia?"

Omar's ears flush rosy pink. Juliana suppresses a smile, and wonders if he has a girlfriend she doesn't know about. Would this be something he talked about with Mahaz if he had been around more?

"Shut up," Omar says.

"Mom, if I don't have a phone, how are you going to be able to reach me when you need to?"

Juliana tries to rub away the tightness forming behind her forehead, undoubtedly the beginning of a headache.

"Leila, let's talk about it later," she says.

Leila pushes herself deep into the chair's cushions with another dramatic sigh and folds her arms over her chest, settling in for a long pout.

Juliana's phone ringing shatters the uneasy silence and sets her heart pounding. On the other end is Ken.

"Are you alone?"

Juliana steps into the hallway. "I'm with my kids right now. He's not here."

"Juliana, I want you to talk to a man named Bryce Ballen. He's with Homeland Security. He's headed over to the hospital now and I hope you'll see him."

"Homeland Security? Ken, I can't believe you got them involved. I thought we were just talking, you know, as friends." This guy really overstepped his bounds, she thinks. But she is also secretly relieved. Having a friend in Homeland Security certainly can't hurt when your husband is threatening to take your children to Saudi Arabia without your consent.

"Just talk to him. Hear him out. I think you can trust him. He's coming with your brother."

"My brother?" Now she is more confused, but knows she can count on Drew for support.

"Look, they'll explain it when they get there."

She hangs up and gazes down the long corridor to where a window looks out onto a garden. A tree branch thick with green leaves scratches at the glass in the light wind. She hasn't felt the wind or sun on her face in two days.

She and Mahaz were married outdoors, in a pretty garden near the San Fernando Mission in October. Bright blue sky, puffy white clouds, and low afternoon sun shone on them. She was so happy that day. To love and cherish one another as equal partners and helpmates. To stay steadfast in this love in good times and in bad. To walk with you hand in hand wherever this journey leads us.

Damn it, Mahaz, what have you done? The headache intensifies, like a spring coiling tighter and tighter between her temples. She returns to the hospital room and digs in her purse for the painkillers the emergency room doctor gave her.

"Sis," Drew says from the door. *That was fast,* she thinks. The relief at seeing him overcomes her and she starts to cry. He takes her in his arms and holds her tight, and she buries her face in his shoulder.

Behind him she hears footsteps, and she lifts her head and pulls away to see a tall man in a cowboy shirt.

"This is Bryce Ballen," Drew says. She extends her hand to shake his, and notices the gun neatly holstered in a black leather sheath on his hip. *How jarring,* she thinks, *to see a weapon of destruction as potent as that in a place of healing.*

Leila leaps up to hug her uncle. Omar, stuck in the bed, takes a half hug from Drew.

"Mrs. Al-Dossari, thanks for letting me come by."

She isn't entirely sure she had a choice in the matter, but she appreciates his politeness. She introduces him to Omar and Leila as a friend of Drew's. No need to mention the Homeland Security bit yet to the kids, even though they are openly staring at the gun on his hip. They don't need any more drama today.

"Why don't we go get a cup of coffee?" she says.

They settle in the waiting room where earlier Juliana and Ken saw the surgeon giving a woman the worst possible news. She wonders where that woman is now. Even though she knows she is about to hear devastating news of her own, she feels detached, her mind blank and seeming to hover just outside her body. She corrects her slouch into more perfect posture, imagining her shoulder blades touching.

Bryce sits across from her, leaning so far toward her that his hands nearly touch her knees. Drew sits next to her, his arm around her shoulders like a protective net.

"Why don't you start, Drew?" Bryce says. Juliana hasn't met many men in law enforcement and wonders if they all have this quiet strength and self-possession. Bryce strikes her as a natural leader, the kind of steady guide that other men rely on in times of crisis. Somehow, she expected more of a cowboy mentality, but the only cowboy trait she sees on Bryce is his boots.

"We've had some computer forensics experts in to try to figure out how the hackers got into the water system," Drew says. "Turns out, I was the dupe who opened the door."

Drew hangs his head for a moment, and she squeezes his arm.

"They found a program on my computer that tracked all of my activities online, passwords, emails, everything. It stored them in a file and emailed all that information right to the hackers."

"How did the program get on your computer?" *Don't say Mahaz. Don't say Mahaz. DontsayMahaz.* But she knows he will.

Drew shifts in his seat. "They think it came from a USB drive Mahaz gave me."

His words hit her like a punch, and she shrinks from him. His arm on her shoulders feels heavier than a sand bag.

"When was that?" She scours her memory for the last time she and Mahaz were with Drew and his family. It has been at least six months. "New Year's Day?"

"Remember he was telling me about a security presentation he had done for a corporation? He said he brought me a copy because he thought I could use it at work. I remember looking at it on my work laptop, but it was way over my head. I could have never pulled off giving that presentation. Way too technical. Anyway, the computer forensics people said that just by inserting the USB drive into my computer was enough to activate the software. After that, he just had to wait for an email with all my activity logs."

Six months ago. He has been planning this for six months.

"Drew, I'm so sorry."

"Not your fault, Jules. How could you have even known?"

"I don't know. It's just…everything is a mess." Her hands flutter to her face and hair. She thinks of the book *Alice in Wonderland*, and little Alice falling and falling through the rabbit hole. That is how she felt, like a child tumbling into a world with all new rules. She wants to get away from them both so she can think, but she knows from their body language that they have more to tell her.

Bryce goes to the coffee station set up in the corner and brings her back a cup of hot black coffee. She takes a drink and nearly gags from the thick bitterness of coffee that has been sitting on a burner for hours and hours.

"We want you to help us get access to his computers," Bryce says. Her hair tickles her cheeks as she shakes her head vehemently.

"I can't do that," she says. "Why don't you just get a search warrant or whatever and get them that way?"

"We don't want him to know that we are on to him yet," Bryce says. "All we're asking you to do is help us get access. We're going to install a piece of hardware in each that enables us to track everything he does. Just like what he did to Drew, but using a piece of hardware that his system won't detect."

Drew nods along, his eyes darting from Bryce to Juliana then back again.

"He'll find out." She knows it with icy certainty.

"Maybe not," Drew says. "You can't be sure of that."

Bryce resumes his place across from her, his elbows on his knees and hands in a steeple in front of his face. "Drew told me that Mahaz has threatened to take the kids to Saudi Arabia. Your seventeen-year-old boy and your fifteen-year-old girl. I'm sure you are aware how difficult it can be to get them back to the United States once they are within Saudi borders. Your daughter, Leila, would have to get her father's permission to travel."

"So the goal would be to make sure they don't leave," Drew says.

"I feel like you're ganging up on me. You're asking me to betray the man I married."

"Julie, you need to think this through. Think about the future," Drew says.

The future. It looms like a black hole, its gravitational force pulling her into the unknown. Everything is changing, fast. Her stomach drops out from under her. It's a sensation of free-fall, the kind you get at the tippy-top of a roller coaster ride. Right before you plunge to the depths. They have some evidence that makes him seem like a likely suspect for the hacking. But Mahaz, working for the Islamic Crusade? A member even? It boggles her mind that he has transformed this way.

"Will he be home tonight?"

"I have no idea," Juliana says, wanting nothing more than to stop time.

"We want you to help us gain access to his office at UCLA and at home."

"Are you kidding?" *You're stalling. Make the decision.*

"I'll stay here tonight with Omar," Drew says. "I've already talked to Cathy."

"We just need you to get us access so we can stay undercover," Bryce says.

She presses her elbows into her sides, trying to make herself as small as possible. "I'm really not comfortable with this," she says. "What if he finds out? What if he tries to hurt me, or the kids?"

Bryce's eyes pierce into hers. "Do I need to spell this out for you, Mrs. Al-Dossari? Your husband and you are still married and share joint custody of those kids. You might have been able to stop him from getting passports for them, but you can't stop him from taking them out of the country. You have absolutely no legal recourse unless you file for divorce."

He pauses for a moment to let his words sink in. She knows what he is saying is true, but she doesn't like it. She suppresses the child-like urge to put her fingers in her ears and sing la-la-la until they leave.

"I am offering you a chance to keep him, and your children, in this country and out of Saudi Arabia. Now, what do you say?"

"Think about Leila and Omar, Jules," Drew says. "You need to do this."

"If I do this, I lose him forever," she says. She is surprised to find hope for her marriage still exists in some narrow crevices of her mind, even in light of all these revelations and his changing behavior.

Drew pulls her to him so their shoulders mash together, and for once, he stops shaking his leg and is still. Her jittery brother transforms into a rock beside her.

"There's not much time left," Bryce says. "The Islamic Crusade has given the U.S. two days to take troops out of Muslim countries before it unleashes its next wave of cyber attacks. We need to get ahead of that attack."

She takes a long breath one-two-three-four-five, resting her head on Drew's shoulder. If someone asked her, when she first met Mahaz, if she ever thought he could do something like this, she would have said, no, absolutely not. He loves America.

"I'll help," she says in a thick voice that to her ears sounds like someone else's. "He might be tracking my phone, though." She tells them about how he found their daughter Leila when she skipped school.

"Leave your mobile phone at home, and go buy a disposable phone at a convenience store," Bryce says. He gives her his business card. "Call me when you have it. That's how we'll communicate."

She stares at the thick white paper with the blue and red Homeland Security logo. Her fall into the rabbit hole is complete. All she needs now is the White Rabbit telling her to hurry.

Chapter 49

G0d_of_Internet has very little to do for *Chrysalide* now except watch it grow and update itself. His creation has come of age, and his last task will be the pleasurable one of sending the final command. Not today, but soon.

He looks at the available flights to Cairo. Buying airplane tickets with two days notice costs a lot of money, particularly when you are buying first-class tickets, but money holds no obstacles for him now. He possesses plenty thanks to the *Chrysalide*.

He books his ticket using the counterfeit Egyptian passport he obtained through the dark web, a criminal's marketplace with anonymous websites peddling stolen credit card numbers, fake documents, weapons and drugs. He charged the tickets to a purloined credit card he bought on the dark web as well. He paid for both in Bitcoin, using its mixing system that shuffles the currency around various accounts before paying it out, shielding his payment and his identity through its virtually untraceable network.

The internet's open architecture creates wonderful opportunities for freedom of activity. But part of him longs for the simple life of his childhood in the seventies, when family was the only network he knew, and games were played in the hot dusty streets rather than on consoles and laptops and phones.

He remembers drowsy afternoons under cedar trees in the desert heat with his uncles and cousins, followed by camel races viewed from the climate-controlled seats of their four-wheel drive vehicles.

Back then, he wanted so badly to be one of the jockeys astride a camel, humping through billowing clouds of sand. But his uncles said it was too dangerous for him to ride. Instead, they made him ride in the car alongside the camels, cheering for the small barefoot Pakistani boys astride saddles made of brightly colored blankets. These were primitive races, more like the original Bedouin sport than the kind held now, drawing tens of thousands of spectators under the white-tented roof covering King Fahd Stadium. But he loved them, and loved being in the desert much more than in the vast antiseptic compound even with its air-conditioned comforts.

He anticipates his return to the desert with the eagerness of a groom approaching his wedding night. He understands now the pull of his homeland soil, the whispers of his ancestors calling him home. His adopted country served him well for many years, and he loved its shiny promise and potential dearly for many years. But he knows now the wisdom of the old ways is what endures, and it is time to return home.

Chapter 50

Juliana parks her car into the garage next to Mahaz's black Mercedes and clicks the engine off. She assumes Homeland Security has their house under surveillance but she saw no sign of it on her drive.

What am I doing? I wish I could take the kids and go far away from all this. She looks at the plastic bins of Christmas and Halloween decorations as though they contain some answers she needs. But they do not. *No use delaying the inevitable,* she thinks.

Purse and briefcase slung on one shoulder, she opens the door from the garage into the laundry room and takes a deep breath of the soapy scent of detergent and dryer sheets. She hasn't been home in days, and despite everything, being there still feels safe and comfortable. The house embraces her as it always does. The familiarity of the furniture, the rugs, the artwork and knick-knacks she and Mahaz collected over the years brings her a sense of security.

In the kitchen, a stack of unopened mail spills onto the granite counter. Mahaz already sorted it by size, putting the large magazines and envelopes on the bottom and the bills on top. They never receive any personal mail, really, just bills and carpet cleaning flyers and Thai food take-out menus. She skips going through the pile and fills a glass with tap water and drinks half quickly.

The door to Mahaz's office is closed, but she can see a shaft of warm electric light pouring onto the floor. She raises her hand to knock on the painted wood but freezes when she hears his voice. He speaks quietly and she only hears fragments of his conversation.

"No, I want a direct…that won't work…"

Flights? Is he talking about direct flights to Riyadh?

Heavy footfall on the carpet moves toward the door, and she flees for the kitchen expecting to hear him behind her.

But the door doesn't open, and he doesn't follow her.

She climbs the stairs to their master bedroom, decorated in muted purples, and gets into the shower, letting the steam clouds rise around her. Thinking about the tasks ahead of her only raises her blood pressure and makes her head pound more, so she lets her mind wander instead to a mental playlist of her favorite memories of her children. Vivid, sharply etched moments in time when her love for them was so absolute that she is breathless thinking about it even now.

Omar at the all-school spelling bee in fifth grade, standing on the stage in his white polo and blue slacks, spelling "oxymoron" into the microphone, smiling before he even hears the judges say he is correct, because he knows he got it right. Leila in her pink princess dress she wore every day of the summer when she was five, holding in her hand a baby bird that fell from its nest in one of the great oaks towering in their backyard. "We've got to put it back, Mom!" she cried, and Mahaz climbed the tree and gently put the bird inside. And had his nose pecked by the mama bird for his trouble.

Mahaz. Her present worry crowds out the memories. No doubt she would lose him. But hasn't he already left her? She stayed with Mahaz for years in a kind of stasis, clinging to the routine of their marriage. Letting their mutual love of their children be the glue holding them together. Hoping that was enough. Had she been foolish or lazy? Did it matter now?

She steps out of the shower determined that she is doing the right thing for her children. She dresses in jeans and a black sweater, the most fitting outfit she could think of for her reconnaissance mission tonight, and uses a little under-eye concealer and blush to hide the fatigue that dulled her complexion and painted dark commas underneath the fringe of her lower eyelashes.

She finds Mahaz in the kitchen, eating carrot sticks with hummus and opening the mail.

"I thought I heard you," Mahaz says.

"Drew came to the hospital so I could get some rest. Leila's there with him."

Mahaz nods but maintains his focus on a credit card bill. Juliana lets her eyes travel over his face and shoulders, scrutinizing him. She knows with certainty he is wrestling with something internally, from the pinched look around his eyebrows and the way his shoulder blades are clamped around his ears.

"We'll need to get Leila a new phone soon," she says in a flat tone meant to be a statement of fact instead of a call to battle over what happened this afternoon. But the words sound false to her ears. If the next two days go as Bryce told her they would, Mahaz will be in custody. She could buy Leila a phone without his interference.

"Uh huh," he says, laying the credit card bill to one side and opening another envelope.

"Are you planning on going back to the hospital tonight?"

"No, not tonight," he says. "I have some things I need to do around here. Are you going back?"

He speaks to her without lifting his eyes from the papers in front of him. She studies the dark curls, salted with grey, on the back of his neck that reach the top of his collar.

"No. Drew is going to stay there with Omar, and that's what

Leila wanted to do as well. She's pretty mad at us. Anyway, I might go the store. We're out of pretty much everything." She clears her throat. "You're not going into the office tonight?"

"No," he says.

Bryce's plan just might work, she thinks with some apprehension. If Mahaz is in for the night, then they can definitely get in and out of the offices at UCLA without too much trouble. And she'll have to rely on their stealth at getting into the house later tonight.

"It's too quiet, isn't it?" she says. "Without the kids around."

"It's nice for a change," he says.

Juliana leans against the counter. In front of her is a bulletin board she installed next to the fancy stainless steel refrigerator as a repository for the bits of paper and photos that collect in the kitchen when you have two kids. Dental appointment reminder cards, a photo of the four of them at Disneyland, the lunch menu for the month at their high school. The detritus of a modern American family.

She stands there for a few moments, closing her eyes and mentally creating a space for Mahaz to talk to her, to confess his plans and ask her to help him turn himself in. But the moments pass with no sound other than the shuffling of paper on wood and the far away yip of the neighbor's Shih Tzu puppy.

She opens her eyes. Mahaz remains in the same position at the table. She grabs her purse and tells him she is going to the store. He acknowledges her with a tilt of the head, nothing more.

Chapter 51

The Center for Information Technology occupies a suite of offices in the modern five-story complex designed to house UCLA's graduate school of management. The architecture is contemporary and stunning, with four glass, steel, and red brick buildings circling a sunny inner courtyard. A famous architect designed it but Juliana can never remember his name.

She drives into the parking structure at the corner of Sunset Boulevard and Westwood Plaza and finds a spot easily on the lower level. Classes are in session, but the school doesn't offer many night classes mid-week.

The evening sky is violet and moonless, and the air so warm that she could substitute her sweater for a T-shirt. Bryce stands on the pathway leading from the garage to the school entrance with Ken and a grey-haired woman whose skin is so rosy she thinks immediately of Mrs. Santa Claus, despite the fact the woman is bony instead of plump. Both Ken and the woman carry duffle bags.

"Everything go all right?" Ken asks. "Did you go to the house? Was he there?" She can sense his concern for her prickling off his skin.

Bryce must sense it too because he tries to lower the intensity with a forced laugh. "Slow down there, Ken. Let her answer one question at a time."

"Yes, he was there, and he told me he'd be in all night. I left my cell phone on the counter so it would look like an accident I forgot it. You have the number to this one now." She holds up the cheap throwaway phone she bought at a liquor store on Van Nuys Boulevard.

"This is Gina Morgan," Bryce says. "She's with the FBI."

Her hand is as red as her face, but cool to the touch as Juliana shakes it. "Nice to meet you," she says. "I didn't realize we'd have such a big crowd though. It might draw some attention, me going inside with three people. And what if one of the research assistants or someone is in there working?" Kendall Sage's pert face pops into her mind. Kendall would probably love an excuse to call Mahaz if she sees Juliana taking a group into his office.

"You'll introduce us as security consultants. Tell anyone who asks that we're coming in to do some after-hours upgrades to the network."

"Okay," she says. "And I'll say Mahaz is at the hospital if anyone asks."

"Just keep it simple," Bryce says. "Don't elaborate unless you absolutely have to."

She climbs the wide stairs with Ken at her side and Bryce and Gina behind. Anxiety claws at her gut as she opens the lobby's glass doors. Most days when she comes in these doors for work, she feels a wash of inadequacy and stress. Today those feelings are compounded by fear.

A dark-haired man rolls a trash bin across the travertine marble floor. He wears huge red headphones and bops his head to some unheard beat pounding into his ears. He doesn't notice them. They climb another set of stairs to the second floor, their footsteps echoing through the open atrium.

"The Center is over here," she says, just to break the tension. She fumbles with her key ring for the right key, embarrassed at how shaky her hands are.

Her worries about Kendall or any of the research assistants working late are unfounded. Perhaps they only work late when Mahaz does, and like her, secretly cheer when he leaves the office early or travels out of town. At work, Mahaz can be very demanding, prone to shouting for staff from his office so he could dictate letters or presentations or request that someone fetch him a cup of espresso from the cafe.

"Which lock do we need to defeat?" Gina asks. *Defeat is a funny word for breaking in,* Juliana thinks. She points to the door leading to her husband's office, then does a quick circle around her own cubicle in the work area she shares with the research assistants. Nothing seems to have changed, except the wilting of her philodendron plant. She grabs a half-full bottle of water and pours its contents into the dry soil. *I'd be relieved not to have to return to this job,* she thinks. She doubts that once Mahaz is arrested that the Prince would continue his funding. And without that funding, she doubts UCLA will keep the Center open. Feeling keenly how much she wanted his approval of her work here, she realizes with startling clarity that Mahaz never expected her to be successful at it. She grasps now that he gave it to her only as a compromise at her insistence that she wanted to work. He probably thought she would grow tired of it and quit, but he underestimated her stubbornness.

Chapter 52

The esteemed professor and cryptologist, Mahaz Al-Dossari, invested a lot of the university's money in technology for his office. He has the latest, biggest monitors, docking stations, bluetooth keyboards and mice and a huge display screen that drops down from the ceiling. Instead of art, his office walls are covered in glass boards with indecipherable handwritten notes, some in Arabic, flowing across in perfectly straight lines.

The glass and chrome conference table looks freshly polished and his matching desk contains just one neat pile of books and papers, organized into a pyramid by size. There are no pictures of Juliana or their two children.

Ken swallows down office envy and watches as Gina and Bryce methodically comb the room. Gina snaps panoramic photos of the office, while Bryce paws through open drawers. There are no computers or laptops in sight. Juliana was right, he thinks. Mahaz won't let his laptops out of his sight.

"Here," Bryce says. "Look through these for anything interesting." He hands Ken the stack of papers from the desk, and Ken sits down with them at the conference table. On the top is an invitation to a cocktail reception honoring a new faculty member, and underneath that a few more invitations to dinners and conferences. A few of the dates have already passed. An estimate from a software developer for a new website for the center asks a staggering $600,000, payable in two installments. Must be one hell of a website, Ken thinks.

Underneath that is a soft-cover book about cryptography, with a handwritten note clipped to the cover. "Thank you so much for your assistance," it reads, signed by the author. No one has even thumbed through the book, judging by its pristine and creaseless spine.

"Not much here," Ken says.

"Bingo," Bryce says. He lifts an old laptop out of the bottom drawer of the desk. "This thing weighs a ton."

"That looks like the machine the Bureau issued me in the nineties," Gina says.

"You probably still have it, don't you?" Bryce says with a smirk. "Budget cuts and all." With gloved hands he lays the laptop on the desk and flips it over to photograph its serial number.

Ken says, "It could be an old machine he keeps around for testing purposes."

Bryce turns the laptop right side up and cracks it open. Gina crowds behind him to look over his shoulder.

"Or it could be a throwaway machine he's using for *Chrysalide*," Gina says. Bryce presses the power button and the machine whirs then chimes the familiar three tones of a well-known chipmaker.

"Don't turn it on," Gina says. "He'll see that in the log and know someone's been here. We'll get our information from the logger hardware."

The machine works its way through a series of set-up windows then comes to a password screen.

"I forgot how long these things take to boot up," Bryce says. "I'll shut it down." He powers it down and carries it over to the conference table. Gina brings out a kit of small screwdrivers and removes the back panel.

Juliana appears in the doorway. Individual strands of her dark hair cling to the metal doorframe from the static electricity she generated by walking to them on the thick carpet. She holds her arms around her middle as if she is holding a live animal that she can just barely keep under control. Ken wants nothing more than to wrap his arms around her.

Gina places the keystroke logger next to the motherboard with a click.

"Do you know anything about this old computer?" Ken asks.

Juliana shakes her head. "Where did you find it?"

"Bottom drawer," Bryce says. "Is there any other place Mahaz keeps things, like a storage closet?"

She hesitates for a moment, then nods. "We have a supply cabinet. I'll show you."

Ken follows Bryce and Juliana to the closet, even though his presence is hardly necessary. He convinced Bryce he should come along to this reconnaissance mission to provide his expertise, but he knows that his real reason for being there has more to do with the feelings he has for Juliana. Unfamiliar territory he is not sure how to navigate. Instead, he is flying blindly and strictly by instinct. And all his instinct tells him is to stick close to Juliana.

The supply cabinet is more of a walk-in closet, stuffed with bookshelves and file cabinets overflowing with papers, books and office supplies. If Ken had to hazard a guess, he would say that a neat freak like Mahaz has never seen the inside of this cabinet. Otherwise, he would have organized it. Or at least told someone else to do so.

Ken scans the chaos. In one corner, a basket holds USB drives with the center's logo on them. Next to that, ten detachable hard drives sit in a neat stack, each labeled with a name.

"What are these?"

"Back-ups for everyone's laptops. Mahaz makes us do it every Friday."

Ken exchanges glances with Bryce. Could it be that easy?

"We ought to take a look at those," Bryce says.

Ken grabs the stack and shuffles through them like a deck of cards. "Here's Mahaz's," he says, holding it up like a trophy.

Though he finds it hard to believe their good luck, Ken isn't surprised to find the backup drives just lying around. Most people, even those who should know better, treat backup drives with really low security. They back up every little file, photo and video, then forget about it entirely. Sometimes people even back up their contact lists and emails. Some hacker made headlines recently for uncovering a corporation's system administrator who stored system passwords in a big Excel spreadsheet titled "passwords." Guys like that make it easy for blackhats.

Has Mahaz made the same careless error?

Juliana backs out of the closet and stands with her hand on the doorknob. "Are you almost done in there?" Her eyes dart back to the door that opens onto the corridor, as though waiting for Mahaz to walk in. "It's been more than an hour. I told him I was just going to the store."

"We're almost done. Give us another fifteen minutes or so," Bryce says. Ken watches as she presses her lips together. *This poor woman*, he thinks. She didn't ask for any of this. She bows her head in acknowledgement and retreats further into the hall. "I'm going to the ladies' room," she says.

Bryce and Ken watch her leave the office. She shuts the door quietly, standing there with her hand gripped around the doorknob until the glass door finally clicks shut.

They walk a few steps in silence.

"How do you do this kind of thing?" Ken says. He feels sick to his stomach thinking of the anxiety and fear coursing through Juliana's veins. "Convincing someone to betray her husband?"

Bryce turns into the open door of Mahaz's office. Gina sits at the conference table looking through the same stack of papers Ken examined a few minutes before.

"You have to use the tools at hand to do the job," Bryce says. "We exploit weaknesses just like the other side does. You know that. Rules of the game."

Ken hands the hard drive to Gina. "We found this," he says. Gina takes it and plugs it into her own laptop for a data dump.

"Onward," Bryce says. "Maybe we'll get a little luckier at the house."

Chapter 53

Proxyw0rm: Nothing is foolproof, my friend. There's always a fool out there who is just a little more creative.

G0d_of_Internet: Yes, but we are far ahead of them.

Proxyw0rm: The error in the encryption implementation was preventable. Our leader says your arrogance clouds your vision.

G0d_of_Internet: What you hear from me is confidence, not arrogance.

The programmer is beginning to think that living among his brethren in the Islamic Crusade is going to consist of daily lectures on humility and enforced Quran study. G0d_of_Internet feels unappreciated.

To be honest, he thinks, *this financial system hack came together faster than I thought it would.* The bank employs what security professionals jokingly call M&M security. Named after the candy-coated chocolate treat, M&M security is hard on the outside, but gooey and soft on the inside. Meaning that once you breach the first line of defense and stand inside the firewall, you can practically do whatever you want.

Over a series of weeks he gained access to the bank's servers and with that, a full set of training manuals on how to use the bank's critical applications. Basically, he has the ability to perform any activity a teller could—viewing and changing customer account information, watching nationwide for ATM activity, checking bank loans and transfers and even reviewing the records of the Department of Motor Vehicles. Most importantly, he has access to the system that wires funds to any bank in the world, and the bank administrator's passwords that allow him to process the transactions.

G0d_of_Internet believes in backup plans so of course he has arranged for his own Swiss bank account to be one of the beneficiaries of a wire transfer, as well as the account of the Islamic Crusade. The group will get the bulk of the money, of course, but he will shave off some for himself as well. He deserves that, and in light of their constant admonitions about his arrogance and lack of humility, he is glad he took the extra steps to ensure his financial independence. He may be on his own sooner than he had planned.

Chapter 54

This is not a week Juliana wants to relive. She's pretty much gone through every emotion possible since she took Omar to the hospital two days ago. The days have been by far the most fearful and anxious she has ever endured, eclipsing each of Omar's previous surgeries and setbacks. Her marriage is unravelling, and she is pulling the thread to make it unravel faster. Not to mention she is physically exhausted and injured.

She hoists the grocery bags onto the kitchen counter with a grunt for emphasis. After all, the bread and milk and paper towels are her proof to Mahaz that she really went to the store. But Mahaz shows no signs of noticing or caring how long she has been gone. His car is still in the garage, and his office door remains shut and impenetrable to her.

Her phone lies on the kitchen counter right where she left it. She picks it up and calls her brother.

"I'm home," she says. The situation feels surreal. Is she supposed to use code words now? She is reminded of the *Scarecrow and Mrs. King* television series from the eighties. Just a normal housewife with perky hair and a can-do attitude, suddenly forced to become a CIA agent on the front lines of national security. It sounds ridiculous and yet, here she is undergoing the same kind of transformation.

"Good," Drew says. "All is well here. We're watching a movie. Something about young vampires in love."

"Sounds like Leila got to make the choice."

"Yeah, we let her pick."

"That's nice," she says. Drew passes the phone to Omar and Leila, and she presses the phone tight to her ear as though it will transport her to their presence. Their adolescent one-word answers and distracted replies are music to her ears, and transport her out of the mess of emotions she faces at home.

"Maybe we should get a dog," Leila says. "My friend Rebecca has the cutest French bulldog. It has these big ears like Shrek. So cute."

Juliana smiles. The most amazing things come out of Leila's mouth sometimes. All this drama today, and she wants a French bulldog. Her resilience is breathtaking.

"I've always liked those fluffy little Pomeranians," Juliana says, closing her eyes and enjoying the distraction. "The ones that celebrities put in their purses."

"Those are chihuahuas, Mom," Leila says. "So can we get a dog?"

"You know you can't get the internet or text your friends on a dog," Juliana says.

Her joke is lost on Leila, who responds in a very serious tone. "I still need a phone, too. Jeez, Mom, I didn't mean I wanted a dog instead of a phone. I thought the dog might be nice for you, too. Omar will be going to college next year and me in a couple of years, so you'll have that empty nest thing."

"We'll talk about it later, sweetheart. I love you. Now let me talk to your uncle."

"I love you, too," Leila says.

"You can have our dog," Drew says. "He doesn't listen to a damn thing I say."

"No, thanks. But maybe I can send Leila over for an hour of poop scooping to show her the downside of having a dog."

"She's welcome anytime," Drew says. "Look, you should be careful tonight, okay? And try to get some rest."

She snorts. "Right. That'll be easy to do."

"You're doing the right thing, Jules," he says before she hangs up.

She powers up the laptop to look for news reports about the Islamic Crusade. Something to tell her why Mahaz chose this group over his life in the states. His life with her. Though news sites have hundreds of stories on the Islamic Crusade, a quick scan through the top stories shows that there isn't anything new to report. Each basically regurgitates the same facts she's been hearing for days on television and radio. The Islamic Crusade takes responsibility for the attacks on American water and power utilities and threatens to do more damage if the United States doesn't remove all of its troops from Muslim countries.

"If one country or group levies a cyber attack on the United States, it is as much an act of war as bombing Boise would be," says one man on CNN who looks as hawkish as his words. "It justifies a military response."

The Islamic Crusade has yet to specify its future attack targets should the U.S. not remove its troops by Friday, but pundits and talking heads are happy to speculate to fill in the blanks.

"The International Money Fund, the Federal Reserve, Lockheed-Martin, Sony. All of these could be targets on Friday," the hawk continues. "Or will they attack air traffic control networks, transit systems, telecommunications? My instinct, personally, is that they're going to go after the air traffic systems. They want to create as much fear and chaos as they did on 9/11, and planes crashing in the air is just about the most horrifying thing I can imagine."

She clicks on a *Washington Post* profile piece on the Islamic Crusade.

The Islamic Crusade is one of the most capable of the al-Qaeda network, operating out of Yemen but actively seeking to expand its reach throughout the world. It is led by Abdul al-Lahem, rumored to have run clandestine terror operations for the CIA in the eighties and early nineties, and said to have deep connections to the Saudi royal family.

Abdul al-Lahem has financed and armed a variety of terror operations, using affiliates of Al Qaeda, the Wahhabi sect and other Sunni Muslim militant groups in Iraq, Syria, and Afghanistan. The Islamic Crusade has training bases in Jordan, Pakistan and Turkey.

"He's vehemently hostile to Iran, and has poured billions of dollars to bolster the pro-Islamic regimes in Tunisia and Morocco to demobilize pro-democracy movements," said Samuel Bally, senior researcher at Alight Foundation for Foreign Policy. "The groups that receive support are encouraged to, among other things, assassinate secular democratic leaders and socialist trade union leaders."

The reclusive al-Lahem has not been seen in public since the Ramadan celebration in the Qatari capital Doha in 2010. Born in Tabuk, al-Lahem is said to be the son of an African-born concubine and was only recognized by his Saudi father as his heir when he was in his teens. He was commissioned as a fighter pilot in the Royal Saudi Air Force in 1978.

Several Westerners have joined the Islamic Crusade, including a few who died in high-profile suicide operations. A Muslim convert from Canada, Michael Deghayes, 32, blew himself up in Jeddah along with a group of seven U.S. tourists and two security guards.

Their latest move into cyber terrorism has been a transformational moment for the group, marking a shift from suicide bombings and military force. By bringing the battlefield to cyberspace, al-Lahem has found another way to strike fear in the hearts and minds of Americans. The industries most likely to be targeted are financial companies, media companies and government agencies, analysts said.

With a click and a whoosh of air, Mahaz opens the office door and steps into the hallway.

"You're back," he says, his eyes on her screen.

She rearranges her face to what she hopes is a neutral expression, and changes her web browser to a cooking and recipe site.

Mahaz approaches her from behind, his hands resting on the chair backrest. She can feel his breath on the top of her head.

"A recipe for pork roast?" he says with a snort. "Are you going to start cooking dinner for us again?"

"I'm just surfing around," she says. She didn't even notice what was on the screen until he pointed it out.

"And here I thought you'd be looking up divorce attorneys."

He pushes the chair roughly, and her head snaps forward with the impact. She tries to push herself out of the chair but he holds her shoulders down.

She goes numb, her eyes fixed on the photo of pork roast on her screen. He wants a fight. What feels like minutes but is probably only a few seconds passes as she tries to determine how to respond. *What did Bryce say? Keep it simple.* She swallows and tries to keep her voice even and calm.

"You made it clear you don't want that," she says. "And I don't want to lose my children."

The pressure lightens on her shoulders and she hears him take a step back. Ads for a cookbook by some celebrity chef flash on the laptop screen.

"I knew you'd see reason. And what would you do if we got divorced anyway? Get a job at the makeup counter at Nordstrom and live in some shabby apartment?"

"I asked if you wanted a divorce. I didn't say I wanted one," she says. She must keep this conversation simple. She must get through this night.

"You don't get to decide what happens with this marriage," he says. "I decide."

She shuts the laptop, swings her legs to the side and contorts her body to get out of the chair so she can face him.

"I'm tired and I want to go to bed," she says. She takes a step toward the stairs but his fingers latch onto her lower arm and hold tight.

"Do you think I don't know?"

She freezes like a wild animal in headlights, adrenalin filling her mouth with the taste of copper pennies. His fingers bite into her flesh. She looks down at his feet, covered in brown silk and cashmere socks that have to be washed by hand. He orders them from Italy. He loves the small, artisanal luxuries that most people don't notice.

It is the first time in a long time they are alone together like this, no kids in the next room. *He could kill me*, she thinks. *He could kill me, and Bryce and his buddies will find my body here on the kitchen floor, just another casualty of the war on terrorism.*

"You're so transparent, Juliana," he says. "Enlisting your family to help you get a bank account, find a divorce attorney. Telling the kids that you'll protect them from me taking them to live in Saudi Arabia."

"Let go of me," she says, realizing that he has been tracking her laptop and phone just as he had Leila's.

He tightens his grip, and steps even closer to her. She can smell his stale breath. His dark eyes flash; he is so angry he is a complete stranger. She isn't sure what he will do next.

"At home, the man runs the family. Women cannot be trusted. Too emotional. Look at you, always crying and demanding, when you have everything you could want. You're like a child."

She yanks her arm but his fingers stay tightly wrapped as if he's cut through her skin right to the bone. She can't believe what he is saying. It directly contradicts everything she knows about him.

"Really? You can say that with a straight face? You, who told me when Leila was born, that you wanted her to grow up as a strong American woman, like me?"

"Isn't that what your friends at the FBI are telling you? That I've joined the Islamic Crusade? Isn't that why you were just reading an article about it?"

His eyes glitter like onyx. His mouth curves into a joyless smile.

She was so scared of him finding out about her betrayal that she feels almost grateful that it is out in the open. Finally she can ask him the question directly, and gauge his reaction for herself. She squares her shoulders and stares into his eyes.

"So, Mahaz, are you the hacker who created the worm?"

"Shame on you, Juliana," he says. "You don't even know what to believe in, so you blow like the wind." With one fluid motion, he drops her arm and brings his fist to her jaw, sending her reeling against the corner of the kitchen table. A second punch to her stomach lands her on the floor, her head bouncing against the wood. She gasps for air, and tastes blood in her mouth.

"I used to love how guileless you were," he says. "The way you just looked at me like I was your god and your lover all mixed up in one. I wanted to fill your head with everything I knew. I wanted to explain myself to you. But you're still just as empty as you were the day I met you, aren't you? A pretty head full of nothing, ready to let anyone fill it. Maybe your new friend Ken won't get tired of you as quickly."

She lies without moving on the floor, letting his words drift over her like clouds. She hears his soft footsteps as he returns to his office, and then after a while, she hears him walk to the garage. She only rises when she hears the car engine rev and fade, then the chut-chut sound of the garage door shutting behind him. *Let Homeland Security deal with him now.*

Chapter 55

What Mahaz says about calling Ken makes her feel like a traitor when she dials his number. But she knows she has to call either Bryce or Ken. After all, there is no reason for them to come to the house now to plant their devices. Mahaz obviously is on to them and took whatever he needs with him. And Bryce is law enforcement, while Ken is…a friend. And right now, she needs the friend more.

She pushes herself off of the floor, trying not to bend at the waist to set her cracked ribs on fire. Pain throbs from her right cheek and molars, where his fist landed. She presses her fingertips on the skin and is surprised to find it swollen and warm to the touch.

"Ken, it's Juliana." Her voice sounds loud and strange in her ears. "Mahaz knows, and he's taken off."

An hour later, Bryce and Ken ring the doorbell of her home. Two Los Angeles Police Department cars park on the street in front, lights and sirens thankfully off.

"Going to be a nasty bruise," Bryce says, his eyes scanning her face. Juliana forces herself to make eye contact, shame bubbling up inside her that she caused this visible violence on her face. And that she deserves it. She tells herself that's not true, but the feeling is hard to shake.

Bryce keeps his face neutral, the hallmark of a man who has seen more than his share of domestic violence, while Ken makes no effort to mask his anger. His hands close into fists at his side.

"Maybe we should take you the hospital, make sure everything is all right," Ken says.

"No hospitals tonight," she says, holding her hand up like a stop sign. "I'm fine. Let me show you his office, but like I said on the phone, you're not going to find anything there."

Her comfortable house is no longer her safe haven. The whole environment is static charged with violence and fear. The kitchen lights burn bright as an operating room and there are small dried blood stains on the floor where she fell. The darkness outside presses on the window glass like a blanket. It is the kind of darkness that can easily conceal someone who does not want to be found. *Is Mahaz out there, watching me lead these men through our home?*

She turns to Bryce. "Do you know where he went? Are your people following him?"

Bryce nods once before his phone rings. The sound makes her jump, blood hammering through her chest.

Ken places his hand on her shoulder gently, as though the slightest pressure will cause her pain. She turns to him and buries her face in his chest, and lets the tears come. She's done so much crying these past few days, she's surprised at her seemingly limitless capacity for more tears.

He wraps his arms lightly around her shoulders and lets her cry into his grey hoodie.

"You can't sleep here tonight," he says. "It isn't safe. We'll get you a hotel room."

She shakes her head and steps back, wiping her tears away with her shirtsleeve. "A hotel…I don't know. I don't think I want to be alone tonight."

They both stand silently for a moment, watching Bryce as he leans in the doorway of the office surveying its contents.

"But I can stay at my brother's," she says. "It will be fine." Her parents' home is obviously off limits tonight; her bruised face will break their hearts. Then she thinks of Mahaz, his eyes narrowed into slits. Is there any chance he'll come looking for her again tonight? Will he come to Drew and Cathy's to find her?

"You know it's past ten-thirty, right?" Ken says.

A glance at the digital clock on the stove affirms it. "I had no idea it was so late," she says. "His wife is home alone with their little ones. I hate to bother them now." She runs a shaking hand through her hair and sighs.

"You're welcome to come home with me," Ken says. "I mean, it's late and—"

An explosion erupts from the office, shaking the wood floor like a major earthquake and knocking Juliana into the refrigerator. A nasty black smoke stains the air as burning embers pelt her hair and shoulders.

The violence of the explosion makes Juliana's entire body feel as though it has been smashed in a vise. The air sucks out of her lungs, and her ears ring with such fierceness she feels sure they are bleeding.

She places both hands over her ears. Thankfully, there is no blood. She holds out her arms, examining them for damage, then scans her clothes for blood. None. She is okay.

Juliana looks up to find Ken, standing at the door of the office, his mouth moving like he is shouting at her but she hears nothing. His eyes look semi-glazed over and he bleeds from an inch-long gash on his forehead. Small pockets of flame burn on the office carpet beyond his feet.

Ken points to the counter behind her, and she turns to see the fire extinguisher she mounted to the wall a few years ago after the kitchen remodel. She snaps it out of the plastic bracket, her ribs screaming as her body twists.

As soon as she catches her balance, she runs to the door, pushing by Ken to see Bryce, still seated in the desk chair but thrown back against the bookshelves. His face is as shredded as his clothes, and the fabric is burning. A horrible rasping sound emerges from his throat. Around him is a perimeter of destruction and black smoke. The blast shattered the glass in the French doors leading to the patio, and hollowed out the wood desk. Only two of its legs remain upright, like soldiers left at their posts.

She aims the extinguisher nozzle with shaking hands and tries to spray it but nothing comes out. Ken mouthes something and takes the heavy extinguisher from her. With a few twists, he aims and shoots the fire retardant on the desk and Bryce's clothing. White, powdery smoke billows over the floor and into the air like a toxic cloud and makes her cough, setting off a galaxy of pain in her side so sharp she sees stars.

The four LAPD officers who were waiting outside rush in with their guns drawn and fan out. Two mount the stairs. A woman officer with dark hair pulled back in a tight bun who looks to be in her thirties passes Juliana, followed by a tall male officer with red hair and acne scars. "We've called for an ambulance," the woman shouts over her shoulder as she examines Bryce, but from her facial expression Juliana can see she knows it is too late.

"Ma'am, we need to get you out of here, now," the male officer says, his arm pointing toward the back door. He looks as young as Omar.

"I'm not hurt. But Bryce…" Juliana says, not sure what to do, but feeling deep in her bones that leaving him in that office is too painful to bear.

"There might be a secondary device," a male voice from behind them says. "We need to get you away from this area."

The other two male officers come back downstairs. The one in his early fifties with short salt-and-pepper hair steps toward her. "Sometimes terrorists wait for help to arrive at the scene of a bombing before setting off another, deadlier explosion," he says. "Let's go outside."

She can hear the wail of sirens as fire trucks race toward the scene. Tears fill her eyes. This officer called Mahaz a terrorist, and it hurts her profoundly, even though Mahaz's actions made the label true. She wonders if the officers suspect her of collaborating with him, and her facial bruises just part of the ruse.

As Ken drives her over the winding Laurel Canyon shortcut, Juliana is silent, staring into the night, its darkness only broken by his Jeep's headlights on the canyon walls and sporadic homes. Spidery side roads lead to neighborhoods Mahaz never wanted to live in, citing the risk of mudslides and fire.

They are silent for most of the drive to Ken's house. She can't stop thinking about Bryce. The horrible rasp of his breathing, his burning clothes, his face. She's seen dead bodies before. Her grandparents, and a neighbor laid out in funeral homes with blush on their cheeks and hands folded over their hearts. But to see someone die such a violent death is crushing. And Mahaz, her husband, caused that death. And probably means for her to die too. Tears start forming a hot cloud in the back of her throat. She bites down hard on her lip to stop herself from crying. *Don't cry*, she thinks. *If you start crying now, you'll never be able to stop.* She doesn't want to melt down in front of Ken, and make this any more difficult for both of them.

Sleep-deprived, she has lost track of time. It is somewhere between dinner time and bed time, with few people on the road.

They pass houses with glowing windows, and she imagines families going about their evening rituals of bath times and homework.

A few fish hook curves and another ten minutes later, the narrow mountain road opens into the wide streets of a posh Beverly Hills neighborhood, with homes set back on spacious lawns like a suburban sub-division. But because these are in a specific zip code, they are priced well out of reach of most Angelenos.

Ken parks the Jeep in a detached garage outside a colonial-style white duplex on Charleville Boulevard.

She follows him down the driveway and through a wooden door with stained glass inset panels of deep red and blue. The ceiling in the front space soars at least twenty feet, with open beam ceilings with track lighting illuminating a huge piece of abstract art dominating one wall. A ficus tree shivers next to a dark green leather couch. A fifty-inch flat screen television hangs on the opposite wall. The overall effect is cold and stark and incredibly clean.

"The guest room is really just an office," he says. "There's no bed. So why don't you take mine?"

"No, I'm not throwing you out of your bed. Give me a warm blanket and the couch down here is fine."

He walks into the open kitchen area. "Are you hungry?"

"No, just tired," she says. He retrieves a bottle of water out of the refrigerator and drinks half of it.

"Let me get you that blanket. I can turn on the heat, too."

"That would be great." She perches on the couch, taking a slow inventory of her bumps and bruises until she notices a dog bed in the corner. "Do you have a dog?"

"Yes," he says. He returns with a thick knit blanket and a pillow in his arms. "Tilly. My dachshund. You're lucky she's at my mom's or she'd be barking up a storm. She likes to tell visitors who is boss."

"My daughter was just talking about us getting a dog."

"They're great company."

Back in the kitchen, Ken extracts a bottle of bourbon from a cabinet and pours two glasses.

"Medicine," he says as he hands her one and sits next to her on the couch.

She presses her swollen lip to the glass and knocks the drink back. Ken does the same. She feels like a foreigner in Ken's world, her senses sharpened by the unfamiliar scents and surroundings. Ken sits so close to her that their knees touch, and she can smell his masculine scent, clean and rich. She glances at him. He looks dismayed, though he composes his face in a camouflage of steely strength. He's worried about what will happen next, she thinks. *So am I. Every minute.* Ken watches her, waiting for her response to the liquor. He seems worried and unsure what to do.

"That tasted awful," she says with a slight smile, to his obvious relief.

His smile creases his cheeks. "This is what you say about 21-year-old sour mash bourbon from Kentucky?"

She shakes her head sheepishly, smiling at his joke. "I've never been much of a drinker," she says. "More the white wine type, I guess. Your fancy alcohol is wasted on me."

"I don't consider it a waste," he says, and his face reddens. She draws her brows together, trying to think what to say. A throbbing pain in her side and her face remind her of her injuries.

"I must look like a mess," she says.

He doesn't reply, only shaking his head a few times. His eyes remain on hers, kind and brown, soft and inviting where Mahaz's were hard and glittering. He moves his hand a little, like he's reaching for hers, then stops himself as if second thoughts flood his mind.

"I have an alarm system," he says. "And a security camera

installed at the entrance. You've been very brave, and you're safe now."

"Brave?"

"Not many people would do what you have done," Ken says.

She wonders if this is true. She also wonders how many women have been so deceived by their husbands as she was. All this time she thought she was swimming alongside him, when really she had been merely pulled along in his current into deep, dark waters. She condemns herself for her weakness, her passivity. These last twenty-four hours are her *mea culpa* to the world for being such a fool.

Without thinking, she leans over and presses her lips to his, and feels him kiss her back so tenderly she feels only a trace of pressure. Waves of heat rush over her, until she remembers again the wrecked state of her body, bruises on her face, a swollen lip. Here she is reaching out to some strange man like a helpless victim in some sappy television movie. She pulls away, shaking her head.

"I'm sorry, Ken. I don't know what got into me. I just…"

His eyes lock on hers and he lets the silence settle around them for a moment before reassuring her it is all right.

"I'm sorry, too, I shouldn't have…"

He plucks the glass out of her hand and stands up. "We should get some sleep." She hears the clink of glasses set in the sink.

To cover her discomfort, she rises to shake out the blanket and lay it over the couch cushions.

"I'll turn on the heat," he says. But she is no longer cold. Just tired. She lays her head back on the pillow and drifts almost immediately into sleep.

Chapter 56

G0d_of_Internet slept in a rental car in a hospital parking lot in Glendale, waking when the first hint of golden light pierced through the night sky.

He taps the dark blue vinyl of his Egyptian passport, and practices introducing himself as Fouad Ibrahim, and his daughter as Sara Ibrahim. The passport, driver's license and university security badge identifying him as Mahaz Al-Dossari should have burned up in an explosion that, *inshallah*, should have also taken out his scheming wife and at least one of her law enforcement friends.

He hates leaving his son behind, but with Omar's surgery and ongoing health issues, it is best that he stays here in the States. Mahaz hopes Omar will come to the Kingdom of Saudi Arabia on his own. He has already mailed a letter explaining all this, along with Omar's passport, to their family attorney.

What freedom there is in this moment. The burdens of his life as Mahaz Al-Dossari have fallen aside like tall grass as he cuts his path to his new life. No more marriage or house or car payments and the end of that relentless cycle of more, more, more that Americans love to live in.

He strides into the hospital without checking in at the front desk.

Only people who look confused or lost tend to be noticed. Anyone moving with confidence through the lobby is left to their own devices. And his confidence is high. *Haven't I already outwitted the Homeland Security agents who were following me?* A sleepy hospital security guard is no obstacle now.

His plan is to wait in one of the adjacent rooms to his son's. He'll wait until there is an opportunity to speak with Leila alone.

He exits the elevator, only to see two policemen in uniform outside his son's hospital door. *The bomb must have worked*, he thinks, his heart racing. Before the doors shut, he slips back into the elevator and rides it to the floor below, where he exits. He needs to think. He slows his breath down hoping it will have the same effect on his heart, which is pounding from the excitement of playing cat-and-mouse. He walks into a room where an elderly man, little more than a skeleton wrapped in skin, sleeps. There is little chance that anyone will question him sitting there. The nurses are too busy during the morning shift change.

Mahaz sits in the tall chair designed with wing-like headrests to support an overnight visitor's head so they could catch a nap sitting up. The respirator pumps and sighs in time with the heart rate monitor, as sunlight glows in the windows.

He extracts the pay-as-you-go cell phone from his pocket and texts Omar.

this is Conner. will u tell Leila to meet me out front? I want to talk to her.

That should get her running, he thinks. He forbade Leila from having a boyfriend, but he knows from his nightly scans of her phone and laptop that she is "in love" with Conner. Mahaz doesn't think her feelings are love. She is a silly girl in the grip of a hormonal obsession, and an excellent example of why young women should be chaperoned until they are married.

An electronic tone shatters the early morning silence of the hospital, indicating a response to Conner's message.

hi Conner. u r here already? thought you were coming around 10.

Smiling at his cleverness, Mahaz types a quick note back: *couldn't wait to see u. come as soon as u can.*

There isn't anything more to do but wait. The plan is in motion. He rides the elevator back down to the lobby, and then walks into the early morning sun to a bench outside the parking garage with a view of the doors.

Ten minutes pass before Leila emerges in the sunlight, her hand shading her eyes as she scans for her boyfriend. Mahaz can see the attention she took with her appearance. Her hair is brushed and shiny, and blush and lipgloss stain her pretty face.

Mahaz rises from the bench and walks toward her. "Good morning," he says as she turns to face him, blinking warily. Does she know about the bomb? He scans her face for telltale signs of fear, but sees only confusion and calculation. Juliana has kept the details of last night's incidents from the children, just as he thought she would. He wonders how they explained away the police presence outside the hospital room, but realizes he can't ask Leila about it without revealing he has been upstairs.

"What are you doing here, Dad?" Leila says. He sees her looking around for Conner, not sure what to do.

"I wanted to take you to get a new phone."

The girl brightens immediately, a smile replacing the teenage pout that has clouded her face for the last day.

"Really?"

It is too easy, Mahaz thinks. Children are so self-centered. The world could crash around their ears but if they get what they want, all is right with their universe.

"But where's Mom?" Leila says. "And aren't you going to tell Uncle Drew?"

"Your mom's still sleeping," he says. "And I'll text Drew in a bit. Now, Leila, let's go."

"But nothing's open yet," she says. "I don't think the stores open until nine." He thinks she is stalling, hoping Conner would jump out of the bushes.

"I want us to be there when they unlock the doors, that way we can be back in time to take Omar home from the hospital," he says. "I'm very sorry that I broke your phone yesterday and lost my temper like that. You know I love you, don't you?"

She nods. "Maybe we can get pancakes on the way? I'm starving."

"Sure, sure, come on."

Leila falls in behind him as they walk to the parking garage.

"You know there is a new version now of the phone I had. I had version five, but they released version six a few months ago. It has a better camera and more memory."

He glances back at the front doors. No one is in pursuit. He just needs to steer Leila to the car without any incident.

"The other thing version six has is a higher-resolution screen. So not only can you take better photos with the camera, but you can also see more detail just looking at it. But you know all this," she says with a giggle. "I mean, you have version six, don't you, Dad?"

"I do." He unlocks the silver Buick with the key fob.

"Where's the Mercedes?" she says, stopping short.

"It wouldn't start," he said. "The dealership gave me this rental car while they fix it." He opens the passenger door for her and watches her get in, worry lines crinkling her forehead.

"Do you want to go to the Galleria?" he says, trying to shift her attention off of the rental car and further conversation about the Mercedes.

The mention of one of her favorite destinations achieves the desired effect.

She smiles and nods with excitement.

"Good." He shuts the car door with his palm, glancing back one last time to see the immediate area is still clear of Drew or the police or Homeland Security.

The plan worked perfectly, seamlessly.

Chapter 57

"Good morning," Ken says, following the smell of coffee into the kitchen. He's cleaned himself up more than he normally would after rolling out of bed, wanting to make himself look presentable for his overnight visitor. He's clad in sweats instead of his usual T-shirt and boxer shorts. Juliana sits on one of the high bar stools, her feet dangling like a child's. Her lip is still swollen on the right side, and the bruise along her jaw purpled over night. Looking at the bruise makes him angry. How can a man hit a woman like that? She gives him a lopsided smile and signals she is on the phone. A residual fear is in her eyes.

Things are more complicated now. He pours a cup and tells himself to keep it light this morning. No need to bring up the kiss. Even though he wants very much to kiss her, and more, again. But talk about preying on the weak—she's just left her husband, who beat her and left her lying on the floor while he went off to wreak havoc on the world's communications network in the name of a terrorist group.

What has he gotten himself into? Last night, he watched a man die in an explosion that nearly took his own life and Juliana's. Cyber terrorism has morphed into real world terror, with bombs and guns and people who aren't afraid to shoot. He is a computer programmer. A geek in front of a screen and a keyboard, suddenly playing in the highest stakes kind of game. A life-or-death kind of game.

The situation is screwed up. And he has no idea how to unscrew it. All he wants to do is lock the condo doors and windows, and cut off the rest of the world. He wants to curl up in bed with Juliana and hold her tight until Homeland Security cleans this mess up and the danger passes. He wants to wake up in the morning next to her, to see her rub sleep from her eyes, her hair messy, and kiss her so she knows that he will protect her always.

Shit. He is in love. He blinks and sits down across from her at the small table. Unspoken words swim around his head, but he holds them there, not wanting to further complicate things.

"If you're sure it is not too much trouble on you and Cathy," she says into the phone, worry lines creasing her forehead. "I know Omar will be happy to leave, but these hospitals are always chasing you out the door as fast as they can."

Ken rarely sits in the kitchen, mainly because he wants to be parked in front of the laptop or the television most mornings. Sunlight streams through the skylight and onto the dark granite countertop, highlighting a thin layer of dust on the seldom-used juicer. He ought to sell that thing online to some other sucker looking for a lifestyle change. He has only managed a half day of the juice cleanse before giving in to a turkey sandwich.

Juliana glances at him before resuming her study of the floor. "I hate to take the kids home and have them see the damage and the crime scene tape. A few nights with you would be great. Omar and Juliana will love playing with Jack and Cissy."

Ken can hear the deep tones of her brother leaking out of the phone but can't make out the words.

"All right, love you too," she says, and puts the phone down.

"Thanks for making the coffee," he says. His voice sounds creaky and congested from lack of use. "It's good."

"I was just so relieved you didn't have one of those fancy espresso machines. They put one in at the office and I swear it had more controls than a fighter jet." Her smile turns rueful, and she seems to wilt a little with the thought of her workplace and undoubtedly her husband.

Her phone rings.

"Hey, Drew," she says. Ken watches as the blood drains out of her face, accentuating the bruised jaw even more. She rocks slightly in her seat, breathing heavily and loudly through her nose and barely blinking. Then, she stands up suddenly. "I'll be right there." She ends the call, staring at the phone for a few beats in naked disbelief.

Ken rises. "What happened?"

"Leila's gone. She slipped out while Drew was talking to me on the phone. Omar said she went to meet some boy I've never heard of named Conner. She's been gone an hour and Omar texted Conner but there was no response. What if Mahaz has her? Oh my God. Sometimes I just want to wring that girl's neck. I don't know what to do…"

The air becomes harder to breathe. Juliana paces the floor, one hand clutching the phone and the other raking through her hair. Her eyes are wild with panic, and her fear infects Ken. She stands directly in front of him, then takes one step toward him. He puts his hands on her arms and gently pulls her to him. Her arms wrap around his waist and she squeezes, tighter and tighter, as though she is drowning and he is a life preserver. He must help her. He cannot sit back and watch her struggle. He feels her pain as keenly as if it were his own.

"I have that woman Gina's card. The woman from the FBI. We'll call her on the way to the hospital," Ken says.

Chapter 58

Leila slumps forward in the Buick's front seat, the sedatives he crushed then mixed into her white chocolate mocha finally taking effect. *The girl talks nonstop*, he thinks, relishing the silence as he speeds to the rental car office in Burbank where another nondescript midsize sedan waits for Fouad Ibrahim to pick it up.

He misses the quiet, smooth ride of the Mercedes, but he'll be in one again soon enough once he makes it safely out of this country, *inshallah*. Now, the most important thing to do is to get Leila on board the private jet that Prince Abdul arranged for him to take to Riyadh today.

He drives past strip malls and around buses and finally parks the car on a Glendale side street where street sweeping has just been done, providing him with relative confidence that the car won't get a parking ticket for at least a week. He parks in front of a mid-century ranch house with a for-sale sign with the words "in escrow" on the top. No doubt someone will buy the house as a tear-down and build a stucco and terra cotta tile monstrosity with a five-foot lawn and wrought iron gates. That's the way Southern California real estate works. The land is worth more than the houses.

He pops the trunk and removes the lightweight, folding

wheelchair he bought at a medical supply store.

He unfolds the wheelchair next to the open door. He lifts Leila from the front seat and puts her in the wheelchair. Even at a hundred and ten pounds, she is dead weight and the exertion makes him stop to catch his breath before wheeling her to the rental car office on Brand Boulevard.

A thick Armenian woman behind the desk at the rental car company looks at him with maternal pity in her eyes as he fumbles with keeping the door open and pushing Leila's wheelchair through. She has kind eyes and is somewhere in that middle-age range of forty-five to sixty-five. He never can tell. She comes from behind the counter to assist, her hands outstretched and her smile wide, but he's already managed to push the rubber wheels over the slightly raised threshold. *Surely that was not compliant with current building standards*, he thinks.

"Are you all right, honey?" the woman asks, her black eyes fixed on Leila. She darts a disapproving glance at him. Mahaz looks at his daughter for the first time since he plopped her in the wheelchair. Her head lolls to one side, and long strands of hair have escaped from her ponytail and pasted themselves on her cheeks and forehead. One arm dangles over the armrest, the other lies unnaturally at her side with the palm facing up.

Mahaz lifts her dangling arm and places it on her lap, and sweeps the hair out of her face. He arranges his face into what he hopes is the weary smile of a loving and worried father.

"She's just so tired," he says. "The chemo treatments take it out of her."

The specter of childhood cancer deflates the woman's distrust like a pin through a balloon. She aims a yellow-toothed smile at Mahaz and waves him toward the counter.

"That poor girl," the woman says. "My sister-in-law's cousin had a daughter with non-Hodgkin's lymphoma. She was a fighter, that girl. Her name was Mari."

Mahaz nods along, pretending to care about this woman's distant relative who, judging by her use of past tense, must have died from the disease. He knows that bringing Leila in like this is a magnet for attention, but they need to move fast and get out of here. Drew and Juliana have undoubtedly notified the police by now. The quicker they get to the airport, the better.

"Terrible thing, cancer," Mahaz says. "I'd really like to get her home though, so she can rest comfortably."

The woman nods quickly. "Yes, yes. Well, let me get you on your way as fast as I can so this little one can rest in her bed."

He smiles at her with honest gratitude.

She types and clicks and stares at some screen out of his line of vision, then asks the usual series of questions about insurance, drivers and how he'd like to pay. He places his credit card on the counter.

"Thank you, Mr. Ibrahim."

A printer behind the counter whirs into life. Leila snorts and rubs her nose, but her eyes stay shut and her body relaxed.

The Van Nuys airport is the rich cousin to the commercial air traffic behemoth of LAX, and Mahaz takes a deep breath as he drives the rental car up to the gate to the executive terminal on the north end of the airport. Not far to go now.

The radio news stations say nothing yet of the explosion in Sherman Oaks last night or an abducted teenage girl, only the usual blend of box office earnings, weather and traffic reports that make up Los Angeles news. He wonders if the police are trying to keep it out of the news for some tactical advantage.

He punches the intercom button adjacent to the security gate leading to the terminal. A high-pitched voice that could be male or female screeches out of the loudspeaker, asking his name. He stops himself short from saying his real name. That is a hard habit to break, but one that he must do flawlessly from now on. "Fouad Ibrahim," he says. To his great relief, the security arm lifts and he drives the car into the parking lot.

A white U.S. Department of Homeland Security SUV rolls past him slowly, heading in the opposite direction. He is relieved when it drives out of the parking lot without stopping. Being a Middle Eastern man at an airport always earns second looks, if not outright suspicion, despite the liberal Americans' hatred of profiling. He runs his fingers over his clean-shaven chin. When he is in Riyadh, maybe he will grow a beard, at least for a little while.

He has it all planned out. He'll launch the final attack shortly before boarding the plane, using a throwaway laptop and layers upon layers of encryption. As the jet soars over America's heartland, money will flow out of thousands of personal and business bank accounts and into his own Swiss accounts. Banking systems are really just giant databases of entries. Most people still have some quaint notion of money sitting in a bank vault somewhere, marked with their name on it, when really their funds sit in massive investment pools. Their money is little more than a figure in some ledger. Erase the ledger, no more money. Casting the world's financial markets into chaos is as simple as that. And filling the Islamic Crusade's coffers—and his own—is a fine by-product.

Leila moans softly and her hand twitches. He pats her shoulder. "It is all right, Leila," he says. He catches his own eyes in the reflection of the rearview mirror. The weight of what is happening is written in the creases around his eyes. It isn't like him to second-guess or question himself, but the cock-up with the encryption shook him. Maybe he needs to reassure himself, not Leila, that this will work. It must.

He pops the door open. A hot blast of valley air, combined with the heat from jet engines, dries the thin film of sweat on his skin. He scans the hangars and terminal for anyone watching him, but sees only lush green plants and those orange and purple bird of paradise plants that mimic the look of flight with their streamlined petals.

Private air travel has significant perks over commercial air travel, such as no security lines, no requests to remove your shoes and no delays. Three shining jets sit on the tarmac like white steeds waiting to whisk royalty away. None have any identification on them to reveal who their passengers are, and that is just as the ultra-rich like it. Mahaz owes Prince Abdul a huge favor for this kindness when he arrives in Riyadh.

He hears a car door open nearby, and sees Prince Abdul's fixer, Jamil, emerging from a black Mercedes S class. He is studying his phone through dark sunglasses with a very gold Gucci logo on the sides. He hasn't changed out of his Western attire yet. Mahaz assumes he will don the *thobe* and *ghutra* in flight, like most Saudis. Jamil waves curtly at Mahaz and gestures toward the hangar ahead and to the right. *He knows I've been here before*, Mahaz thinks. Leila and Omar would call him a poser, always trying to act like a royal instead of an employee.

Mahaz slips his hands under Leila's arms and lifts her into the wheelchair. She stirs and coughs, but her eyes stay closed as though lead weights line her eyelashes. He pushes her wheelchair ahead of him as he follows Jamil into the hangar. Though he has been inside twice before, Mahaz still marvels at the luxury touches given to just the hangar itself. Dark blue carpet stretches for what seems like miles under twenty foot ceilings, and dark wood paneling absorbs light and harkens back to the glamorous days of air travel. A Boeing 737 with a Cayman Islands registration rests in the middle of the hangar, maintained with such attention to detail by the mechanics of Royal

Jets that it wouldn't dream of dripping oil onto the carpet.

"We can put her in here for now," Jamil says, stepping to a glass door covered in wood blinds and unlocking it.

The room is lined in wooden crates and cardboard boxes, and smells musty. Dust flies in mini-cyclones through shafts of sunlight as they enter. Mahaz scans the room for escape routes Leila could use, but is satisfied to see the windows are too high and narrow for her to access or climb out of. The door is the only feasible route out. She could break the glass, he supposes, but that would only draw attention to her escape so they could easily stop her.

"This will work," he says with a nod to Jamil.

He parks Leila in her wheelchair against the wall, out of the sunlight, and watches as Jamil locks the door behind them.

"Now, it is time, yes?" Jamil says. He points to a second glass-fronted door further inside the hangar.

The royal family obviously uses this space for relaxing pre-flight, Mahaz thinks, though he has never been invited inside this room. The Prince only invited him into his small office instead. Inside this larger living space, a wrought-iron chandelier hangs over a mahogany coffee table. One wall is consumed as a complete entertainment area, and a comfortable-looking couch at least twelve feet long faces the enormous flat-screen television. A stainless steel refrigerator hums in the background.

"You're not going to use their wi-fi, are you?" Jamil says nervously. Mahaz snorts. *What an imbecile.*

"I take more precautions than you can even dream of. You don't even know the right questions to ask," Mahaz says.

He sees Jamil roll his eyes before turning to the refrigerator where he takes out a sparkling water, then collapses onto the sofa without offering Mahaz a drink.

Mahaz sets the laptop on the low coffee table and turns it on, then as it rolls slowly through its start-up cycle, he opens the internet radio application on his phone. Soon the sounds of French chanteuse Juliette Gréco pour out of the tinny little speaker. He sings along with her in a loud voice, pretending to be oblivious to the sidelong glances Jamil sends his way, along with an amused, if not patronizing, smile. Mahaz knows that Jamil would never act that way around the royals, and he wonders why the young man feels emboldened enough to do so in front of Mahaz. Has something shifted in his own status with the Prince? Impossible, though. The Prince assured him of his support, most tangibly with the use of his private jet today.

Put it out of your head, Mahaz tells himself. The computer finishes its cycle. Time to get to work.

Chapter 59

"What's going on, Mom? Did you find Dad?"

Ken stands behind Juliana at the door to Omar's hospital room. Drew sits in the visitor's chair looking at his phone, his work boot tapping the floor in a fast staccato. When he sees them, he stands up.

Omar sits upright in bed, his color nearly back to normal and his eyes bright and wide.

Juliana shakes her head. "The police are looking for him now, Omar," she says. "I'm sure he won't be trying to find me." She hopes her words are more reassuring than they sound to her ears. She isn't sure what Mahaz is doing right now.

She bends over to kiss her son, and sees the FBI agent Gina Morgan on a folding chair along the wall, talking in a low voice on her phone. A tall black man with a beer gut so pronounced he looks seven months pregnant leans against the wall next to her, wearing a blue windbreaker with FBI printed in yellow letters over his heart. Gina holds up two fingers, indicating she needs a few more minutes to wrap up her call.

The man stretches out an enormous hand. "I'm Agent Theo Kantis. You must be Juliana Al-Dossari?"

She places her hand limply in his. "Have you found my daughter yet?"

"We got a hold of this Conner kid finally, through one of the social media sites," Kantis says. "He never texted Leila or Omar. The text that came to Omar's phone for Leila, supposedly from Conner, was sent from a burner cell phone."

Deep inside her, Juliana knows something terrible has happened.

"I don't understand," she says. Dread rising in her chest, Juliana racks her brain trying to remember her daughter mentioning anyone named Conner, but no memories emerge. "I didn't even know she had a friend named Conner."

Her brother steps toward her, his eyes sympathetic. "Omar said that Leila had just started spending time with him in the past month or so. You can't know everything."

Gina finishes her call and stands up. "Juliana, we think Mahaz has her. We've put out an Amber Alert for the Mercedes. Omar sent us some recent pictures of her and Mahaz from his phone that we're sending out to all airports."

Nononononono. Her heart beats so hard in her chest she feels the pulse in her fingertips. Her arms feel hollow, as though Leila were an infant snatched right from her hands. This cannot be real.

"He's taking her to Saudi Arabia," she says with deadly certainty. She remembers the tracking software on Leila's phone. The software that told Mahaz where to find her that day she ran away. If only Leila still had her phone, they could find her. But Mahaz has taken care of that as well, destroying it yesterday.

"We're aware that your husband has threatened to take your son and daughter to Saudi Arabia before. We're taking that threat very seriously."

"But he left me here," Omar says. His eyes are liquid pain. He wipes away tears Juliana can't see.

She puts her hands on his shoulders. "He knows you are too sick to travel," she says. "And your father…he's in a lot of trouble. I don't know how much your Uncle Drew has told you."

Juliana sees Drew shaking his head softly in her peripheral vision. Omar looks so much like his father. How do you tell a boy that his father killed a man?

She sits on a corner of the bed and takes his hand. She doesn't have the strength to stand to deliver this news. She takes a deep breath and begins.

"The police think your father may be behind the computer hacks that shut down the power grid," she says.

Omar's eyes widen. "Is that why he took Leila?"

"Partly," she says, squeezing his hand. Now for the difficult part. The part that involves her own betrayal. "Your father figured out that I was suspicious of him, and he set off a bomb in his office. He figured out I was going to let the police search the house."

Omar takes his hand from under hers and folds his arms over his chest. "You were working with the police? Against him?"

"Yes, I was helping them," she says with some difficulty.

"But you thought they were wrong, didn't you? You were trying to show them he was innocent," Omar says. The hopeful look on his face breaks her heart. Telling him this story about his father's violence and his mother's treachery crushes her.

Her face hot, she continues. "There's more. That bomb your dad set, it killed a Homeland Security agent. It almost killed me. That's why the police are looking for him."

Omar pauses and takes some deep breaths. Juliana waits for him to respond, but he only presses his lips together and shuts his eyes. She touches his wrist softly. "I know this is hard," she says, choking back tears. "I'm doing my best."

The front door of Drew and Cathy's dark grey bungalow in Eagle Rock flies open as Drew drives up the sloping driveway into the garage. Ken maneuvers the Jeep into a space on the street between trash cans already emptied by the early shift of trash collectors.

Juliana watches the early-morning sun bounce off of her sister-in-law's blonde hair and turn it into a halo of golden glow. Cathy, a former bodybuilder, is tall and maintains an impressive athletic physique even after two pregnancies. She holds her youngest, Jack, easily in one arm, his bare feet kicking the air, and their daughter, Cissy, runs ahead to wrap her arms around Drew's legs.

Ken turns off the Jeep's ignition and yanks the parking brake. "Omar's just in shock," he says. "He'll come around."

Mahaz has torn us apart, she thinks. He's taken Leila as a hostage and left her and Omar behind like collateral damage. She can barely process the pain herself as an adult. How will her children cope? And what if he takes Leila to Riyadh? What if Omar never forgives her? It is as if her life as she knew it has shattered into pieces, and in picking up the shards she found herself in a bizarre new reality where nothing is as it seems.

Omar stayed silent throughout his hospital discharge, then opted to ride home alone with his uncle rather than spend any time with her in the car. His body seemed to shake with waves of anger, all directed at her, reminding her with every dark look that half of his blood is her husband's. His anger is like a proxy for Mahaz's.

Juliana snaps the door latch open and breathes deeply into the pain signals firing through her arm and side as she pushes the door open. In the few places where she doesn't have pain, she feels stiff. The rearview mirror reminds her just how awful she looks.

"What happened to you, Auntie?" Cissy says. She gapes openly at the bruising on Juliana's cheek.

Juliana bends down to get a hug and wet kiss from the little girl.

"Omar and I were in an accident," she says. "In an ambulance."

The girl's eyes widen and she nods seriously.

"This is my friend Ken," she says as he comes around the front of the Jeep.

"I like your car," Cissy says, then turns and runs to Omar, who is getting out of Drew's SUV slowly.

"We need to talk," Cathy says, looking around as though she expects someone to be hiding in the lantana shrubs. "Some more stuff has happened."

Juliana nods, and refocuses her attention on Omar. She isn't sure how much more "stuff" she can take today, but maybe Cathy's cryptic comment means they heard from Leila or Mahaz.

"I thought Omar could take Cissy's room," Cathy says. "Thank goodness she's moved into her big girl bed, huh?"

Juliana gives her a wan smile, and Cathy holds her left arm out to the side. Juliana walks in close, inhaling the baby's soft, powdery scent. A deep cry shudders through her as Cathy wraps her free arm around her. Hot tears plop onto Cathy's grey hoodie. Jack fidgets and coos.

"It's going to be okay with Omar," Cathy says. "He just needs time to process. And you need a cup of tea and a shower, if you don't mind my saying so."

Juliana moves her head back to catch Cathy smiling at her. "Yeah, a hot shower sounds good. It's been a while. Can you help Omar get settled in? He's not going to let me anywhere near him."

"Sure, anything," Cathy says. "But like I said, there's more."

Juliana pushes off of Cathy, wiping her nose with the back of her shirt sleeve. "Well, what is it?"

"There's been another computer hack," Cathy says. "The news stations are saying this one is related to the others. This time it's the banks."

Twenty minutes later, with wet hair wrapped in a fluffy towel and clothed in a pair of Cathy's yoga pants and a loose top, Juliana enters the living room to find Cathy, Drew and Ken huddled on the blue plaid sectional. Cissy sits on the floor coloring with a pink crayon, oblivious to their conversation. The flat-screen television on the wall flashes with the happy, smiling faces of some couple delighted to be taking cholesterol medicine.

"Look," Ken says. He points at the television screen, where the newsreader speaks from behind her desk, the words FINANCIAL MELTDOWN dominating the lower third of the screen.

Drew hits a button on the remote and sound blares out of their surround-sound speakers so tastefully mounted on the ceiling.

"The New York Stock Exchange has suspended trading after a series of anomalies occurred on its trading platform, causing companies to buy and sell shares without proper authorization. Experts think the shutdown could last as long as a week.

"The last time the stock exchanges were closed for six days was after the terrorist attacks on 9/11. Before that, the longest shutdown had been during the Great Depression. After the markets opened on September 17, 2001, the Dow Jones Industrial Average had fallen by 684 points, a 7.1 percent loss.

"Freedom Bank, the U.S.'s largest bank, has released a statement that its financial system security has been breached by hackers claiming to be with the Islamic Crusade, and that they've shut down their website and customer access to ATMs."

Cathy squeezes one of the throw pillows and clutches it to her chest. "That's our bank," she says. "How is this even possible?"

Ken clears his throat. "It's easier than you think. You can buy software on websites like Pirate Bay to break down and take full control of online banking systems. A few years ago, a criminal gang in New York stole something like $45 million by hacking into the companies that process online payments for prepaid MasterCard debit card accounts. They had people withdrawing money with stolen cards all over the world."

"But we do everything online now. I haven't written a check or gone into a bank in years," Cathy says. "You mean our money's not safe?"

"Calm down, Cathy," Drew says. "The banks are the ones liable if there's a security breach on their systems, not us."

"But still…how long will it take to sort it out? And what about our retirement investments?"

Juliana sits frozen on the arm of the sofa, fear pinning her in place. Mahaz's powers seem endless. Is any system secure from his hacks? Dread rises in her like floodwater. If he can hack into banking systems, what would stop him from clearing out their joint account? That would be child's play in comparison. Would he be so spiteful?

Leila has been missing for nearly two hours now. Has she missed the FBI's call? When they left the hospital, Gina said she would be in touch.

Suddenly frantic, she searches her purse for her cell phone with no luck, resisting the impulse to dump the contents on the floor and have yet another good cry. Frustrated, she unwraps the towel from her hair and lets it drop to the floor, her wet hair falling on her shoulders. Then she remembers leaving the phone on the kitchen counter of her house.

She figured taking her phone was a risk since Mahaz could track her with it. However, she still has the disposable cell phone Bryce told her to buy in her purse, along with Gina's card. And of course Gina has the cell phone number. She remembers swapping text messages with the agent at the hospital. Her mind is playing tricks on her. She needs to calm down and focus on one thing at a time.

Using the burner phone, she logs on to her bank's mobile

application. Her fingers shake as she punches in the username and password.

Checking Account Balance: Zero dollars. Savings Account Balance: Zero dollars.

He's cleaned them out.

The U.S. President appears on the screen behind a podium, giving the cameras and the reporters behind them a grave nod. Then he looks into the television eye for a silent moment. His face is lined, but not unattractively so, with deep square brackets crasing down past his mouth and into his broad jaw. His hands rest lightly on a sheaf of papers, big veins running from his wrists to his knuckles.

He begins to speak in his usual, calm and customary My-Fellow-Americans style, but Juliana sees a hard anger in his eyes. He is urging them not to panic, but she finds herself filled with fear and anxiety. It is her husband behind these acts. It is Mahaz who is being hunted now. "We do not negotiate with terrorists," the President says, and she knows they will kill him if given a chance. "Let our enemies take warning."

Beside her, Ken drops his smart phone to his lap with a sigh. "Looks like my accounts are still okay," he says.

"I'm calling Mom and Dad," Juliana says.

Her father answers the phone. She doesn't even need to ask if they have seen the news because she can hear the same CNN program in the background.

"Our money's gone, too," her father says. "But like I said to your mother, we shouldn't worry. They're going to straighten this out. This is like a computer glitch. The money is still there. It has to be. They couldn't turn it into real cash that fast."

Juliana shakes with a black rage. Mahaz took Leila, then made sure the institutions where her family banked were among those targeted.

Family. We are a family. Her brain plucks a memory of a dinner long ago, in a private room at a posh Beverly Hills restaurant with Mahaz and his friend Prince Abdul. Champagne was flowing, which was unusual for the Prince who was a devout Muslim, and Mahaz cautioned her to only sip at it. "Watch his wife," he whispered in her ear. "Don't drink faster than her." Juliana thought of it as a game. This dinner was before Leila was born, before the trips to the Kingdom had worn her down and made her want to keep her feet firmly in the United States.

"Nothing is more important than family," Prince Abdul told her. "And Juliana, you are like one of us."

He said you are like one of us, she thinks now. Not one of us. Just "like" one. How had she not heard that statement for what it was? She was an interloper in Mahaz's life. He has returned to his real family. Was it all a lie?

From Cissy's room, the shrill ringing of Omar's phone startles her. She holds her breath for a few beats until Omar shouts for her.

"Mama Yalima is on the phone for you, Mom," he says.

Yalima. She hasn't talked to her since Mahaz brought Leila home from the modeling gig. She rises quickly from the sofa only to find her steps slowed by doubt. Yalima is family. But whose family? Is she calling to get information for Mahaz? Or maybe to deliver a message from him? Who can she trust? Juliana's mind spins round and round, as she stands still as a mannequin in Cathy and Drew's living room, all of their eyes on her.

"You have to take the call, Juliana," Drew says.

"Mom, are you coming?" Omar shouts.

She walks through the hallway, her arms folded tight across her chest, a knot of anxiety in her stomach. Despite the warmth of the house, she shivers. Omar holds out the phone to her without making eye contact.

"Juliana, are you all right?" Yalima's voice through the phone is tense and tight.

"Yes," she says. "What do you know?"

"What do I know? What kind of question is that? I've been trying to reach you all morning. I've left you many voicemail messages and texts. Did you not get them?"

"I don't have my cell phone," Juliana says. If Yalima was in contact with Mahaz, won't she know that already?

"My friends have told me what my son did," Yalima says. Juliana hears tears in her voice and it makes her angry. She wants to shake her mother-in-law and ask her why her son did these terrible things. But she bites her tongue and says nothing. She needs to listen and think carefully.

"He's gotten involved with bad people," Yalima says. "But things are coming to an end now."

"What do you mean, coming to end? Where is Leila? Is she safe?"

"She is safe. I have it on very good authority," the older woman says. "I'm calling to tell you where to find them."

Juliana gasps. "Where?"

"He's at the Van Nuys airport. Prince Abdul's private jet. The authorities have been notified as well. But I thought you'd want to know so you can be there for Leila."

Time slows down as her mind and body flood with adrenalin. Fight or flight. Her maternal instinct to save her daughter is so strong she can taste it. But can she trust Yalima? Is this a trap?

She is so lost in thought that she hands Omar the phone without ending the call.

"What did she say?"

"She told me where your father and Leila are, Omar," she says. "Now I have to go get her."

"You're going to get her? Shouldn't you call the police?" Omar says in disbelief. She shakes her head.

"This is what I have to do," she says.

She walks back into the living room to four sets of worried eyes. Someone muted CNN. Even little Cissy detects the tension in the air. Her big blue eyes follow Juliana as she crosses to the sofa.

"Mahaz is on Prince Abdul's private jet at the Van Nuys airport," she announces. She picks up her purse and runs her fingers through her damp hair. "Where are my shoes?"

"We should call Gina," Ken says.

"That's fine," she says. "But I'm going there now, Ken. I can't sit here and wait."

Chapter 60

The tall and slim flight attendant offers Mahaz a glass of mango juice the same color as the silk scarf knotted around her neck. Blonde, olive-skinned and beautiful, with a faint dimple on her right cheek. Prince Abdul loves the blondes.

Thirsty, he takes the cut crystal glass from her, noting her long manicured nails are painted deep green with white tips. *How is that not sacrilegious for this Western woman to mimic the Saudi flag on her fingernails?*

He drinks half of the juice quickly. It has been many hours since he ate or drank anything. He scans the empty couches and armchairs of the first cabin, a sterile but comfortable sitting area outfitted in someone's version of modern elegance. Clean lines, dark wood and a thousand shades of light neutral in the upholstery, paint and trim.

"Where is my daughter?"

The woman smiles at him, and sets the tray of juice down on a table. "Come this way," she says. She leads him to the second cabin, which looks more like a traditional first-class cabin on a commercial airline, with its rows of wide leather seats, two by two. Leila sleeps in one of the window seats, seatbelt over the black *abaya* and *hijab* she has been dressed in.

Jamil comes up behind them. Mahal watches him exchange a long glance with the flight attendant, and he wonders if they are sleeping together. That may be something he points out to Prince Abdul when he lands in Riyadh.

Jamil turns back to him with a smile. "It is a glorious day for Islam, brother. This is the day when their truth shall benefit the truthful ones," he says.

"Most surely this is our mighty achievement," Mahaz says.

"Our friend Abdul al-Lahem asked me to have you call him," Jamil says, extending his phone. "I've put the number in for you."

Mahaz hits the send button and listens as the phone lines connect. Abdul picks up on the second ring.

"Mahaz, my son," he says. "I am watching the BBC now with my smile stretching from ear to ear."

"Yes, *inshallah*, the plan worked beautifully. I hope you find your faith in me well-placed."

"It is not I you should think of, but Allah. I am one of his servants, as you are. We do our work to restore to this world the light of divine justice. Allah demands no less."

"Yes, we have sent the call out today for all to hear."

Abdul clears his throat. "Mahaz, you must remember that your sacred duty is to carry the message of Islam. What happens to that message once you deliver it, that is in Allah's hands. You must pray for Allah to accept your sacrifice in His name."

What sacrifice? Mahaz can only imagine the man still thinks of his leaving the United States and his wife behind as a sacrifice, although Mahaz moved well past mourning that loss months ago. He is ready for his new life in the Middle East, and more importantly, his Swiss bank account is ready as well, thanks to this morning's transfers.

"*Ma'a salama*, my son," Abdul says, and the line falls silent.

Mahaz hands the phone back to Jamil. Leila's eyes flutter open and her fingers grope for her hair, now covered by the black cloth.

"So, when are we taking off?" Mahaz says. He hates to give Leila any more of the tranquilizers. He already gave her far more than a normal dose.

"Abdul spoke to you of sacrifice, yes?" Jamil says.

Mahaz blinks with surprise. "Yes," he says.

"Unfortunately, my friend, this is the sacrifice part," Jamil says, pointing out the plane's windows. Mahaz bends over for a look, and sees four Los Angeles Police Department cars parked outside.

"The plane will not be leaving today with you as its passenger," Jamil says. "You'll have to pay for your crimes here in the United States."

"What?" Mahaz spits out, advancing on Jamil as if to throttle him. "Don't you know who I am?"

"I know who you are, all right," Jamil says, stepping back a few steps and putting his hand on his hip, where he carries a small pistol. Mahaz is nearly certain Jamil has never fired a gun anywhere but on a gun range.

"The Kingdom can't be associated with this bomb blast that killed the Homeland Security agent, or your willingness to abandon your wife and son. They don't want you anywhere near Riyadh."

Mahaz rushes Jamil before he can pull out the weapon and knocks him against a row of seats. He easily pries the small gun from his thin fingers. It is a subcompact Beretta, sold for personal protection, though this idiot probably only carries it as an accessory. He pops the magazine out, sees it is loaded and shoves it back in.

Jamil starts cursing him in Arabic, the whole "son of a donkey, son of a pig, son of a fart" routine. Arab insults tend toward the PG rating. Mahaz gives him a hard right to the stomach, and Jamil folds in half like a newspaper.

Then he hears another man's voice telling him to freeze and the distinct sound of a gun's safety being turned off.

He shoves Jamil, and slips into the seat beside Leila. His meticulous plan has failed him. He points the gun at her head, a last resort move that he knows makes him as much a hostage to the situation as his daughter.

"I'll kill her," Mahaz says, his mind in chaos, hoping they believe him.

Chapter 61

Ken drives through the runway overpass and makes a right turn into the Van Nuys airport. "That's the driveway," Juliana says, recognizing it from a previous trip with Mahaz to see the Prince off. "The second one from the left. The executive terminal. We can get to the hangar from there."

Ken turns the Jeep into the parking lot, separated from the runway by chain link fences draped with black fabric. Rocks ping the Jeep's underbody as loud as popcorn popping.

A woman in high heels and a tight red skirt strides ahead of two men in dark suits and deep conversation to the tinted glass doors of the pristine white terminal building. A security guard stops them, and after a few minutes of conversation, admits them inside.

Ken parks the Jeep next to two white sedans marked with the seal of U.S. Customs and Border Protection. "See, they're already here," he says, hoping to reassure her, but she swings the passenger door open and leaps to her feet. She runs to the terminal entrance but is blocked by the security guard, whose mirrored sunglasses reflect her worried expression.

"That's my daughter in there!" she says, little bits of saliva hitting the officer's glasses.

"I can't let you in, ma'am," he says.

She considers body slamming him—her daughter's imminent danger has her roaring on adrenalin and feeling no pain. But she is saved from it by the door opening and Agent Kantis coming out, his forehead shiny with sweat.

"We've got a situation," he says. "Come in."

Chapter 62

A round woman with white hair and reddish skin replaces the LAPD officers in the plane's entrance to the cabin where Mahaz sits with a gun pointed at his daughter's head. Her broad chest heaves from her charge up the plane's stairs, and she stands framed by the arched doorway, gold curtains on either side. Her hands are open, palms facing him. He doesn't see a weapon on her, but he isn't fool enough to think she doesn't have a gun. Nor is he fool enough to think he has a realistic way out of this situation. He just needs time to think, to clear up this dark cloud forming at the back of his skull.

He presses the gun into Leila's temple. The girl shifts in her sleep and smacks her lips. Her eyelids flicker a little, then rest again. *She's starting to come out of the sedation*, Mahaz thinks. Things aren't happening as they are supposed to. He has to think now. Improvise. Improvisation was never his strong suit. Think. He can't get more tranquilizers into Leila at this point. What will her reaction be? Confusion, followed by fear. She may move, try to get up, but he can overpower her if he has to. This can work to his advantage. Maybe her fear will escalate the police's willingness to cooperate with him. His arm wraps around her shoulder, pulling her tightly to him, her head falling like dead weight on his upper arm. The white-haired old bitch moves an inch forward, not even a step, just the barest lean forward toward him across the space.

"Stay where you are!" he shouts. He must show this woman who is in control here, but the dark cloud feels like it is expanding, bringing a heaviness to his head and to his limbs. Is that Jamil staring at him with big black eyes in the background? Is he using his phone to shoot video of this standoff to send back to the Kingdom? Mahaz tries to shake off the cloud and focus on her. She begins speaking again through pale lips.

"I'm not armed," the woman says, holding her arms out to the side and rotating her hands so the palms face the floor as some kind of proof. "My name's Gina. I'm with the FBI. I just want to talk."

"Keep your hands up, where I can see them," he says. "Who's behind you?"

"The LAPD are in the other cabin. It's just me talking to you. Is that Leila with you? Your daughter?"

"You sound like you already know the answer to that question," he says. The dark cloud is taking over his brain, fuzzing up his senses. He can hear the blood pounding in his ears. He can't think clearly at all. Was Jamil still shooting video?

"You know you don't have many options," the woman says. What is her name again? "Why don't you put the gun down, Mahaz?"

Time slows down. He needs to think about this situation like a flowchart. What are his options? Option one: Convince this FBI agent to leave the plane and allow him to fly to Syria, leaving the Prince and his people blameless in his escape. Is that what they wanted when they set him up like this? Option two: He could shoot the FBI agent, then hold a gun to the pilot's head and make him fly the plane. Both options sound impossible. The stuff of American movies.

He listens to Leila's shallow breathing, while holding his own breath. Option three: A soldier in an impossible situation like this would kill himself. Put the gun in your own mouth, and pull the trigger. The voice of al-Lahem. *You have served us well, but your time has come to an end.*

He feels very cold, and a wave of nausea overcomes him. Everything blurs. The woman continues to talk but her voice seems a long way away, almost like she is under water. The darkness swells in his brain. His tongue feels thick and odd. The mango juice. What was in the mango juice?

A woman's hand with long green and white nails plucks the gun from his loosened grip as he slumps back in the chair.

Chapter 63

Mahaz is handcuffed. At first, Juliana's instinct is to punch him in the face, but her daughter's absence from the scene makes her fear the very worst. Hot tears trail down her cheeks, as the image of Leila on an ambulance stretcher floods her mind's eye, a picture so certain it becomes the truth in her head.

She was mistaken to think they were partners, she knows now. He dropped clues for years that their marriage was far from ideal, but she refused to see it clearly. She thought she was protecting her kids by holding this marriage together. And look at the toll it took on her, and her children. *I will do better*, she promises herself. *Just let Leila be all right.*

"Where is she, Mahaz?"

He spits at her feet. She feels nothing but fury and revulsion, but she refuses to stoop to his level of violence again. He took her daughter with the intention of moving her to Saudi Arabia. He made real his threats, and with that act, he killed her love for him. He declared war, and her heart became armor-plated. She feels panic for Leila—panic that the girl is out of sight still. She whirls around to find Mahaz watching her as the police lead him away, and she believes he is enjoying her display of fear. He's feeding off of it somehow.

She darts out the open door in time. There, she sees through the window another officer carrying Leila down the steps of the plane. Her daughter is covered head to toe in black fabric with only her face showing. Juliana shudders with relief, the image of her daughter covered in a sheet banished back to the corner of her mind from which it sprang. Leila looks all right. From that moment on, she thinks of nothing else but taking her daughter in her arms, despite how surreal the situation is with police and paramedics and her husband in handcuffs. Leila is all right. Juliana is nearly bursting with thankfulness.

The receptionist rises from behind her circular desk and leans forward. "Can I help you, ma'am?"

Juliana walks past her without responding and pushes open the glass doors leading to the runway. She hears Ken's voice behind her, explaining something to the woman in his deep voice.

"Leila! Honey!" Juliana isn't sure her feet even touch the ground as she runs to her daughter, kneeling beside the wheelchair where Leila now sits and pressing her face to her daughter's cool cheek. Her hand fumbles for Leila's underneath the full sleeve of the *abaya*. Leila's hand lies damp and lifeless in her own, and something hard knots and swells at the bottom of Juliana's throat. She pulls away, wanting nothing more than to see her daughter's face, as beautiful as a princess under a spell. That's all this was. Just a spell, baby. You never need to think of it again.

She starts unwinding the *hijab,* her fingers finding the pins that secure the cloth and flinging them to the ground until she is able to push the scarf down to the girl's shoulders. She then unties the under scarf to reveal Leila's pretty dark hair. Seconds turn into lifetimes while she waits for a response from her youngest.

Leila's eyes open slowly. "Mom?"

A wave of happiness sweeps through her and she smiles and cries at the same time. "Baby," Juliana says. "You're okay, now. I've got you."

"Dad said I could get a new phone," she says, her eyes closing again.

The fear and panic and relief swirl into absolute joy and an ear-to-ear smile that blossoms on Juliana's face as she realizes in a flash that Leila is all right. *Leila doesn't even know what happened*, she thinks. The spell is broken and Leila is as she was.

Juliana rocks back on her heels on the cement, bumping into a solid set of male legs, and feels someone's arms grip her shoulders. "I'm right here," Ken says, and she leans into him, taking her first deep breath in what seems like hours.

"What's going on?" Leila asks, and for the first time in days Juliana feels in control of what happens next.

"We're going home," she says.

Chapter 64

Leila and Omar have been home for a week. Juliana has kept them close to her, not letting them return to school yet. She wants them near to her. It feels like when they were babies. She's careful around them, watching for signs of trauma, and waiting for the right time to talk to them about what happened. Not that there aren't reminders every day. A blue tarp covers the door to Mahaz's office, and she avoids looking at it whenever she is in the kitchen. She needs to find a contractor to start cleaning it up, but she must first find the energy.

Today is the first day her kids have complained about being cooped up in the house. *They are resilient and ready to go back into the world.* But she is not. She tells them she helped the police catch Mahaz. She tells them how scared she was that Mahaz would take them away from her. She tells them she plans to file for divorce. She says she wants them to hear all this from her first.

They know most of the story, she realizes as they nod and speak over her.

"Was he really going to take me to Riyadh?" Leila asks.

"Yes, I believe so."

"But not me," Omar says.

Leila's face is pale, and she can see tears rising in her eyes. Omar's are dry.

"Your father changed from the man I married," she says, as if that is an explanation. She hasn't been able to make sense of his actions herself.

They talk a little while longer before they dive into their social media to tell their friends they'll be back at school the next day.

When they go upstairs, Juliana lies on the sofa and closes her eyes. She thinks about Mahaz, trying to understand what sort of person he is. It is hard to admit that you do not know your own husband. That perhaps you never knew him.

She fell in love with him decades before and never looked back. She saw the man she fell in love with, not the man she was living with these past years. People say love makes you blind. But sometimes, it is more like you are blinded by love.

Her mind is an endless loop of if onlys. If only she had stood up to Mahaz about his infidelities. If only she had tried to look beyond what she wanted to believe and see the real him. If only she hadn't stayed on the surface without looking closely at what was going on underneath, worrying about appearances more than reality. She had been sleepwalking.

Her parents want to help her, and they urge her to talk to someone, a psychologist, who can guide her through this trauma and lead her to a normal, well-adjusted life. They've even given her the name and phone number of one, leaving it on the kitchen table after dinner one night. But she's still in shock. She's sickened at the thought of telling the story to a stranger. What she wants to do now is concentrate on her children and her future.

Chapter 65

Ken sits in the recliner his father loved, next to the couch where his mother has stretched out under an afghan, Tilly and Maxie snuggled next to her. They are watching a reality show about ballroom dancing, joyful, easygoing, mindless television, both with a bowl of mint chocolate chip ice cream in their hands. Ken's phone rings. It's Juliana. He sent her an email weeks ago, asking her to call, but when she didn't respond, he figured she never would. Her voice on the other end of the phone makes his heart leap.

"How are you?" he asks. His voice sounds high-pitched and excited, and his mother turns her neck, eyebrows raised in question.

"Good, good," she says, and he presses the phone to his ear, trying to detect her mood. She must be depressed, he thinks. Lonely. He does not want to prey on her.

"They've let me go," she says. "UCLA is closing the center. I gather the funding has dried up from the Prince."

"How are your kids?"

"They're coping," she says. "Probably better than I am. Look, I want to thank you for your help."

He rises from the chair and walks into the kitchen. "You don't need to thank me," he says. "Not at all, and if you're worried about what happened when we, uh, kissed that night, listen, I totally understand. You were emotional, it was a crazy time..."

He knows he is blabbering but he cannot stop himself. He is grateful when she cuts in.

"Look, Ken, I was calling to see if you wanted to have dinner some time."

For a moment, he is not sure he heard her correctly.

"Yes," he says. "I'd love that."

Chapter 66

Juliana drives home from her lawyer's office with a copy of her divorce filing papers resting on the front passenger seat. When talking heads on the radio news channel start jabbering about the trial of Mahaz Al-Dossari for the murder of a Homeland Security agent, she swiftly changes the channel to jazz for the rest of her drive. Leila and Omar have followed the trial online since it began a few weeks ago, but they rarely bring it up to her, knowing she doesn't want to hear about it until it ends. Until they find him guilty.

She pulls into the driveway, noting that the brochure holder on the For Sale sign in her yard is empty once again. She hasn't received a serious offer yet, just looky-loos who have somehow connected her Valley home with the hacker-slash-murderer, but her real estate agent says it is only a matter of time before someone makes an offer. "It's priced to sell!" the agent chirped at her, perennially perky and optimistic.

She no longer cares. The house is nothing more than a hollow shell to her now, a burden she can't wait to get rid of. The crime scene tape is long gone and a team of carpenters and drywall guys made the walls and bookshelves of the office look better than ever. It bears no evidence of the explosion that took the life of Homeland

Security agent Bryce Ballen. Even Mahaz's scent has faded from most of the rooms, except for their bedroom.

She looks at the house and tries to imagine its next life. A young couple, small children, could make their home here. Fill the walls with laughter and game nights and birthday parties. She still has these memories of herself and Mahaz and Omar and Leila. What happened later has not erased them. Omar spraying Leila with the garden hose, their shorts and T-shirts soaked, gleeful. Leila dancing with a broom. She thinks of Mahaz as a different person now, almost a man possessed. Old Mahaz, new Mahaz. She has found no other way to understand his actions.

She sees Ken's Jeep in her rearview mirror, another example of his perfect timing. He's come over to set up her new laptop. UCLA took away her work laptop when they fired her, and she needs a new one for the college courses she's enrolled in at Los Angeles Valley College.

She kisses him in the driveway.

"Aren't you afraid the kids will see?"

"They're at school, silly," she says, and kisses him again. The time is coming when she will want to tell them about Ken, but not yet.

Chapter 67

In a tiny, dark apartment in Paris, Proxyw0rm scans the electronic attachment that his newest partner, Pharm$duke, has sent him. Satisfied with it, he types a message on his disposable laptop into the TorChat interface.

Proxyw0rm: You have made fast progress, my friend.

Pharm$duke: It is a matter of days now. Access was the easy part. Anything connected to the internet can be hacked.

Proxyw0rm: Yes. Time and effort is all it takes. The honorable fight continues with your help.

Proxyw0rm allows himself a moment to enjoy their progress before bringing his hands back to the computer keyboard to write code.

And the botnet continues to sit inside millions of computers, waiting for its next command.

CPSIA information can be obtained at www.ICGtesting.com
Printed in the USA
LVOW11s1716190916

505260LV00005B/1206/P